John Riha

Incident 395

RT3 Media
Ashland, OR
2022

Copyright 2022 by John Riha
Print Edition
All Rights Reserved
Published by RT3 Media, LLC

ISBN 978-0-9911579-4-5

This book is the copyrighted property of the author and may not be reproduced, scanned, or distributed for any commercial or non-commercial use without permission from the author. Quotes used in reviews are the exception.
No alteration of content is allowed.
Your support and respect for the property
of the author is appreciated.

Cover image: ©cannon | Adobe Stock
Kayaker: ©Madamelead | Dreamstime

For the Siskiyou Rappellers

and Craig

Rookie training is designed to prepare rookie rappeller candidates with the necessary mental fortitude, logic and reasoning skills, and physical capacity to succeed in highly dynamic and arduous work environments.

The desired physical fitness goals for the crew are as follows:

- 1.5 mile run 11 minutes or less
- 25 push-ups 1 minute
- 45 sit-ups 1 minute
- 7 pull-ups
- 110-pound pack 3 miles 90 minutes

INCIDENT 395

Early Spring

IN THE THINNING space between the dream and the awakening he can't tell what is true and what is figment. He is kneeling by a small campfire and Martin is there sitting with his legs drawn up and his arms around his knees and he is smiling. Nearby is a river running fresh and clean under a bright morning sky and it's good to see Martin and know his friend is not dead. An osprey comes along and hovers over the river, paused in her hunt as she scans the river below, wings moving in big loping circles as she holds herself in midair, going neither forward nor back. Then she folds her wings and plummets and hits the water with a silent explosion of white and silver and emerges with a wriggling redband in her talons. As she pulls her way back into the sky he marvels *Wow, how about that?* and Martin nods but says nothing, just looks at him smiling.

Now Martin is outboard on the skids of the Huey leaned out against the rope in his yellow Nomex and gloves and his helmet with the visor down so all that's visible of the actual Martin is the smile, the white grin hovering, floating. Then the harness breaks and Martin is spinning away, there is no sound except the cry of a raptor oddly coming through the headset. Martin falls for a long, long time twirling down like a yellow autumn leaf beneath a smile that's a hopeless parachute and at last he comes to rest on the indistinct forest floor of greenery and crisscrossed downed snags which mimic his outstretched arms and legs, his red belly bag is a dollop of bright color so far below.

Bowden comes fully awake and for a clear pure moment he is relieved because the part about the campfire is real and the fiction is the idea that Martin has fallen and died. Then things in his room—the chair where he has draped his jeans, the old chest of drawers—take shape in the pale light of early morning and in his mind as well and the truth begins to rearrange itself.

THERE WERE nearly two years of inquiries and accusations between the harness manufacturer and the Forest Service and he was dragged into the mire of it because he had been the spotter. In the end he and the Forest Service were cleared of any error and liability. The harness company paid a settlement to Martin's family but that of course did not make his friend undead, it only seemed to trivialize how completely gone he was, composted to dirt beneath a fetid mound of legal wrangling.

It took Lucas Bowden more than four years before he could think about climbing back into a helicopter. He asked for and was granted a transfer into the service branch of logistics at the Geographic Area Coordination Center in Portland. He worked wildfires from a computer monitor, making sure the commissary tents arrived at the staging areas and that the rows of Porta-Pottys were adequate to the task of handling the waste of several hundred firefighters. He did the job well enough but he was listless and there was a darkness inside that Zoloft couldn't open up and Ambien couldn't push down. He finally quit the job and took a gig as a fishing guide on the Snake River, showing wealthy clients the deep holes where steelhead lurked. On the water gliding through the towering canyons he felt safe, folded deep away in nature's pocket with the sky winding as a blue river far overhead. But the pay was mediocre and the Idaho winters were cold and lonely, and after the second season when the summer steelhead runs dwindled he went back to the Forest Service and they gave him his old job at the GACC in Portland, sitting in the exact same chair at the exact same desk.

Fifty-two months after Martin Shires had fallen to his death Bowden saw a position open up at the Rogue Rappellers near Grants Pass and he thought about it long and hard before applying. He'd have to give up the pills, at least for the three weeks needed to clear his system before any drug test. Part of him hoped they'd turn him down but they didn't and so he gathered up his television and inflatable mattress and his meager furniture and put everything in the back of his Ford F-150 and with a duffle of his clothes riding shotgun he drove south down I-5 to face whatever thing it was he needed to face. Waiting in the bottom of the duffle were bottles of Xanax and Vicodin and Adderall. Whatever that was, down there in the bottom darkness of his duffle, it was temporary. He didn't really need it. He knew that. But somehow it needed him.

On the first day of live practice they all stood in their gear on the tarmac near the yellow-and-white UH-1. Bowden was on the second stick and was going through safety checks with his partner, a guy named Danny Cravell. He was tugging at Cravell's harness straps so hard that his partner lost his balance and stumbled and said, *Hey, take it easy bro!* When Bowden was done he didn't give a thumbs up but turned to the spotter and said quietly, "Check him, would you?"

The spotter was also the base commander and he knew the backstory on Lucas Bowden and about the helicopter accident. Normally a second check or any kind of hesitancy would be a red flag, but he simply nodded and walked over to Cravell and gave him a similar working over, pulling extra hard on every strap and buckle so that Danny finally said, *What's with you guys?* Then the spotter gave the thumbs up and looked at Bowden in the eyes and said, "Are we good?" He stood there staring hard until Bowden nodded and returned a thumbs up, hoping that this was the end of something and the beginning of something else.

They climbed into their seats while the turbines spooled up and the blades thumped fiercely through the morning air. The vibrations shuddered up Bowden's legs and into his gut and thrummed inside his eyes. His mouth was dry. He wished he'd taken a Xanax.

They strapped in and Bowden looked at the faces of the other three rappellers on the bench seat next to him and the spotter sitting opposite, their expressions easy, confident. They all knew each other from previous fire seasons. He was the new guy; the outsider. Then his pre-flight check buddy Cravell reached over and gave him a slap on the knee and said, *Lucas Bowden, welcome aboard!* and the helicopter eased forward and began to lift into the sky.

Monday, June 8
National Weather Service Station
Medford, Oregon

STEVE PAPACEK had been on the wildfire desk for eleven hours straight, taking double duty because the station was short-handed—one of the staff meteorologists had been requested by CalFire to a burn near Sacramento, and another IMET was on loan to the Forest Service for the Entiat fire complex in Washington.

Papacek didn't mind the extra shift. He liked the hours before the sun came up. The station was quiet—it was only himself and another meteorologist in the big room with the dozens of glowing screens. The entryway and most of the offices were dark, and they were cocooned in the warm glow of data. The five monitors arrayed across the wildfire desk shimmered with wind speeds, humidity levels, fuel potential, and satellite images of southern Oregon.

For now, the area was relatively sedate. Although it was the heart of fire season, there were only two fires burning in the southwestern district, both under ten acres, each more than seventy percent contained. Calm winds prevailed.

Papacek was monitoring the screens and thinking about his kids. A son, Ryan, was enrolled in the Wildland Fire Ecology program at Oregon State as a junior, and their daughter, Bonnie Jean, had just begun freshman classes at the U of O, her major TBD. He and his wife both worked but with kids in school the Papacek bank account was hemorrhaging tuition. He was gratified that Ryan had decided to study fire ecology, he just hoped there would be a decent job waiting for his son after graduation. Hopefully, somewhere on the West Coast. His daughter was still figuring it out, but he knew whatever Bonnie zeroed in on, she'd kick butt. She had plenty of time for that

It was kind of strange in the house with both kids gone. Nice and calm, but strange.

Papacek looked at the wall monitors and a screen displaying the energy-release model. It was a simple data set that combined three factors—humidity, temperature, and the dryness of forest combustibles—into a graph that indicated the amount of heat a forest fire might produce if ignited. It was the kind of data Ryan would eat up with a spoon.

Three jagged lines made their way across the XY axes. A pale gray line ran roughly through the middle of the graph and showed day-by-day averages recorded by the Medford station over the course of the current year. Above that, a red line indicated the historically highest levels ever recorded on those same days. A third line was blue and tracked the year-to-date conditions. The blue line was significantly above the other lines. Papacek stared at it. Five straight weeks of the highest energy-release potential ever seen at the Medford station. The driest May and June ever. It was a botanical bomb waiting to go off.

His colleague, Eddie Johns, had earbuds inserted and Papacek could hear the muffled sounds of rap. Johns once explained it helped him focus. Papacek believed it. The guy took to computer modeling and data sets like breathing. Papacek tapped Johns on the shoulder. "I'm going to launch the balloon," he said.

Johns straightened and took out his earbuds and pointed at one of the screens. "Still got this upper level trough forming off the coast," he said. "And a southeast flow aloft, so we're definitely getting a negative tilt."

Papacek leaned close to a monitor displaying swaths of colored pixels coalescing over the Pacific Ocean. He nodded. With fire conditions on edge, they'd want to stay well ahead of this one.

"Chaos," Johns remarked.

"Note it for the morning conference," said Papacek. "We'll issue a watch. If this looks to form up by tomorrow night, we'll contact the agencies, let 'em know something's coming."

"Bad time of year for anything to start popping off." Johns gave a little shake of his head.

"Amen," said Papacek.

Monday, June 8
Medford, Oregon

"WHY DO YOU want to do it?" asked Cora.

"Because it's going to be great," said Kal. "I'll be with my dad. It's going to be incredible."

"I mean, why do you want to do it if you can't *see* it?" persisted Cora. "The mountains, duh. The rivers. Big trees and shit."

Cora Franklin was not one of Kal Spencer's best friends. Cora was loud and nosy and had a knack for asking about things you didn't necessarily want to talk about. Kal didn't hang with her much—Cora was a year older and in a different grade at school—but they lived in the same neighborhood, which made walking home together from summer dance class sort of inevitable. As usual, Cora was being annoying and Kal was practicing tolerance, zenning out while Cora babbled. Despite their differences, there was something awkward and a bit desperate in Cora that Kal understood. To be an oddity, to have kids whisper about you. So Kal put up a serene smile and nodded as the unlikely pair walked along—the cringe-worthy chatterbox and the blind girl with the round retro sunglasses and white cane.

"I've been hiking with my dad before," said Kal, "and it's very cool. There's just so much there. It smells so *alive*. I can feel it. The bigness. And there's so many freaking birds! And the wind in the trees!" She almost added how much she loved "campfires," but Kal didn't want to jinx the possibility. Her dad had said campfires might not be allowed this year on account of the forest being so dry. Harsh realm. Campfires were the best. The snapping firewood, the heat along her arms and face, that sweet smoke mixed with the cool night air. She loved campfires.

"I've been hiking and all I got was sweaty." Cora wrinkled her nose as she said it. "Anyway, we've got birds and wind here, in case you haven't noticed."

"It's not the same," Kal tried to explain. "Out in the forest, all the background stuff goes away. Lawn mowers, cars, everyday stuff. We won't even get cell service. It's going to be sweet."

"Ugh. That'd drive me crazy."

"Short drive." Kal couldn't help herself.

"Ha ha. So, how do you even hike? How do you stay on the path? Don't you trip on rocks and fall on your face and smack into trees and stuff?"

"Yeah, I fall. But not as much as I used to. I use trekking poles and Dad and I have this method where he walks in front and I follow the sound of him. I hear his boots and his poles and he wears nylon pants and they make noise so it's easy to track him. And if there's something in the way he just calls out *Rock in the path, left!* or *Tree roots to the right!* and if there's anything really hairy he just takes my hand and guides me through."

"But you're going into the *wilderness,*" Cora emphasized. "Aren't you freaked out by cougars and bears? You should be."

Kal shrugged. "We're fine. Dad knows all about that stuff. He used to work for the Forest Service."

"Sorry, he doesn't sound that reliable. I mean, he left you and your mom and took off for like what, Iraq?"

Kal flinched. She mostly could take Cora's dumb remarks but not when it came to her dad. She knew exactly where Cora's big mouth was and she dearly wanted to punch it. But she tamped down the urge and replied, "He didn't leave us, really. He and Mom got divorced a while ago and last year he got this big job—it was in the Emirates, by the way, not Iraq—and he went over there and made a lot of money. I mean a lot. And now he's back and he's going to buy a house so he can be nearby and next week we're going on an adventure."

"Sounds flaky. Who goes to a stupid place like the Emirates? Is that even a real country? Don't they have a lot of terrorists there?"

Only the last sidewalk intersection kept Kal from really losing her cool. Thankfully, this was where they parted ways. Kal smiled and readjusted her backpack. "Later," was all she said, and headed off toward her house.

"Hey!" Cora called after her. "Take some pictures. Well, I mean, have your dad take pictures!"

Eleven-year-old Kal hardly needed her cane on this block—she only used it in case somebody had left something on the sidewalk. She knew every crack and bump on the way to her house, every driveway intersection, all the places where tree roots had lifted the concrete. She knew just when to swerve to her left to avoid the Pomquests' overhanging maple tree branches and she knew exactly how long it would take the Olsens' labradoodle to come bounding up to the fence to greet her. Like, four seconds. *One-a-thousand, two, three, four* and sure enough she could hear the big dog loping through the grass.

"Hi Addie," said Kal, putting her hand down to feel the dog's wet nose sticking between the fence slats and to get a sloppy kiss against her palm. "Good girl!"

At her own house she turned in and followed the curving brick path to their front door. Years ago she had helped her father lay the bricks, as much as a five-year-old blind girl could help. She conjured the feel of the rough edges of the pavers on her small fingers, handing her dad brick after brick, the dusky smell of stone and wet sand, the hot summer sun on her head and back. She missed having her father here at the house. Divorce was stupid, and certain people should just keep their mouths shut about it all.

She shook her head to clear the feeling. Things were different now. Her dad was back from the Middle East, so that was great. And soon the two of them would be going on a wilderness adventure, which would be awesome. And who knew what the future might bring?

She hopped up the three concrete steps to the front door. The path and stairs would never have any stray objects on them—a folded up shopper newspaper or a package from Amazon—because her mother was totally anal about that kind of stuff and would never allow it. The front door gave a jingle as it opened. Kal had hung bear bells on the latch months ago when her dad had first brought up the idea of a hike in the Kalmiopsis Wilderness. They were good luck charms, and their jingle was a reminder of what was ahead.

Inside she could hear her mother, Joss, talking on the phone. From her mom's stiff tone, she knew immediately her dad was on the line. She dropped her backpack and headed into the kitchen.

"Here she is," her mother said to the phone and then to Kal: "It's your father."

Kal followed her mom's voice and took the phone. "Hi Dad!"

"Hi kiddo, what are you up to?"

"I just got home from dance class."

"Ah. They teaching you to jitterbug?"

"No! It's ballet. First position, promenade, fourth position *en avant*. Don't you know anything?"

"I know I don't know much about ballet. You going to teach me?"

"When are you coming over?"

"I'll be there at the end of the week. I've got an apartment in Grants Pass and I'm going to be looking for a house."

"Yay! And we're still going next week, right?"

"Yeah, sure. I'm getting all the gear together. You still have your backpack?"

"Yup."

"You sure you can handle twenty-five pounds all day?"

"No sweat."

"Look, I've been watching the weather, and they say there may be a chance of rain next week."

Kal's heart sank so fast and far that it thudded into her toes. "Oh shit!"

"Kallie!" warned Joss.

"Hey, we're fine. Doesn't look too bad. The worse that could happen is we have to hold off for a day or two."

Kal relaxed. "You sure?"

"I'm sure. Okay?"

"Okay."

"Put Mom back on, please."

Kal held out the phone. "Back to you."

Joss took the phone and said to Kal, "Go put your leotard in the wash."

Kal smiled and Chaines-turned down the hallway, exactly four turns to the laundry room where she put her outfit in the washing machine, another three turns to her bedroom door where she paused. Her room smelled faintly of evergreens and she knew her mother had put a fresh bouquet of cedar boughs on the small side table. Cedar was one of her favorites.

When Kal was out of earshot, Joss said, "Will, the closer this all gets, the more uncertain I get. I mean, the *wilderness*. Are you absolutely sure? Why don't you just go to a state park and hike around?"

On his end of the conversation Will Spencer shook his head. It would be just like his ex-wife to start throwing some last-minute shade. "Don't do this, Joss."

"Do what? Care about my child's life?"

"Look," he said, "we're going to be fine. Like I've said a million times, we're only going in a few miles past the road. We're on the trail or close to it. I'll make a map of our exact location and leave it with you. C'mon, you know it's something Kal's been wanting to do for a couple years now. She's eleven and strong and smart. We know how to hike together. Nothing bad is going to happen."

"Jesus, Will. What if you fall off a cliff and she's out there alone?"

"Nice thought. But come on, Joss, I'm not going to fall off a fricking cliff. You need to take the paranoia down a notch. We're going to be fine."

"You swear you got that emergency locator thing?"

"I do. I'm bringing it with me."

Joss sighed. "Damn you."

THAT NIGHT Kal got into bed with her iPad. "Hey Siri," she said, "play *Wilderness Survival*, chapter sixteen."

The device dutifully responded, *Playing the audiobook Wilderness Survival, by A.J. Cochran. Chapter sixteen.* The narrator came on, a warm, grandfatherly voice that began:

Chapter Sixteen, close encounters with wildlife. [pause] Perhaps no other animal in the North American wilderness is more rightly feared than the American mountain lion, also known as the cougar, Latin name Puma concolor. A fierce and silent predator, the mountain lion is a solitary animal, establishing a jealously guarded personal territory of up to fifty square miles. It is selective in its prey, preferring deer and other medium-sized mammals, although mountain lions have been known to kill and eat rabbits, foxes, pet dogs, cows, horses and even porcupines.

A mountain lion relies on keen eyesight and sense of hearing to detect prey and, once a potential meal has been identified, the big cat will silently stalk its quarry, slowly gaining ground and waiting for the opportune moment to launch a lightning-fast attack. When it strikes, usually from behind, it wraps its front paws around its victim with an inescapable hold, then proceeds to eviscerate the prey with its back claws while seeking a swift execution by biting the prey's neck or crushing its skull in the lion's powerful jaws.

Although attacks on humans are extremely rare, it's essential to know what to do if you should ever encounter one of these...

"Kal, time for bed." Her mother was in the doorway.
"Siri, pause book. Mom, just let me finish this chapter!"
Pausing the audiobook, Wilderness Survival *by A.J. Cochran.*
"How long is the chapter?"
"Maybe another ten minutes."
"Okay, then get to sleep."
"I will, promise. Siri, resume book."
Resuming the audiobook, Wilderness Survival *by A.J. Cochran.*

When the chapter had finished, Kal turned off her iPad and slid it into its familiar spot on the small table next to her bed. She reached down for the power cable and plugged into the power port. Her windows were open and the cooling evening air floated in. She heard crickets strumming and the frogs trilling from down at the Murphys' backyard pond. The leaves of their big ash rustled in the mild breeze.

Two houses away Addie the labradoodle barked with her distinctive *r-r-rolff!* and set off a chain of neighborhood dogs yipping and yapping in response. Perhaps Addie had smelled a cougar that had slunk down from the hills and now wound its way quietly through the backyards. Kal knew that in years past mountain lions had been sighted several times inside the city limits. She could almost detect the soft, deliberate footfalls of the big cat outside her window. Massive shoulders flexed, ears scanning, thick paws quietly pressing the lawn. It would hear her breathing, small and helpless, despite her attempts to keep each breath as shallow and noiseless as possible. It would stop, consider the angle to her bedroom window, whether to jump inside, seize her and leap back out. But it wouldn't attack; couldn't attack. Because her father had come home, and together with her mother, they now formed an impenetrable shield around her. Any intruder, any threat, would slink off into the beyond. She was completely safe.

Tuesday, June 9
Rogue Rappeller Crew base
Grants Pass, Oregon

ON TUESDAY morning Craig Conner busted out a window from inside the tree cooler.

The tree cooler was a barn-like structure that stood near the helicopter pad. In fire season the tree cooler housed rappelling gear and in winter it became a cold-storage nursery for thousands of conifer seedlings used for reforestation projects. The rappellers had added a makeshift weight room at one side, furnishing it with six strength machines, three pull-up bars, jump ropes, exercise bands, and barbells and free weights of all sizes. An hour of PC—physical conditioning—was a daily requirement for every one of the twenty-two crew members stationed at the base.

At the time of the mishap, six men were in the tree cooler weight room, hanging out with towels around their necks and grins on their faces, watching Conner do an impression of a Swedish Olympic discus thrower. Conner had a wiry build and he did the impression in shorts and without a shirt and his gangly body wasn't close to the physique a real discus athlete would have, which was funny all by itself. He did the whole bit, winding up and then spinning around, his arms and legs flailing, all the while making an enormous guttural roar, a ten-pound plate in his hand as a prop. At the end of each pantomime, balanced unsteadily on one foot, he'd bellow *Vass a tass! Sven Anderson! Vass a mahn!* to appreciative laughs from the guys in the room. It was somehow inevitable that after several *tasses* the plate slipped out of Conner's hand and—spinning flat and hard and on a rising trajectory—sailed across the room and out a side window, punctuating its exit with an explosion of glass. There was a brief moment of stunned silence, then everyone except Conner burst out laughing. The really funny thing was that Conner had actually made a respectable discus toss.

Conner yelped, "Shit!" and ran outside to make sure he hadn't killed anybody as guys called, *Way to go, dumb-ass!* and *Nice toss, Sven!*

As he came sprinting around the corner of the tree cooler Conner found Lucas Bowden already at the crime scene, standing underneath the broken window with his hands on his hips. He was looking down at scatterings of glittering glass. The plate had missed him by a good twenty yards, but he was clearly disturbed. Without looking up Bowden said, "What happened?"

So Conner explained about his Swedish discus thrower parody and how because it was hot his hand must have gotten sweaty and the plate slipped and it was a stupid accident. Conner shook his head and said *Sorry about that* figuring the new guy would see it as dumb but funny.

Bowden scowled. "Where's the plate?"

Conner looked around and spotted it thirty yards away in the hands of crewmate Trey Ebbets. Ebbets was turning the plate over in his hands and squinting at it like it had fallen from Mars. He walked over to where Bowden and Conner were standing. "I heard the window break," said Ebbets, "and then I saw this thing rolling along the ground, coming right at me." He glanced over his shoulder. "Might have rolled into the next county if I hadn't grabbed it." He held the plate out. "This belong to one of you?"

Conner took the plate and explained the whole Swedish discus thrower thing again and when he was done Ebbets looked up at the broken window and grinned appreciatively and said, "Nice toss."

"Vass a tass," agreed Conner.

Bowden stood there unsmiling and set-jawed. He said

to Conner, "Clean up the glass. Make sure you get it all."

Conner shrugged. "Sure, yeah. Of course."

"And don't play around with the equipment anymore, right?"

Conner and Ebbets exchanged a look. "Look man," said Ebbets. "He was just horsing around a little. Lettin' off steam."

Bowden's upper cheeks twitched under a sheen of perspiration. He pointed a finger at Conner. "Don't be a fuckup."

"Hey now," Ebbets took an intervening step toward Bowden. Bowden might have been four inches taller and twenty pounds heavier, but Ebbets was the team's top sawyer and was in no way intimidated. Swinging thirty-five-pound chainsaws all day without a break will do that. "It's just an accident. He'll clean it up."

"Yeah, sure," agreed Conner, who'd gone stiff from Bowden's reprimand and held the plate in front of himself with both hands like a shield.

Bowden gave Ebbets a long, hard look. "Everybody leads by example. Everybody." Then he turned and walked away.

Conner and Ebbets stared after the man until Bowden had disappeared into the headquarters. "Is it me," said Conner, "or is this guy Bowden wound kind of tight?"

"Yeah," said Ebbets, shaking his head. "Some guys are frustrated IC wanna-bes."

From that day on everyone at the base called Craig Conner *Sven*. But they were less sure about what to call Lucas Bowden.

INCIDENT 395

FROM THE AUDIOBOOK, "Our Awesome National Forests," by Steven A. Harbaugh:

Although not as large as most of the western National Forests, Oregon's 628,000-acre Rogue River-Siskiyou National Forest includes more than 564,000 acres of designated roadless wilderness and some of the most rugged, remote lands in the Pacific Northwest. The Rogue River-Siskiyou National Forest is composed of two smaller National Forests that in 2004 were combined under a single jurisdiction in order to simplify management and save administrative costs. These two National Forest areas straddle the small towns and private lands of the Interstate 5 corridor in southern Oregon. The Rogue River National Forest is to the east, where big Douglas-fir and sugar pines dominate the high elevations of the Cascade Mountains. To the west, the madrone, cedar and pine forests of the Siskiyou National Forest stretch almost to the Pacific Ocean. Tucked inside the Siskiyou National Forest, the 180,000-acre Kalmiopsis Wilderness hosts some of the rarest and most biodiverse flora and fauna in the lower forty-eight.

Wednesday, June 10
Rogue River-Siskiyou National Forest Headquarters
Medford

FIRE AND AVIATION Officer Ken Hudek picked up on the first ring. "Dispatch, this is Ken."

"Ken, it's Steve Papacek at the Weather Service."

Hudek nodded. He could guess what this was about. "Hey Steve."

"I wanted to give you the heads-up. That storm forming off the coast should be here Friday night. It's going to be significant. Sustained winds at twenty to twenty-five gusting to fifty all the way across the Siskiyous and into the Valley."

"Yeah, we've been watching."

"It's going to be a dry storm—not a lot of moisture—but plenty of lightning. It's red flag all the way. We're changing the 'watch' to a 'warning' for Friday and Saturday for Curry, Coos, Josephine, Jackson, and Douglas counties. I'll update at the agency briefing Monday."

"All right. Thanks for the heads-up."

Hudek rang off and put the bridge of his nose between his thumb and forefinger and began to rub. *Here we go.* The driest year on record. Ninety-one straight days without rain from January through March, only a scant half inch measurable since then. Snowpack in the mountains at an all-time low for this time of the year. Humidity cratered, fuels parched. Now add to that a dry storm with the potential to unleash hundreds of lightning ground strikes.

So far they'd been lucky—no major wildfires in any of the southern Oregon jurisdictions. But you couldn't bet on luck. The climate was whacked-out, drought and wildfires all over the country. In addition to burns in other parts of the Northwest, there were big wildfires in Minnesota, North

Carolina, New Mexico and Florida. Every agency was crying out for crews and equipment. Resources were tapped out. Hudek speed-dialed the Forest Supervisor.

FOR OLYMPIA OATES, being Supervisor of the Rogue River-Siskiyou National Forest was like parenting dissimilar siblings who were always trying your patience in their own particular ways. The Rogue River, with its big timber and towering mountains, was the wealthy offspring. Its rich natural resources brought revenue but also the drama and headaches of big lumber lobbyists, unhappy environmentalists, and the avarice of federal oversight. The Siskiyou was the wild child—untamed, unpredictable, flawed, sometimes dangerous and often broke. Able to charm its way with a devil-may-care magnetism. Each no less deserving than the other of her stewardship, devotion and affection.

She didn't consider herself as having career aspirations. Her rise to Supervisor seemed more like a steady unfolding that was always happening in front of her, pulling her with it. Unlike many agency managers, she didn't have an advanced college degree. She'd started out on a gritty path, signing on with a Bureau of Land Management hand crew in Billings. After a year of outhustling everyone she was made squad leader and eventually a task force manager. It was there that she learned how to negotiate with men who viewed female leadership as inherently suspect. She counseled herself that the bottom line was to perform well and make smart decisions. And if they called you *bitch* under their breath, respond with tight smile and remind them it's *Boss Bitch*.

After Billings she moved to Spokane, got a bottom-rung job with the USDA as a Forestry Technician—the glorified term for a grunt who checks the conditions of the vault toilets at public campgrounds. The low-pressure position let her squeeze in an undergraduate degree in Environmental Policy via the distance learning program at Purdue. After graduating, Oates got hired as an Assistant Fire Manager for the Six Rivers National Forest, and in two years was practically handed the job as Assistant Supervisor. Somewhere in there she and her husband had two sons.

When the Supervisor job for the Rogue River-Siskiyou came up, she applied at the urging of her husband, a crisis-management consultant who specialized in wildfire incidents. He was also a steelheader, and he was stoked on the idea of living close to the Rogue River and taking his sons fishing on a regular basis. She thought she'd pretty much tanked the job interview but, nope, they offered her the position and now—so many years later—she was one of only three female National Forest Supervisors in the country.

And right now there was a shitstorm on the horizon, and it was all hers.

Back in March, Oates had the foresight to request severity funding from the Geographical Area Coordination Center. There wasn't an active wildfire in the area to use as justification, but she'd made a good case: six straight years of extreme fire activity in southern Oregon; one-hundred-sixty-thousand acres of timberlands burned; two-hundred thirty-seven homes and buildings destroyed. Five lives lost—a sawyer crushed by a fire-weakened snag and a stubborn family in a mountain cabin who refused to evacuate and tried to stave off the inevitable with creek water pumped through a garden hose. Husband, wife, and two sons. The familial parallel was not lost to Oates.

Two city-wide evacuations in the last three years alone. Businesses in the valley had closed because of smoke; people were selling their houses and getting out. The communities weren't going to stand for any more big wildfires, and the Service couldn't take another public beating.

It was a good early move, hitting up the GACC before

fire season officially began, and they'd been allotted an above-budget quarter million dollars to beef up resources at all six of the forest's ranger districts. Now, with a storm bearing down and wildfires likely, she'd needed to let them know she was about to dip into the kitty.

She called Portland on her cell and was put through to the Station Manager, Bob Yates, a Forest Service lifer with a woodsmoke-tinged voice. Yates had started his career as a ground-pounder on a Boise crew and had worked his way up the ranks, and he knew what a Supervisor was up against.

"Bob," said Oates, "the situation down here is extreme. No humidity, fuels under five percent. And now we've got a red flag storm moving in—winds, lightning, not much rain."

"Yeah, we're keeping our eyes on it."

"Dude…" Oates began and instantly regretted saying *dude*. Must have picked it up from her teenage son and his friends. Nothing to do but plunge ahead: "I'm going to stage more resources at the districts ahead of this, so I'll be submitting request forms and getting the districts geared up."

There was a pause on the other end, as if the station manager was deep in thought. Then Yates said, "You know right now we've got major fires all over the country. We've got crews in California and Minnesota and the Dry Nines in Arkansas. Plus, the Elk Creek complex is almost into the Teton National Park and the Rocky Mountain GACC is bringing in engines from Canada. National is just about tapped out. There's not much available."

"You know we put in for severity. Four months ago."

Again, there was silence. Then Yates said, "There may be new guidelines on that."

"You mean they're going to cut the allocation?"

"They're trying to spread it out as best they can."

Oates swallowed a curse. "What's that mean for us?"

"I'd say you'll end up in the hundred fifty range. What

all are you after?"

"Another three engines at each of the five districts, any and all types, two hotshot crews, one in the Siskiyou, the other in Rogue River. Two more type one helicopters, same split, and an air crane. And I'd like to make sure we can get two more air tankers."

"That's a probable 'no' on tankers right now. I can ask NICC, but there's requests stacked up from out east. Helicopters, I think there's a couple type twos in Montana that're due to go green. I'll try like hell to grab those. Hotshots, they are just gone and gone. I can find you maybe five or six engines, maybe ten hand crews. With the aircraft and the engines until the end of the season I'd say you're close to your hundred and fifty K."

Oates nodded. The budget game was always give-and-take. Mostly give. "Well then..."

"Submit the forms. This is the government, you know. Nothing moves without a form. Ask for everything you want to start out. Then we'll get you what we can." There was a short pause, then Yates added, "Dude."

Okay, she deserved that. Good old Bob Yates. She'd have to find him at the next fire summit and shake his hand.

Oates stood and walked to the big, eight-foot-tall map that covered an entire wall in her modest federal office. The map included lands under the management of the Oregon Department of Forestry, the Bureau of Indian Affairs, the Bureau of Land Management, and the National Park Service at Crater Lake. The entire southwest fire district covered more than five million acres. She stared at the map as if she could divine how many wildfires would break out, and where they'd be located. What district, if any, was most susceptible? Which would need the most resources? She took a deep breath, then sat back down at her computer and began filling out request forms.

Saturday, June 13
Rogue River-Siskiyou National Forest Headquarters
Medford

FOREST SERVICE DISPATCH ordered fixed-wing reconnaissance flights at 0800 hours and again at 1500 for the Saturday and Sunday following the storm. FAO Hudek contacted each of the agencies and let them know the Forest Service was going to have aircraft up. The manager at the Oregon Department of Forestry said ODF would be launching a helicopter and suggested all the agencies touch base Saturday morning to analyze the lightning strike report and coordinate the search patterns.

The storm officially made landfall at 11 pm Friday night, turning the skies above the coastal towns of Bandon and Gold Beach into a riot of lightning and thunder. True to the forecast, rainfall was moderate as the storm hunkered eastward, and by the time it had crested the Coast Range it had lost much of its moisture but none of its ferocity. It was now a dry storm, with occasional rain pelting down in random bursts. Lighting cut through the clouds and stabbed into the forests and struck among the farms and towns of the Rogue Valley. High winds snapped limbs and downed power lines. Sirens called into the night. By four a.m. the storm had rolled into the high Cascades, finally exhausting its energy and petering out over the Klamath Basin.

The first morning light of Saturday appeared as muted pewter staining the bottoms of low clouds. By 6 a.m. the National Weather Service had recorded 437 ground strikes across southwestern Oregon.

At 0800 the fixed-wing recon plane was in the air and by 0900 had called in twelve smoke columns in Forest Service jurisdiction. Ten were described as small, single-tree fires and two noted as quarter- to half-acre in size. Winds were light and the danger of airborne embers spreading new fires was low, but the Weather Service had predicted winds to increase toward evening.

Each of the smaller fires and one of the larger burns were accessible to the district stations, and engines and crews were mobilized. The other of the larger fires was deep in the Kalmiopsis Wilderness. The remote location automatically made that fire a low priority—it wasn't endangering property or lives. Committing resources was a judgement call.

For Supervisor Oates, there was no doubt about the right call: attack. As her husband liked to say, *Small fires are easier to put out than bigger ones.*

She went to the wall map and plotted the Kalmiopsis location that recon had called in. She knew it well. It was an area that had been repeatedly scourged by wildfires, including the notorious Biscuit Fire—the inferno that decades ago had torched half a million acres.

It would have been logical to assume that the massive loss of fuels would subdue subsequent fires, but that proved not to be the case. Hundreds of thousands of big trees killed by the Biscuit Fire had fallen and rotted, creating a thick, fuel-rich forest floor. Over the years, other significant wildfires had gotten their start in the duff and scrubby underbrush that grew rapidly on the old burn scars. Fire science was beginning to acknowledge that regenerative growth, in the right conditions, burned hotter and faster than big stands of old growth timber. Currently, the madrone and manzanita and young conifers up in the Kalmiopsis area were bone dry. This year, given a little wind, even a small fire could bust out.

It was steep terrain with no direct road access and no trails—no easy way in or out. They'd get after this one from the air. She called dispatch and had them ready the rappel firefighting team stationed outside of Grants Pass.

Saturday, June 13
Roseburg, Oregon

"COME BACK to bed," said Mason, patting the sheets. "It's too fucking early."

"Nice try, bud," said Corby Jones, pulling a gray tee-shirt over her head. "Gotta get going. You know that." *God, she thought, he looks so good, with those wild blue eyes. How did I end up with a guy with eyes like those?*

"I'll be quick," Mason said, "promise."

Okay, tempting. The flesh was weak. Sometimes Mason could be like riding a Cadillac from here to LA; other times it was like ripping around the block on a fire engine. Actually, a tear around the block sounded pretty good, given that she hadn't slept much and was all hyped up. She looked at him and grinned. "I'm up for a rappel, I know it. There's going to be smokes."

"That smoke," drawled her blue-eyed boyfriend, "is from frictionous encounters with yours truly."

Oh Christ. "Anywho, I'm going to be there dirt-early and get geared up. It's going to be a hell of a day."

By 6 a.m. Corby was motoring south on I-5 as the morning sun flared across the ridgetops. It was sheer willpower to keep her old Jeep Grand Cherokee under seventy miles an hour. It was almost as if she wanted a fire to start. Okay, nothing outrageous, nothing beyond control. But damn! She was so ready. She'd finished the training protocol in eighteen months—a slight hitch in Supervisory Concepts notwithstanding—had two dozen live practice rappels, could do fourteen pull-ups and the mile in under six minutes and she could hump sixty pounds three miles over rough terrain in under forty-five minutes and Goddam, she was *Ready* with a capital R. She'd made the move from temp to full-time GS-

5 Senior Firefighter at the beginning of the season and she was itching for a live operation.

As she drove, Corby was getting hyped up, tapping her left foot to an arrhythmic beat that only she could hear. Dispatch probably had already sent fixed-wing reconnaissance to look for smokes and the reports were already being radioed in. What if Danny Cravell had gotten posted for the first load instead of her? Danny was only a Med Two but he'd been at the base for three years and she was still the untried rookie. Maybe the base manager, Matt Murphy, would just automatically post Danny first, which would be a travesty. But maybe Matt hadn't even finalized the up board yet. Maybe she could get there and plead her case. She inched the old Jeep up to seventy-four miles an hour. *Only nine miles an hour over the limit, officer. Anyway, you don't want to stop me. I'm a Rogue Rappeller on the way to put out a wildfire!*

Corby was the only female on the Rogue Rappellers Team. Twenty-one guys and her. Twenty-one of the nicest, sweetest, hunkiest men she could imagine. They were endearingly wooly clones of each other: medium height, ox-strong, short-cropped hair, lots of beards, clear-eyed behind their wraparound sport sunglasses, beat-up smudged and stained baseball caps with the Rappellers' logo. Totally fearless or, as they liked to say, too stupid to be afraid. She adapted the look herself: sport shades, her ponytail stuck out the back of a Rappellers baseball cap that she deliberately aged by stomping on it. How did she end up with someone like Mason when each and every one of her workmates was right up her alley? Was it all about the sex? Well, could be a lot worse.

Corby Jones was a local, born and raised in Roseburg. She was the second youngest in a family of seven kids—five older brothers and her, plus a sister, Kiki, the youngest of the brood by six years, known to the siblings as "the accident."

Her mother, Millicent Gray Owl Jones, was full-blooded Cow Creek Umpqua and a shuttle bus driver for Seven Feathers Casino in Canyonville. She ferried hopefuls from nearby hotels to the gambling tables and slots, then transported disappointed drunks and sometimes obnoxious winning drunks back to their hotels for a few hours of sobering before hauling them back to the casino for more of the same. Millicent was round plump-cheeked and wore her raven hair in a single long braid and when she drove the shuttle bus she wore bracelets and feather earrings and a vest beaded to look like a bone breastplate. She wore her tribal affiliations not because the casino was owned by the Umpqua Tribe of Indians and she felt obligated to play some kind of role, but simply because she was happiest walking in her Native truth. Occasionally inebriated white women would take a look at Millicent and refuse to ride in her bus, citing concerns about alcohol abuse and Indian drivers, to which Millicent would shrug and close the folding doors of the bus and drive on.

When Millicent died of cervical cancer at the age of forty-two, she left her seven children in the charge of her husband, Bruce Jones, a logging truck driver for Boise Cascade. Jones worked hard but was given to periodic absences, sometimes disappearing for days before returning to their small, rural house on the outskirts of Roseburg where he would sit on the couch drinking Red Hook and playing video games. His peregrinating-and-sedentary lifestyle held fascination for the brothers, who'd gather around the small video monitor and cheer and fetch beers for their dad and jockey each other for the right to continue play when their father would get up to take a leak. Every one of the children except Kiki had their mother's glossy black hair.

The family dynamic made Corby de facto mother to all. She made toaster waffle breakfasts and mended ripped seats of jeans and tried to encourage homework and, although school rarely made the family's top priority list, there was a semblance of order and normality to the drift of their days.

In summer she organized rides to the annual Southern Oregon Tribal Pow Wow on the South Umpqua River. The boys would balk on account of they weren't full-blooded anything and she would guilt them about how their mother would want them to have a connection to Native culture and the fact that half their blood was Umpqua and that was still a lot of blood. They caravanned with friends and other tribal members and when they got there Corby would take Kiki to make pine needle baskets while the boys scattered into the woods to throw rocks at the river and each other while the drums beat crazy-ass everywhere and dancers strolled around in full regalia. Eventually the Jones clan ended up at the salmon bake where rows of pink fillets were spread before open fires, the cooking sticks canted in the holes of concrete building blocks. Every year the boys swore they'd never go again but every year they went.

When she was eleven Corby learned that the small metal box attached to the siding near the side door controlled all the electricity in their house. The first time she opened the box and experimentally pulled down the big red switch at the top she could hear the boys moaning inside and then moving about as they wandered through the rooms, trying light switches and calling out items that no longer functioned. After fifteen minutes or so the older boy, Garth, came outside and saw Corby standing near the open service panel and he walked over and peered inside the panel and said, "You little dumb shit. Do you want to get electrocuted?" Then he flipped the switch back on and closed the panel door and said, *Dumb shit* once more and went back inside.

It didn't take Corby long to figure out that this could be a source of amusement. So one school-less day when their father was out hauling boles of Doug-fir to the mills in

Roseburg and the boys were engaged in an especially rowdy session of Grand Theft Auto, Corby put an old folding chair off to one side of the yard and had Kiki sit in it. "Watch this," said Corby, and she went to the service panel and opened it and pulled the main switch and immediately there were agonized howls from inside the house and in two shakes the side door flew open and out came a livid Garth.

"Dammit!" said Garth and he immediately went after Corby.

Corby, however, was ready for this eventuality and had a plan. She ran straight to the big Ponderosa pine that towered some one hundred and fifty feet above the backyard. Years ago they'd nailed boards in the side of the trunk as a ladder to reach the lower branches, but the paternally promised treehouse never materialized and the novelty of sitting in the tree quickly wore off. After a black bear sow and her cub started to use the pine as a hangout, their father had taken down the makeshift ladder boards to make it less inviting for local wildlife. He took down only the boards he could easily reach, leaving one last board about eight feet up. Corby knew that if you timed it right and had on your good sneakers you could run full bore at the tree and at the last instant plant your right foot about three feet high on the scraggly bark and use your momentum to vault up and catch the last remaining ladder rung. If you calculated correctly you could swing your whole body onto the lowest set of branches, and from there you were safe because none of the boys knew the trick that she'd practiced almost daily.

Corby hit the tree perfectly and grabbed the ladder board and in moments was sitting calmly in the lower branches, grinning down at Garth who tried in vain to grab onto the vestigial ladder, sputtering and saying *Dammit all to hell*—a favorite family epithet—about a million times.

"Yay!" yelled Kiki, clapping her hands.

When their father appeared two days later the boys explained the incident and the patriarch, standing in the kitchen in his trademark flannel shirt and Carhart jeans with red clip-on suspenders, holding an Oly that he dearly would have preferred to consume in lieu of offering parental wisdom, looked at his daughter and shook his head and said, *Dammit all to hell, Corby. Do you want to get electrocuted?* The next day he put a small padlock on the service panel box.

The lock was only a temporary setback. Corby was quick to discover that the key was conveniently stashed on top of the box where their father was sure he could find it. Corby bided her time, lulling the boys into thinking they'd solved their little sisterly problem. Then she took the key and opened the panel and pulled the switch.

This time all the boys came pouring out of the house like ants when you turn over a rock and expose a nest to the sun. Corby gave them a tempting half a beat to get started after her, then she sprinted to the pine and executed a perfect vault into the safety of the big tree's branches.

This time, however, the boys also had formulated a plan. They got an old stepladder from the back of the garage and carried it *en masse* to the base of the Ponderosa like a ragtag bunch of juvenile Medieval knights coming to storm the castle walls.

With the ladder in place the boys elected the second oldest, David, to climb up after their sister. David was on the high school wrestling team and although he was an anemic third-stringer, within the Jones family he had the reputation of being an athlete. What kind of punishment David was to administer to Corby was undetermined, but certainly the terror of the chase would be enough to frighten off any future electrical shenanigans.

"We're coming for you, shithead!" yelled Garth.

"Climb, Corby, climb!" screamed Kiki.

By the time David reached the lower tier of branches Corby was already a third of the way up the tree. Climbing was relatively easy in the big horizontal branches, but the higher she got the more challenging it was to squirm through an increasing number of smaller limbs. Her hands were accumulating sticky pitch and pieces of loose bark, and every so often she paused to rub her palms together and rid them of the pungent pitch.

For Corby, the excitement of the arboreal chase soon changed to a different kind of feeling, a sort of marvel at moving higher and higher, of finding her way through the maze of branches, of making the right decisions—hand here, foot there—that were taking her upward. She was fifty feet off the ground, then seventy-five, then more than one hundred. It was way higher than she'd ever climbed, a dreamy place, so far up in the lofty reaches. Where the branches opened and offered views, she could see down the entire length of their street and the tops of the neighbor's roofs and out to the far hills and the dark blue ridges of mountains beyond.

As she neared the very crown she paused. A breeze was making her perch sway and slowly rotate in a wide circle. The wind whispered through the needles. She was so high up that birds flew below her. Far off in the distant sky a helicopter moved above the ridgetops and from her perch the aircraft seemed to be at her eye level. The sound of the thrumming rotors appeared and vanished and then came again.

Her brother was nowhere near. She looked down and realized David had stopped climbing. Now his voice came floating up, "Help, I'm stuck!"

"Did you get her?" the boys called from below, oblivious to David's plea. "Fucking punch her in the stomach!"

"I'm stuck!" repeated David, a tinge of panic edging his voice.

Dammit all to hell, thought Corby. She climbed down and found her brother sitting on a narrow branch, holding onto the main trunk with both hands, his palms and fingers coated with bits of bark, his legs dangling free. She shook her head. "How did you get over there?"

"I don't know," he said sorrowfully.

"Can you stand on that branch?"

"I guess."

"Get up and then climb up to that branch there and come down over this way."

With careful coaching Corby guided her older sibling down and followed him to the ground where the other boys were waiting.

"Corby you little shithead you ruined the game don't ya know?"

Kiki came running up and threw her arms around Corby's waist to form a protective shield. "Leave her alone!"

"Yeah," said David, looking down at his shoes, "let's just leave her alone. She's just our dumb-shit sister."

The next time Bruce Jones appeared at home Corby intercepted her father as he made for the refrigerator. She planted herself in front of him and said, "I know what I want to be when I grow up."

"Oh yeah?"

"Don't they have people who jump out of helicopters to fight fires?"

Her dad wrinkled his nose and opened the refrigerator door. "Um, sure. Where the hell's all the Red Hooks?"

"Do they let girls do that?"

Resigned to an Oly, Jones closed the door and twisted off the top. "They got girls doing just about every damn thing these days. They got female truck drivers if you can believe that." He took a swig and a bit of beer ran its sparkling course down his beard. "Why the hell do you want to jump out of helicopters?"

"I'd like it," she said, putting her fists on her hips, "saving trees and being way up high."

"As long as I don't have to pay for nothing," said Bruce Jones, "it's fine with me."

CREW CAPTAIN Matt Murphy arrived at the rappellers' base early. The helicopter pilot, Lance Fernandez, was already inside the low-slung headquarters building and was scanning the weather report on one of the computers. The radio was tuned to the dispatch and there was light chatter going on between dispatch and the fixed-wing pilot and the spotter who were getting ready to take off from the municipal airport. Murphy knew the rest of the crew would be in shortly. The official starting time was eight, but after a lightning storm everyone came by seven. You didn't have to tell them to do it.

"Hey Lance."

"Hey Matt. Looks like we might get some action today." Fernandez was definitely the most reliable pilot they'd had in the past eight years. He was on contract to the Forest Service from a helicopter outfit in South Carolina that also supplied a fuel truck, a mechanic, and a yellow-and-white Bell 205 helicopter. The mechanic was always a new guy from year to year, but Fernandez had been assigned to the Rogue Rappellers for three years in a row. Murphy knew they were lucky to have him again. The guy was good.

"Yup. Quite a show last night. We had a strike near to the house that just about made the cat shit her tail off. Probably still under the bed." He pointed his chin at Fernandez' screen. "Have you seen a ground-strike count?"

"Looks like about four hundred on the Siskiyou side, a hundred in the Rogue. Maybe another hundred across BLM and in the Valley."

Murphy nodded. "I'm going to check the up board."

Murphy left the headquarters and headed for the tree cooler. He was halfway across the compound when a twenty-year-old Jeep Grand Cherokee came barreling through the entryway. Ignoring the small staff parking lot, the Jeep skidded to a halt at an awkward angle by the headquarters entryway. For a moment the SUV was shrouded in a cloud of summery dust, then Corby Jones spilled out.

"Matt! Hey Matt!" she called.

Murphy stopped and turned around slowly, shaking his head. "Corby," he drawled. "You can't park there."

"Matt," she said, not bothering to shut the Jeep's door, hustling up to get in his face. "Just making sure I'm still on first load. You're not headed to the board to switch out anybody, right? I'm here early, I should get a head start and get my stuff in the ready locker, right? I mean, there's going to be smokes today and I'm the second most-experienced woofer you've got."

"We only got two."

"My point exactly. So, I'm first load, right?"

"Yeah, you know you're on. Go put your Jeep in the lot like a normal person and get your stuff in a bug-out locker."

"All right," she grinned. "Hot damn." Her woofer training was absolutely going to pay off. With only two certified wilderness first responders on the crew, she was definitely going to get her share of ops this summer.

By 7:30 all the on-duty rappelers had arrived and were in the weight room working out or jogging around the base in the cool morning air. At 8:30 Murphy called everyone together for an early roll call and a weather briefing. He emphasized the hot temps and winds light out of the southeast. Low humidity and the lack of rain from the storm would keep the energy potential off the charts. Five hundred ground strikes meant there were going to be fires. Now, they just had to wait for dispatch to call in the locations. The first four-person team on the up board had stashed their gear in the ready lockers. Fernandez was out on the pad with the mechanic going through pre-flight. The distant mountains had begun to waver with the growing heat of the day.

THE RECONNAISSANCE plane was over the Siskiyou National Forest, flying west along the Oregon-California border. The spotter had uploaded the latest Weather Service data including a ground strike map and was directing the search toward areas of high probability. It wasn't long before sightings were being called in. *Smoke column in the southwest portion of the Wild Rivers Ranger District, small narrow column, headed straight up with a slight turnout moving north.* Coordinates followed. Another pair of smokes along the California border. Two more six miles north.

Dispatch notified the Forest Service districts but everyone, including the rappellers, had been eavesdropping on the communications anyway, and the districts closest to the fires were already mapping out road access and attack scenarios and crews were getting the engines ready to mobilize.

At the rappelling base the first load crew split up, two to check lines and hardware in the helicopter, and two to work up a load manifest. When the manifest was complete pilot Lance Fernandez calculated maximum flight elevation and carrying capacity based on temperature, humidity, and wind speed. Then everyone waited and made small talk while watching various weather service maps and listening to recon chat with dispatch. Around nine a.m. recon called in coordinates for a smoke in the Kalmiopsis Wilderness. They could hear dispatch in Medford questioning size, accessibility, and potential. The pilot remarked, *It's right on the edge of a healthy stand of trees.*

Fifteen minutes later Forest Service dispatch called Matt

Murphy on his cell phone and let him know a Tactical Air Response Order was on the way and that they were to attack the burn in the Kalmiopsis.

"Roger that," said Murphy. He'd trekked out of the Kalmiopsis before. Hornets, poison oak and steep terrain came to mind.

Murphy and the pilot went to the dispatch room where a six-foot-tall map of the area hung on a wall. They plotted the fire coordinates and Murphy stuck a big red pin at the location and noted the closest relay tower for radio communications. Fernandez did a mental calculation for flight time and fuel, then went out to ready the helicopter. Murphy stared at the pin. Moments later the fax chattered out the TARO with coordinates, channel frequencies, and a brief description of conditions. On the form the fire had been designated as "Incident 344."

LOU PEDERSEN had brought an heirloom to the rappelling base—a three-and-a-half-foot-long Viking-style horn that he'd inherited from a Danish uncle. This massive instrument was hung on a peg in the outdoor porch area, and Lou Pedersen was the only one who could get a sound out of it. The other crew members had tried, but the most they managed were a couple of flatulent toots. Pedersen, however, could make the old horn give a great mournful bellow that rattled the windows and certainly could be heard miles away. It was because, said Pedersen, only people of Danish descent could make the proper embouchure. It was a genetic thing.

"So," mused Tom Su, "you gotta be Danish to sound like a constipated cow?"

It was Lou Pedersen's self-appointed, unofficial duty to sound the big horn whenever a mission got called in. That fit right in with his designation as the crew's Chief of Party, which meant making sure everyone got going in the right directions whenever an operation was activated.

When dispatch called the base to give them official authorization for the operation in the Kalmiopsis Wilderness, Pedersen overheard the call. He immediately went outside and got the horn down from its perch, rested the bell on the small table set out for the purpose, puckered up and, with inherent Danish virtuosity, produced a tremendous braying that resounded through the compound. When the horn echoes subsided Matt Murphy, who was a stickler for more official protocol, got on the broadcast PA and announced, "First load!"

No one needed the PA announcement. At the sound of the horn, Corby and the other three rappellers listed on the up board headed for the tree cooler to get into their gear. Pedersen, Matt Murphy and the pilot Lance Fernandez met in the map room. They plotted coordinates and studied the topo map of the area as the Tactical Air Response Order came in by fax.

"Steep," commented Murphy. He poked the map with a forefinger. "Here's a repeater."

"About thirty-eight-hundred feet. Light winds," noted Fernandez.

"Looks like FS 405 is the closest road," added Murphy. "Going to be a long hike out." He turned to the pilot. "Do a load calc for four and thirty-five."

Fernandez was a step ahead, already having calculated load capacity for a variety of temperatures and altitudes. "At four thousand feet and thirty-five degrees C, we're good for a full load. All the AI boxes. But we can't take the bucket if it gets any hotter."

"Leave the bucket," said Murphy. "We're fifteen minutes out, we can come back for it. Anybody see anything to worry about?"

"Tell 'em to bring their bug spray," said Pedersen. That

got a chuckle from Murphy. The last time they had humped out of the Kalmiopsis one of the sawyers, Chuck Hammond, had stumbled onto a nest of yellow jackets. With his hands full of gear and a chain saw, Hammond couldn't protect himself. Everyone was a bit loopy from a tough, six-day op and all they could do was watch with morbid fascination as Hammond yelped and danced. It didn't help poor Hammond when they all started laughing.

The first load crew was standing near the landing pad with their yellow Nomex shirts and red belly bags and were buddied up doing safety checks. Fingers tugged at straps and snaps and fittings, front and back. Nobody cracked jokes during safety checks—no distractions. When they were finalized they exchanged thumbs up and walked to the helicopter.

Corby Jones had definitely scored the A-team for her first live operation. She was buddied with the team IC, John Deluth, a guy with a rep for being a steady and unflappable squad leader. Deluth and Jones would be first to rappel, one from each side of the helicopter. They'd be followed by the second stick—Trey Ebbets and weight-room legend Tom Su. Murphy preferred that the first load include somebody capable of carrying an injured teammate to safety, and Tom Su was a plank-holding, squat-thrusting beast. Murphy designated himself as spotter—he'd stay in the aircraft and oversee the rappel.

Murphy joined the team wearing the spotter's harness and John Deluth gave him a top-to-bottom safety check and a thumbs up. Everyone climbed aboard. The four rappelers sat on a backwards-facing bench, looking at the spotter. The first team of John Deluth and Corby Jones occupied the outer seats, the second team sat inboard. Matt Murphy climbed inside and did a final check—restraints, gear, rigging. He clipped himself into the spotter's tether ring and Ebbets confirmed the connection was good with a nod and a thumbs-up held right in front of Murphy's face. The initial attack boxes with tools, ropes, chainsaws, and food for seventy-two hours were stashed in the hold. Everyone plugged in their headsets so they could hear each other over the whine of the engines.

Murphy reached out and closed the doors on each side of the aircraft. "Doors are closed," Murphy spoke to the pilot Fernandez via his headset. "We've got four and one souls back here, all clipped in and thumbs up. I'm clipped in. Gear is good. We are leaving the bucket."

"Four and one good to go," Fernandez repeated. "Spotter clipped in. Gear is stashed and the bucket stays behind. I've got the coordinates plotted, looks like seventeen minutes." The copter quivered as the turbines spooled up and the big blades started to swing. The air inside the cabin began to thrum.

"Roger that."

The helicopter gave a hard shudder, lifted, paused a moment, tilted slightly to catch forward thrust and headed for the mountain peaks.

Corby had done dozens of practice drops, but heading out for her first live mission was a different kind of thrill altogether. Did the other rappellers feel it, or were they so used to it that an active fire was just another day at the office?

Fernandez came on the headsets talking with dispatch. "Rogue dispatch, this is eight hotel x-ray, we're off and en route to incident three four four. Six souls on board. Two hours twenty minutes of fuel and looking at a seventeen-minute flight. Over."

"Roger that, eight hotel x-ray," dispatch responded, "you just turned green and you're positive AFF." Dispatch was now monitoring the flight via a satellite linked to an automated flight-following computer.

Murphy turned to the four rappelers who sat facing him.

"All right, we're heading west into the Kalmiopsis, we got what looks like a half-acre burn. There're whole lot of snags and a whole lot of steep."

Corby nodded. She'd heard the wilderness could be a bitch. Unsure footing, poison oak, hornets, lots of dangerous snags from previous fires. *Bring it on.*

Murphy brought up a topo map on his iPad and held the screen so the team could see. "Here's the burn. Ridgeline here, the drainage runs all the way to the Illinois River. Grade is variable to fifty degrees with loose scree. Light winds so we shouldn't have spots but keep your eyes open. Closest road is over here. Five miles. That's our exit. We'll follow this ridge down and then over."

The four rappelers all nodded. There was not much else to say until they got to the fire and could assess it from the air. The team eased back on the bench seat.

They flew northwest across miles of national forest, waves of deep green trees swept along the bottom edge of the window, flowing past and then disappearing from view. All those trees. The serrated horizon etched against a pale blue sky.

"Six minutes," Fernandez came over the headsets.

Corby took deep breaths. A seventeen-minute flight was an *effing eternity.*

Ebbets nudged her with an elbow. "Ready, rook?" He had his visor up and she could see his grinning eyes. Ebbets was always on her case, calling her "rook" every time he got. She had to smile. He looked so happy, like a puppy that had just been let loose to romp around in a big backyard. His question came over the headset, meaning they all had heard it, and now the crew was looking at her and every one of them had a shit-eating grin.

She gave a double thumbs-up, and the whole crew replied with double thumbs up, and she knew she had stepped onto some new level. This was real. *One-hundred percent focused.*

Ebbets winked at her. "This never gets old," he said. "Never."

The chopper slowed. "Coming up on left side," said Fernandez. "Less than forty and one minute."

"One minute and less than forty," repeated Murphy. "I'm opening the left-side door." He unlatched the door and slid it back. Even with all the missions he'd been on, both as a rappeler and spotter, there was always that rush as the side of the aircraft gaped open, that vertigo sensation, and Murphy reflexively eased forward to feel the reassuring tug of his spotter's harness holding him back.

The Kalmiopsis Wilderness sprawled, vast, uninhabited, scarred and scabbed from the ravages of historic fires. Whole sweeps of land were skeletal forests of standing dead trees, their trunks charred black or, having lost their bark years ago, bleached ghost white. But the apocalyptic past was already being renewed—the snags poked up out of a green layer of regenerating growth that was thick with manzanita and buck brush and young conifers. *Nature won't give up*, Murphy thought, and then, *Remember: manzanita burns hot.* The land heaved around with rocky ridges and abrupt valleys and here and there were giant swaths of pristine, healthy trees—massive pines and spruce and cedar that fires of the past had by chance skirted.

"Left-side door open," announced Murphy. "Reset the master caution."

"Left-side door open, master caution is reset," responded the pilot.

The burn appeared, five thin columns of smoke snaking out of the land like the fingers of a ghostly hand. It was burning in one of the intact stands of old trees where the crowns of unburned conifers formed a mass of green spires.

"Let's take a tour," said Fernandez, and he guided the

helicopter along the edge of the burn so Murphy could check out the terrain from his doorway perch. Harnessed into their seats, the rest of the team craned their necks to look out. The fire had stretched vertically, and there were active flames on the upper edges and along the left flank.

"What's everybody think?" asked Murphy.

"Rollouts," said Corby, pointing at the elongated pattern of individual smokes that indicated burning debris had tumbled down the slope, starting new fires along the way. Everything she'd learned in training was sizzling vivid in her head. "Looks like the head's up top. Flanks are stable."

"You sure about that, rook?" Ebbets had put his visor down and was looking past Corby out the door, but he was still grinning.

"That's what I see, old timer."

"Depending on where we camp, looks like we can go in from either side," said Tom Su. "The ridge is pretty rocky, it'll probably hold a control. We set anchor just off the ridge, work down the left flank and size it up from there."

Ebbets said, "There's some hazard trees along the lower edge. We can approach like Corby says, the team goes up and starts a line. I'll go down and take down the hazards, stop any more rollouts. Then I'll head up."

Murphy nodded. "Take Tom with you to keep an eye out." Everyone nodded. The crew was good, the rookie was ready. "Everyone okay?" he asked and got thumbs up all around.

"All right, we've got light winds from the south, so we'll approach from the left flank. Let's check out a drop zone. Looks like there's one about a quarter mile south. We can spike on the ridge and from there looks like a pretty clear shot to the exit. Lance, you catch that?"

"Copy that," responded the pilot, "heading one quarter mile south." The helicopter banked right into a U-turn and headed for the opening that Murphy had spotted.

It was a good zone, free of trees for a fifty-yard circumference, and the nearby terrain flattened enough to set up their overnight camp. Close enough to the fire but far enough away for safety. Squatting in the open doorway, Murphy guided the pilot over the center of the zone.

"Bring it to two hundred feet," said Murphy.

"Lowering to two hundred feet." The aircraft settled.

"Let's come left thirty feet." Murphy glanced toward the rear of the helicopter to make sure the rotor was clear of treetops. "Tiller is clear."

"Left thirty feet."

"Left three, two, one and hold," said Murphy, giving the pilot a verbal cadence to help judge the distance.

"And hold."

"How's your power?"

"Power is good. Winds are good."

"All right, I'm getting ready to drop ropes."

"Standby on ropes," said Fernandez, "I'm seeing a gust come through the smoke."

"Standing by on ropes," Murphy responded as the aircraft bounced and rocked slightly. He peered out the doorway. "Let's center up again. Forward twenty feet and hold."

"Forward twenty feet and hold," replied Fernandez.

"Down fifteen and hold."

"Down fifteen and hold."

"Three, two, one."

The nuances went on for another two minutes. Corby could feel perspiration crawling down her back. It was probably ninety degrees already, and deep inside her Nomex shirt her heart was pumping. She took in slow, deep breaths through her nose.

"How's this for you?" Murphy asked the pilot.

"Power's good. Wind is good. Drop the ropes."

"Dropping the ropes." Murphy reached up and gave a tug on the rope connection even though he'd checked it four times already. Then from a cubby he pulled out the bright orange rope bag with the two-hundred-foot line. He tossed it overboard and leaned out to watch it unspool as it plummeted to the ground. "Left side rope is on the ground."

"Holding steady."

"Moving to the right-side rope."

With both ropes deployed Murphy said, "First team rappelers hooking up."

At last. From her seat Corby reached up and brought down one of two descender devices attached to the rope. She snapped the descender onto her harness and gave it a hard tug. At the other end of the bench the team IC John Deluth had done the same.

"All right, disconnect," said Murphy and the rappellers unplugged their headsets. From now on it would be hand signals. He came to Corby, gave the descender connection a close look, then pointed at her seat harness and gave her the hand signal for unbuckling. Then he pointed outboard toward the skid.

"Rappellers to the skids," Murphy said to the pilot.

"Rappellers to skids," acknowledged Fernandez.

Corby stood awkwardly, her thirty-pound BD bag with all her essentials—helmet, gloves, headlamp, fire shelter, space blanket, two quarts of water—had gotten wedged between her knees. It happened to everybody. During training, people getting hung up in their belly bags seemed funny. Now, not so much. *Stay cool, it's no problem.* She tugged the bag out with her free hand, then turned around so her backside was toward the opening. She held the descender in her left hand and her right hand gripped the line trailing below. She set her boots on the grip edge of the door and leaned back out of the helicopter to put tension on the rope. Her breathing slowed, her heart had stopped racing. She felt rock solid. Then she stepped down onto the skid and leaned way out, nearly horizontal, and she could smell the baking-pine scent of the forest in summer mixed with pungent woodsmoke. Straight above her the rotor blades cut a gray circle into the pale blue sky and then Murphy was looking down at her from the doorway of the helicopter and he stuck his arms out, palms down, and made a sweeping downward gesture and she squeezed the release lever and the rope played out and she rocked back nearly upside down and then swung free and she could see the IC John Deluth opposite her going down at the same rate as the ground reached up to meet them.

Saturday, June 13
Medford, Oregon

"OKAY, LOOKS GOOD," said Will, peering over the top of his iPhone. "No more storms and no precipitation for the next seven to ten days." He held up his cell so his ex-wife could see the screen, although from across the room all she could see was a tiny colored graph displaying God-knew-what information.

"Yah!" yelled Kal.

"Are you sure? Did you check the National Weather Service?"

"Mom!"

Will pointed at his phone. "This *is* the National Weather Service app. So yup, all clear. We're good for adventure!" He looked at his daughter who greeted this latest info with a clumsy pirouette precariously close to the coffee table followed by a dramatic collapse, hands clasped and poised over her bowed head.

"What am I?" she called out.

"A swan," said Joss.

"Jeez, Mom. Give Dad a chance."

"Good one!" said Will. "But I probably wouldn't have said *swan.*"

"What then?"

"Um, like maybe a praying mantis?"

"Ha ha. Nice try. *Swan* is correct," replied Kal, still head down, facing the floor, holding her pose for dramatic effect.

Joss eyed her ex-husband warily. She'd come to view his time in the Middle East as a convenient dereliction of parental duty. He could have found a job nearby. Portland. Or Seattle. At least he would have been around to occasionally be a father at a time in her life when their pre-teen girl certainly could have used one. Putting some distance between the exes after the rigors of divorce—she got that. But it had been too far and too long for their special girl.

And now? After all that time, who arrives like a caped hero, ready to scoop their daughter up on some goofy outback adventure? Enter the man who announced at the settlement hearings that his wife had the sexual warmth of a sack of dead mice. Exact words.

Okay, the Dubai offer had been too lucrative to pass up. Joss got that, too. A fourteen-month stint analyzing seabed stabilities around Dubai's aging tanker docks and he got paid more than he would have made in six, seven years with the Forest Service. Now the job was over and he'd returned to make up for lost time. A mixed blessing. She was glad for Kallie but was apprehensive about having Will back in their lives. Between her work-from-home job as a CPA and Kal's school and outside classes, Mother and daughter had forged a good rhythm. They stayed upbeat. Joss didn't want that to be upended.

But she couldn't deny the two of them the opportunity to go camping. Kallie was thrilled down to her toe shoes and to tell the truth, Joss figured a few days with the house all to herself would do a world of good, just listening to the sound of her own bells.

Joss was less sure about the idea of a wilderness adventure. Will and Kal had hiked various trails before—fairly gentle ones—with various amounts of success and various amounts of cuts and bruises. Kal proudly declared that she'd fallen a total of seven hundred times and was looking forward to seven oh one. Will had assured Joss that their hiking pace was slow and deliberate, that they'd developed a hiking synergy based on sounds and verbal cautions, and that the last time they'd hiked there had been no falls at all. Joss knew all that. But she still had reservations. Parental paranoia, thank you very much.

Theirs was a quest. Will and Kal were going to hike into this particular wilderness to search for the plant that gave the wilderness its name—Kalmiopsis—a rare little wildflower shrub unique to southern Oregon. Years ago before they were married Will and Joss had been part of a group doing a guided day hike into the Kalmiopsis. They'd come across sprays of the plant in full bloom, sprinkles of pink and red amidst stands of dead, charred timber, a painterly impression of hope. The image had always been part of their language, their early bonds, and they conspired to indelibly share that bond by naming their daughter Jane Kalmiopsis Spencer. Over time the middle name became too insistent to deny, it had so much resonance, and it slowly overtook the plainer *Jane* and eventually emerged into their day-to-day as *Kal*.

Everyone called her *Kal*. Friends, teachers, her grandparents. Some asked if *Kal* was short for *Caledonia* or *Kalista* and Kal would give a sly reply, like *Maybe it's Calamine?* so that the real name remained a shared secret, like a magic charm that would lose its power if spoken too often. It was an overly romanticized notion, sure, and Joss had twinges of regret about it. But a person only comes to understand over-romanticized notions in retrospect, right? Here, in fact, was Exhibit A: ex-hubby Will Spencer. The Indiana Jones of soil compaction. She should have married a hardware store owner instead of this starry-eyed geologist. She would have done well with a solid, basic guy who understood ceiling fans and degreasers. *Jane Kalmiopsis Spencer. What were they thinking?*

Kal's blindness had been a wild card in the stacked deck called Life. Stargardt disease, childhood macular degeneration. Joss probably knew more about the disease than anybody on Earth. A genetic abnormality, handed down from some distant great great grandparent. A defective PROM1 gene; a mutated ELOVL4; an accelerated formation of toxic vitamin A dimers in the retina, too much lipofuscin in retinal pigment RPE epithelial cells. There was no shortage of medical acronyms and explanations. Joss had spent countless hours online, searching professional ophthalmology journals for signs of a cure, a new miracle eye drop medicine, some off-the-radar eye doctor in Spain or Sri Lanka with a possible surgical cure. There was nothing. It was uncurable, untreatable piece-of-shit thing to happen to a child. To her child.

At first it wasn't total blindness. It was a progressive blurring of vision, loss of acuity and color perception, hypersensitivity to light. Her visual world reduced to vague blobs and patterns. Corrective lenses didn't help; surgery was not possible. Most people with Stargardt retained some vision, but Kal had gone almost completely blind by age five. One in ten thousand, they said. Nothing helped except her daughter's uncanny ability to accept and move forward. As if she had deliberately chosen to become a rarity as opposed to an abnormality. She picked up Braille and could read it in both French and English. She danced. She had a B-plus average. Her school had given her permission to wear sunglasses in class and the look had conferred upon her a special cool status that she loved. She'd gotten sunglasses with round lenses and insisted on wearing the most flamboyant scarves Joss could find and with her unruly, untamable hair she looked like a miniature Janis Joplin.

Will stood and said he had an appointment to look at a couple of houses for sale in Grants Pass and Joss ushered him to the front door and closed it slowly behind him. She stared at the little mound of gear that Kal and Will had assembled in the hallway—two dolphin-gray backpacks sat amid little hills of freeze-dried food, rain ponchos, maps, sleeping bags in stuff sacks, trekking poles, socks, water bottles, rolled-up foam matts, fire starters, compasses, bear bells and the canisters of bear spray that Joss had insisted they take. The excitement was palpable, and Joss felt a pang for being left out of an adventure with her daughter. Instead, she found herself being the cautious voice of reason, better known as *the wet blanket*.

She sighed. "Damn you Will Spencer."

Saturday, June 13–Monday, June 15
Kalmiopsis Wilderness / Rogue Rappellers Team base

IT WAS TEXTBOOK. The crew stayed two nights and most of three days and the plan went off pretty much as they'd sketched out in the helicopter. Tom Su and Trey Ebbets took the chainsaw down to the heel of the burn to work on hazard trees while Corby Jones and John Deluth made their way up to the head to start cutting a line in the hard ground. After a couple hours Su and Ebbets joined the line, cutting, sweeping and pulling brush. Dust rose out of the dried duff and crumbly mineral soil and swirled with the smoke and they put on dust masks. The fire was twenty yards away, moving slowly like a stalking animal, eyeing the humans who were trying to contain it. It crackled and snarled with flames three and four feet high, occasionally leaping up into manzanita and tanoak branches with showy bursts of sparks. Although the air movement was light and favorable, every now and then a breeze backtracked and rolled smoke into the crew and they had to pause until their watering eyes cleared.

In the afternoon Deluth radioed the base for another stick and the helicopter brought Mike Zelinski and Lucas Bowden. It was the first fire for Bowden as a Rogue Rappeller and his wide-eyed, maniacal pace seemed to infect everyone and the control lines grew rapidly. Murphy and Fernandez flew back to the base and rigged up the 275-gallon bucket and were able to make a couple of runs that first day, dousing the head and shoulders of the burn to keep it from creeping over the top of the ridge. By the late afternoon the rappelers had cut a line across the head and down the left flank and had begun work on the bottom. By nightfall two-thirds of the fire was boxed, including a defensive line between their spike camp and the burn.

At camp after the sun had gone down and the air started to cool they sat on the ground and ate canned tuna and peaches by the light of headlamps. Tom Su told a story about the time he was working a burn in northern California and a fire-weakened Douglas-fir "the size of a fucken 747" came down, missing him by a scant twenty feet and it was like a bomb going off inside his head and it wasn't until he'd made camp that night that he discovered he'd shit his pants. Everybody laughed and Su asked the new guy, Bowden, if he had any stories and Bowden just shook his head and the beam from his headlamp wagged back and forth and he said, "No, not really."

Off to the east they could see the remains of their fire as bits of orange winking in the dark.

An hour after sundown with a blush of pale light still clinging to the western horizon, they readied their beds. Corby took off her boots and laid on top of her sleeping bag in her clothes. She was too amped up to go to sleep and the little mattress pad was too hard and she stared up at the stars and the blue-black night and before she knew it John Deluth was shaking her gently and telling her to get up and a sliver of dawn was etching the ridgeline to the east.

They ate protein bars and gulped water and got moving while temps were still cool. Despite the steep ground they made good progress. The lines were holding and the lack of wind was keeping airborne embers from setting spot fires. The helicopter made six more drops and by the end of the second day John Deluth radioed that containment was good, the fire was well damped down and another stick wouldn't be needed. They'd check the area in the morning to make sure it was out and head for the exit point.

On the morning of the third day they ate a leisurely breakfast and went out to scrub the blackened burn area, getting down on hands and knees, no gloves, riffling through the soil with their bare fingers, searching for lingering hot spots. Everybody was streaked with ash and mud from the bucket drops. On the hike out they looked like a platoon of the apocalypse, coming down out of the wilderness with their sooty clothes and their faces smudged and Pulaskis in hand like primitive weapons. Ebbets was striding downhill with the big chainsaw, the flat of the blade resting on his shoulder and the weight of the engine behind countered by his gloved hand on the front of the blade.

Nearing the exit point they could see a big green Forest Service Chevy Suburban waiting for them by the side of the road. As the team made their way down the last stretch of mountainside Trey Ebbets came up to Corby and said, "You did good, rook."

Corby squinted at him. "You can't call me 'rookie' anymore."

Ebbets brought the smell of gasoline with him as they walked. The sawyer grinned and the soot on his face turned his smile all lopsided and goofy. "I just might always call you that. Rook. It kind suits you. Your personality."

"What's that mean?"

"You're all eager and get-up-and-go all the time."

"That a putdown? You're talkin' to a woman with a dangerous weapon in her hand." She held up the Pulaski and gave it a shake.

"Hell, we all kind of have it to some degree. The go juice." He gestured with his free hand at the crew.

"Yeah, you got some of that yourself, Ebbetts."

He nodded, pleased. "You think?"

"Yup. You get near a wildfire and you're like a puppy just had his kennel door opened up."

"Well then," he said, their boots crunching in rhythm through dry leaves and needles, "birds of a feather."

AT THE END of the shift Ebbets was waiting for her by her Jeep. "So," he said, looking down and tapping the tip of his boot in the gravel of the parking lot. "I was wondering if possibly we could, you know, like go out sometime."

Corby couldn't keep a smile from creeping up. Now this was a surprise. Trey Ebbetts was asking her out. Holy shit, will miracles never cease? Too bad she'd have to turn him down. Trey was a great guy and not bad looking and his apparent shyness about it all was completely adorable, but it wasn't in the cards. There was her boyfriend, Mason, back at the house. Nevertheless, she didn't get many flattering moments like this and she didn't want this one to end. Not just yet. So she said, "What do you mean, *go out?*"

"You know," he said, lifting his head to look at her with eyes the color of burnt clay. "Like, go out to dinner? Or coffee? Or herbal tea, if that's what you're into. Is that what you're into, Rook? Are you a hipster?" And here came that shit-eating grin.

Okay, this was getting to be too much fun. He probably knew she'd say no, hell everybody on the base pretty much knew she was involved. But here he was anyway, waiting for her by her Jeep. And he was drawing out the moment, too. *The devil.*

"Look, I'm with a guy," she said. "We live together up by Roseburg. So no, you and I can't go out."

"Uh-huh," he said, nodding and looking off. "Sooo," he drew out the word, "what you're saying is, that you'd go out with me if you weren't with some other guy, right?"

How did Ebbetts get the upper hand here? She was turning *him* down, wasn't she? "Trey, look, thanks for asking. I appreciate it. But we're workmates. So let's be good work buddies and leave it at that, okay?"

He nodded and hooked his thumbs in his front jean pockets like some firefighting cowboy. "Sure, Rook. Ten four. Understood."

"Thank you, though."

"Yeah, okay." He smiled. "You let me know when you ditch that guy, right?"

Maybe she shouldn't have said it, but she said it anyway, "Friend hug?"

"Sure."

They hugged and as they came together she thought, *He smells of fresh-cut pine and armpit stink and damn he feels good!*

Tuesday, June 16
Siskiyou Rappeller Crew base, Grants Pass

THE NEXT DAY Corby Jones and John Deluth walked into the tree cooler and found Trey Ebbets and Lucas Bowden practically nose-to-nose with a rope bag on the floor between them. They leaned toward each other with hardened eyes and clenched fists.

"What's going on, guys?" asked Deluth quietly.

"He won't check the rope," said Bowden.

"Bullshit." Ebbets shook his head. "I checked the rope already. There's no pitch. It's totally clean."

"Regs say check it every time." Bowden said. "That's *every* time."

"I don't know where you're coming from, pal, but if I say the rope is good then the rope is fucking great."

"Jeez, yuck" said Corby Jones, waving a hand in front of her face. "It reeks of testosterone in here."

"All right, guys. Let's damp down the fuels, okay?" Deluth made a placating motion.

"I know guys are all hyped up because we got a smokin' hot woman on the crew," said Corby. "That's me, in case you hadn't noticed."

There was a long moment with Bowden and Ebbets still in a stare-down, then Jones' comment registered on Ebbets as a twitch of a smile and Bowden's shoulders came down a notch and it was over. Bowden shook his head and mumbled, "Hey." Then he reached down and picked up the bag and said quietly, "Well, if I'm so bent about it then I should be the one to check it."

Ebbets shrugged. "Okay, look. I'll check it again. It's my job." He held out his hand for the bag. "Serious, man. It's cool. Safety on."

Bowden nodded and handed the bag over and Ebbets went out the open barn door to inspect the rope. Bowden looked at Deluth and Jones and then without a word turned and went over to the weight room, sat on one of the benches, picked up a 25-pound dumbbell and began doing curls.

Walking back to the office with John Deluth, Corby said, "The new guy, Bowden, seems kinda tense, don't you think?"

Deluth, who was the team's second in command and was aware of Bowden's back story, took a deep breath. He tried to keep the personal shit out of the day-to-day, but maybe in this case a little clarity would be helpful for everybody. "Yeah. Lucas has had some tough luck."

"How's that?"

"The guy's done a ton of rappels. He's the real deal on the ropes. But awhile back he was on a rappel team over in the Wallawas and they lost a guy during a descent. Totally a freak accident. Equipment failure. Bad harness clip or something."

"Oh, man. I remember hearing that. And Bowden was on the operation?"

"He was the spotter."

"Shit." A spotter would be in position to witness the whole thing from the door of the helicopter. She shook her head to clear the thought.

"Anyway, I think it got to him somehow and he takes all this..." Deluth gestured around at the base site, "...really seriously. That's not a bad thing."

Corby nodded. The crew liked to play it loose, joking around, keeping it upbeat. It was healthy; it made bonds. But every so often you got a reminder, and the thing that lurked in the back of your head made itself known. And you'd better pay attention.

RIGHT BEFORE quitting time Corby found Bowden sitting at the old picnic table somebody had dragged under an oak tree so the crew could eat lunch outside in the shade. Bowden was watching the pilot and mechanic hose down the helicopter. The yellow-and-white Bell shimmered wetly in the late afternoon light. Jones sat down in the opposite built-in seat and said, "How's it going?"

Bowden seemed transfixed. "Quite the machine."

Corby looked over her shoulder to follow his gaze. "Pretty amazing."

"Got a good pilot there in Fernandez."

"One of the best I hear."

They were quiet for a minute, then Bowden said, "Do you ever wish you could just disappear? I mean, not be part of the Big Matrix anymore. Just find your own space. Screw money. Fuck it all."

"Jesus, Bowden, what have you been smokin'?" When he didn't respond, Corby said, "You need to get out. You know, socialize. Have some laughs."

Bowden shrugged. "Not necessarily my thing."

"What? You got something against enjoying yourself?"

"I mean hanging out. Not really me."

"Well listen, I came over to tell you that a couple of us are stopping at the Tin Chicken for a beer or two before heading home. Feel like it?"

"The what?"

"The Tin Chicken. It's a pub right outside Merlin. Out front they got a big goddam statue of a chicken that's made out of automobile body parts. Hard to miss. Take a right onto the frontage road I forget the name just before the interstate and it's down that road a bit."

Bowden squinted. "Maybe." He looked over at her. "We'll see."

"Free peanuts."

"Thanks, I'll think about it."
"No problem." She got up. "Hope to see you there."

BOWDEN STOOD naked in front of the full-length mirror attached to the back of his closet door. He'd just gotten out of the shower. The reflection showed an athletic young man with thick shoulders and a shadow of dark hair across his chest and a square face wrapped in a cropped-short brown beard. Chest, arms, and legs dimpled with shadows of muscles. But the eyes—the eyes leaked. They betrayed the inside him. The weakness that had found the hole and squatted there and refused to be evicted. He looked fit and strong, but he was not.

It was unfair. To others. People depended on him, assumed he lived up to the code of the craft. But he jeopardized them, added risk. That was part of the struggle.

He didn't use all the time, only as necessary. And yet… he was such a better person when he did. That was the irony. He became focused, involved. He became committed to the task at hand. The noise and the churn inside his head subsided and was replaced by simple clarity. Willpower. Complete engagement.

He kept his pills in his underwear drawer. He'd read somewhere that underwear drawers are among the first places that burglars search. Not of course for the titillation, but because so many people kept their valuables in their underwear drawers with the mistaken belief that underwear was a natural repellant. Burglars knew better. If someone would break into Bowden's crude apartment—and rummage through the underwear drawer—that thief would be rewarded with a pharmacopeia of stimulants, opiates, antidepressants, sleep aids. Perhaps that was why he kept his stash there, with the small hope that the temptation—the need—might be swept away when he wasn't at home.

But no. It would be too easy to replenish everything. A phone call, a quick trip to the Bay area, and his drawer would be restocked. The thing inside of him would demand it, and rationalize it, and find a way to obtain it. The real reason he kept his pills in the underwear drawer was that the drawer was easy to reach and he really didn't give a shit.

Bowden put on his clothes and swallowed a Vicodin and got into his Ford truck and drove to the Tin Chicken and parked on the outer edges of the gravel lot. The music falling out of the windows was studded with shouts and laughs and the chime of pinball machines. Three people stood outside smoking cigarettes and their smoke wavered in the neon lights. Cars and trucks came and parked and as they did their headlights cut across his face. After a while some people left the building and got into their vehicles and swung onto the frontage road to return to their homes, their partners, their dogs, their televisions. He sat in the cab of his truck for nearly an hour with the windows open and the night air moving softly around him. Then he started the engine and swung out onto the frontage road and drove back to his apartment.

Inside the Tin Chicken Corby Jones threw darts with Craig Conner, Lou Pedersen and Danny Cravell. The Tin Chicken served free peanuts in the shell and they let you throw the husks on the worn wood floors and there was something soul satisfying about drinking beer and crunching peanut shells underfoot. It wasn't long before the area around the rappellers' table was carpeted with crushed shells. She had two beers—followed by a tequila shot that was heartily encouraged by her companions. The laughs were coming easy and time eased by and then Corby's cell phone buzzed. It was Mason calling, wondering when she'd be home. She didn't answer, just wrinkled her nose at her phone and said, *Oh shit! Got to go,* and she fist-bumped her crewmates and headed out, with Lou pleading for her to have one more shot of tequila. It was only as she was walking out into the parking lot that she realized Lucas Bowden had not shown up.

THE NEXT DAY at roll call Jones sat next to Bowden. "Hey, you didn't make it last night."

"I guess not."

"You missed out. Danny throws a bullseye on his last dart and the only way Sven can beat him is to throw another bullseye and the son of a bitch does it and Danny had to buy everybody's beer." She shook her head. "Only two bullseyes the whole time and they go one-two for the win."

"Sounds like a time," said Bowden.

"You shoulda come."

Bowden shrugged. "I'm not much of a bar guy."

"You don't drink? You a Mormon or something?"

"No. I like a beer now and then. Just not that into bars and the noise and everything."

"Well then, where do you like to have your beer if I might ask?"

Bowden rubbed his chin. "I like to hike. Some technical climbing. I river kayak. Then afterwards I might kick back at home, have a beer. Nothing too elaborate."

"Well, the Tin Chicken is not at all elaborate, let's be clear on that one."

"Okay. Maybe next time." He turned and gave a brief smile. "And if you ever want to go kayaking, let me know. I got a couple rafts."

Bowden had caught her so off-guard that the only thing she could think to say was, "Hell yes I want to go kayaking."

"Okay, then how about tomorrow? We're both off the schedule."

Corby was curiously pleased that Bowden knew her day off. "That," she smiled back, "sounds like a time."

Thursday, June 18
Klamath River, California

FOUR DAYS AFTER her first live rappel Corby Jones told her boyfriend, Mason, that she was going to spend her day off with an old high school girlfriend who she'd run into at the Tin Chicken.

"You know," said Corby as she rummaged noisily in the refrigerator, keeping her face hidden behind the open door, "Trish and me got to talking and after a beer or three we swore we'd do a raft trip, nothing too strenuous, probably rent a couple of torpedoes in Shady Cove and do the easy part of the Rogue. Hang out on the river and do some catching up."

"Mmm," responded Mason, engrossed in his iPad.

In fact, she had not run into an old friend, and she was not going to do an easy section of the Rogue—she was going to do whitewater on the lower Klamath and she was going to do it with Lucas Bowden. She felt a bit guilty lying to Mason, but she figured a fib in the service of peace and tranquility on the home front was a decent bargain. After all, she wasn't into Lucas Bowden, but when he asked her to go kayaking a big *Yes* came out of her faster than she could rein it in. She figured kayaking with another guy wouldn't have the best optics with Mason, so a little truth-stretching was in order. The bottom line: She just wanted to get in the big river and get wet and have some fun, and river rafting was not a pastime that interested Mason. Bowden was into rivers and had the kayaks and she wouldn't have to rent one so here we go. She hadn't done much kayaking, but enough to know running a river was damn good for the soul.

She was up with the sun and headed south on I-5, up over the Siskiyou Pass and down into California. The grassy hills were parched and sun-scorched but the early light softened the harshness and the cattle-country rolled golden and shadow-draped out to a mountainous horizon. At the Highway 96 turnoff Corby found Bowden waiting by his truck at the side of the road. That definitely put him in the plus column—he said he'd be there waiting for her and by God there he was.

They car-caravanned along the curving, twisting road, following the canyon as the big river rolled alongside. They dropped off Corby's Jeep at a take-out downriver, then drove back up to launch the rafts. On the drive they made small talk about water levels and haystacks, pointing out routes through the class 3s as they passed them. Views of the whitewater from the passenger seat of Bowden's truck got Corby grinning. "This will be so cool," she said.

They launched in Bowden's inflatable Sea Eagles, stout boats he assured would handle well and take some punishment. Corby let Bowden's experience lead them through the bigger rapids and Corby echoed his strokes and movements and she only got wrapped once, sliding sideways against a big knob of granite, hung up as the water pummeled at her over the lower edge of the kayak, but she twisted her weight and dug in a huge forward stroke and the boat came free and bucked downstream in a righteous blast of spray. On the slow water they ran side-by-side and didn't say much and once an osprey with a trout in its talons flew directly overhead on its way upriver. Bowden stopped paddling to watch for a long moment and he said something quietly and when Corby said, *What?* he just shook his head and started paddling again.

At the bottom of the last easy water before their takeout was a wide bar of fist-size gravel, each rock time-polished to silky smoothness, some oblong and some round as billiard balls. They pulled the Sea Eagles up on the gravel bar and took off their helmets and sat in the sun leaned back on their hands and turned their faces to the sky and closed their eyes and let the sun dry their clothes. They didn't speak. The sound of the hurrying river filled everything up. After ten minutes Corby took off her shades and set them aside and turned over and stretched out on her stomach to let her backside dry. She laid on the warm smooth stones, her folded hands a pillow. She said, "They oughta make this some kind of therapy, lyin' on hot rocks. Like a massage. You could charge money. Thirty bucks an hour. Hell, fifty. People would pay."

Bowden followed suit, took off his sunglasses and laid down with his back to the sun, his face facing hers. They closed their eyes. Their elbows touched and they left them that way. They were tired and content. Corby was half-dreaming about the river run and stacks and rocks floated toward her in random flashes of recall and even on the warm rocks she could sense the steel-cold spray lashing her face, fresh and brilliant. After many minutes Bowden said, "They should take out the dams. This one here on the Klamath, the Snake. The Applegate."

"What about these nice reliable summertime flows? Pretty good stuff for kayaking."

"Let the rivers run free. Let them be wild. Spring runoff blowing through here like a freight train. You could have some incredible rides."

She opened her eyes. Bowden was looking at her. She nodded sleepily, said, "That would be fucking amazing."

Bowden sat up. "People settle all the time. For whatever it is. Jobs. Marriage. Shitty lives. Dammed rivers. What do you do? Have kids? Get a mortgage. Drink too much. Gamble. Save up a four-oh-one-kay. Go to church. Buy a Harley and ride off into the sunset. Do drugs. Jump off a bridge. It's crazy shit, man. Crazy."

Corby lifted her head slightly and looked at the silhouette of Lucas Bowden, burned dark into the bright, thin-blue sky. He seemed to be talking to himself more than her. She didn't reply; there was nothing to say.

WHEN THEY GOT back to Corby's Jeep, Bowden took out one of the packed kayaks and set it by her vehicle.

"What are you doing?" she said.

"Take it. It's yours."

She shook her head. "Jeez, Lucas. I can't take your kayak."

He shrugged. "Take it. Use it. Take your boyfriend out, it'll hold two. I go out by myself mostly anyway. If I need it, I'll borrow it from you."

She stared at the stout square bundle of de-inflated kayak. "You put me in an awkward place, Lucas."

"It's nothing."

"No, it's not nothing. I'm part Umpqua Indian. The part that says giving has to be a two-way street." She gestured helplessly. "I don't have anything that's close. I can't take this."

"Don't worry about it."

"Jesus, Lucas, I'm culturally obligated to worry about it." There was a long moment of silence, then Corby dug into her pocket and pulled out something that she held in her closed fist. "I do have something, but it's stupid."

"I like stupid stuff. What is it?"

She opened her hand. In her palm nestled a stone. Oblong, smooth, five inches from tip to tip. It was a pure, silver-gray color bisected by a single vein of pure white. "I got it off the beach where we hung out. I like it a lot. It has power, if you believe in that stuff. I was going to keep it as a talisman and a reminder of, you know, a great day on the river. Um, I'd like you to have it. She held it out. "I told you it's stupid."

He took it, examined it, smiled and put it in his pocket. "I don't think it's stupid. I think it's cool. And I think that makes us even."

FROM THE AUDIOBOOK, "The Planet Earth: Amazing Natural Phenomena," by Dr. Jessica Shai Nusbaum, PhD:

A bolt of lightning is one of nature's most primal and violent forces. A bolt can be five times hotter than the surface of the sun and carry up to one billion volts of electricity. It's the exchange of energy between positive and negative electrical fields that occur naturally in the Earth's surface and atmosphere. It's nature struggling with itself, trying to come into balance, attempting to equalize forces that can never be equalized.

Lightning is a common occurrence—more than one billion lightning bolts occur around our planet every year, and a single storm may produce thousands of bolts. About eighty-five percent of all lightning occurs inside clouds, where electrons—jostled about by winds and turbulent air—build up positive and negative charges. The result is a burst of electrical energy that appears as a giant spark arcing across the sky.

The other fifteen percent of lightning—the portion that doesn't happen inside clouds—strikes the ground. Again, this is the result of fundamental electrical forces, the enormous quivering attraction of positive and negative energy. In the case of ground strikes, the exchange occurs between clouds and the surface of the Earth. But here something strange occurs. Overall, the surface of the Earth is negatively charged. But the negative charge that can build up inside a storm cloud can be so rowdy and powerful that it causes the ground below to flip to a positive charge. The result is an explosive exchange of electrons—a lightning ground strike.

Because electricity seeks a path of least resistance, a ground strike may connect via the tallest object it can find. In some instances, that would be a building or a tower. In the forest, it's often a big tree. When lightning strikes a tree, it can vaporize the moisture inside the tree, turning that moisture into steam with such sudden violence that the tree literally explodes, sending lumber-size shards of bark and wood flying in all directions. Lightning will also spiral down the outside of the trunk, leaving a charred, corkscrew burn mark on the bark. In rare instances the outside of the tree may remain intact, but the wood deep inside the tree ignites. There are reports of firefighters finding trees that look normal on the outside but have cracks in their bark that reveal flames boiling inside. At the base of the tree, where the massive electrical charge flows into the ground, it vaporizes organic matter and fuses dirt into solid, rock-like masses of silica crystals.

In forested areas, the arboreal floor is made up of thick layers of organic matter—years of accumulated needles, leaves, twigs and decomposing plants. This organic duff can be up to two feet deep and—in the summer—bone dry. When a ground strike hits a tree, the surrounding duff may briefly ignite but often is too densely packed to provide adequate oxygen and any fire burns out.

Sometimes, however, this duff holds just enough oxygen that an embryonic fire survives, smoldering quietly and unseen for days and even weeks. It emits very little smoke, working its way through the duff like a network of tiny glowing worms—a fibrous ember on the end of a long, slow-burning fuse. At some point, this nascent fire may come upon looser duff that contains more oxygen. If it does, it gets brighter and hotter, coring its way up to emerge into the open air where it finally flutters into outright flames. Nearby grasses, twigs and leaves catch fire and the flames begin to spread.

These are called "sleeper fires."

Sunday, June 21
Siskiyou National Forest

THE ILLINOIS RIVER ROAD out of Selma swung past modest rural development houses and then spacious, open farmland before the asphalt road narrowed to a single lane and trees closed in on either side. Scorched bark evidenced past fires. In the distance blackened spires of dead pines and firs serrated the horizon.

After eight miles the asphalt turned to gravel and Will's thirty-one-year-old Land Cruiser skittered and rattled over the relentless washboard ridges.

"My guts are shaking," said Kal.

"Yeah," said Will, "it's probably going to be this way all the way up."

"I doh-oh-oh-oh-n't m-eye-eye-eye-ind," she said, letting the rutted road make her voice quiver. "The road is t-aw-aw-alking."

"What's it sa-ay-ay-ay-ying?"

"*I'm an old Forest Service roh-oh-oh-oad and I've got wrin-in-in-kles.*"

For Will, it was a joy to be in the mountains after so many months in the endless deserts of the Middle East, to liberate his beloved Toyota from the storage facility and hear its throaty grumble as he and his amazing daughter made their way up the battered Forest Service road. The SUV ground its way steadily upward, passing stands of oak and madrone at the lower elevations, the grasses pale and dry and scattered through with crisp leaves that the madrones had shed during summer. As they drove higher the conifers began to dominate. They switchbacked up the flanks of ridges, occasionally cutting through swaths of thick forest that the capricious wildfires had spared. Beyond the untouched areas were the skeletal remains of thousands of fire-killed trees, most scorched black and those that had lost their bark bleached gray, all with naked limbs drooping in apology. Yet the feet of the big snags were swaddled in new green growth, manzanita and tanoak and conifer saplings fifteen feet high. The mountains in their tireless will to regenerate.

The Land Cruiser smelled of aging leather laced with whiffs of oil and hot machinery and the scents of the vehicle swirled in Kal's mind as a comforting, mottled tapestry of brown and cream and brilliant gold. Her hands took in the aging leather seat, its tiny cracks and fissures running as a network of rivers beneath her fingers, crisscrossing the enchanted, unexplored territory of their adventure. There were rattles and mechanical squeaks—metal-on-metal, a loose rear window, a pencil in the glove box—as the truck jostled over the road. Shadows of the big trees passed over the windshield in sudden waves of light and dark, and when they emerged from stands of timber into open areas the sapphire smell of the forest changed to the purple scents of stone and sunbaked earth.

"Why do you like the Kalmiopsis?" she asked. "I mean, besides my name. I know you like mountains and rocks. But..."

Will nodded. "I've thought about that. I mean, it's not necessarily the prettiest place. A lot of it's been burned pretty bad over the years. But I used to come up here quite a bit when I was younger, before I met your mom and before you were born. It's a place not many people go just to visit. It's too strange, too foreboding..."

"What's foreboding?"

"Meaning sort of scary. Intimidating. But I think that's what attracted me, it was like my private place. I could come out here and not see anybody else. It was like I had it all to myself. Miles of just raw planet. I'd bring a tent and hang out for days. Then I started to learn more about it and realize how amazing it really is and that's pretty much the reason I got into geology in the first place."

"With the Forest Service?"

"Yup. As a soil scientist."

"Did you still come out here?"

Will gave a short laugh. "Well, I didn't have as much time. Seems like there was a lot going on. I married your mom, and then you arrived, and you kept us pretty busy."

Kal sighed. "I'm glad we're coming out here."

"I think this place has a soul, a living soul. Maybe it's not everyone's idea of the coolest place to backpack, but it's got a good soul and deserves some love. And we're going to give it some love. Does that make sense or just sound goofy?"

"It sounds goofy but it makes sense." She was quiet for a moment, then said, "Is it still bad?"

"The burn scar?"

"Yes. The burn scar."

"Things are coming back. The young trees are getting big, there's a lot of pine and cedars and some firs starting to fill in. There's tons of manzanita and buck brush everywhere, some of it is ten feet high. It's super dry, but things are definitely coming back."

"Any Brewer's spruce?"

Will slowed the SUV to a stop and turned off the engine. It was a relief to pause the bone-jarring ride. "There's one right here by the road," he said. "Do you want to say hi?"

"Yeah!" she said, unbuckling her seat belt and climbing out. She stood for a moment and let the sun settle on her face and she took in the heat of the day as it teased evergreen scent out of their surroundings. A sprawling, enormous quiet was all around. No human busyness, just a comforting tick from the Land Cruiser's engine.

"Here," said Will and he took her hand and led her to the side of the road where a large Brewer's spruce let down its shaggy branches. He lifted her up and was amazed at how light she was. He knew she wasn't big for her age but cradling her in a chair made of his arms it was like she was made of air, as if she would float away if his attention strayed for a second. He put his chin gently on her shoulder to keep her from sailing off. He brought her to the long drooping fronds and she reached out and found one of the branches and she held it and shook it gently as a greeting.

"Picea breweriana," said Will.

"Native to the Klamath and Siskiyou Mountains and one of the rarest trees in North America," recited Kal.

"You remember."

"Yup, I remember," she nodded, twisting free a few needles and holding them up to her nose to take in the pungent, turpentine smell. "Mmm, nice."

Will said, "Really nice."

"How big is it?"

He leaned back and looked up. "A hundred feet or so."

"So it lived through that big fire?"

"It did. It's kinda charred on one side, but it looks healthy."

They got back in the truck and Will started the engine and put the truck in gear and they made their way up the road.

Will smiled at his daughter. For their trip she'd switched out her granny-type sunglasses for a very cool pair of wraparound sports shades and an outdoorsy khaki-colored chamois shirt with button-down flaps on the shoulders and button-down flap pockets, the tails hanging out over bright yellow hiking shorts. The fingers of her right hand were moving lightly over the door handle, exploring. She had a dreamy look on her face and Will felt a wrench of regret for the lost time between them. But they were here now, and he was doing the right thing, being a dad, being present.

The road ended at a small campground that was nothing more than a wide, flat grassy area nestled along the banks of a tributary creek that fed the Illinois River a quarter mile away. Will and Kal got out and stretched and shook their bodies to re-settle their bones after the long, bumpy ride. The plan was to spend the night at the campground, then set out the next morning when it would be cool.

They put up the tent and Kal helped. She loved the tactile certainty of the shock-corded poles snapping into place and the slick sensation of sliding the long poles into the nylon sleeves sewn along the outer seams of the tent. When the tent was up and staked Kal scrambled inside to set out their air mattresses, sleeping bags, and stuff pillows. When she was done she was very pleased with herself—it all felt very snuggly and Hobbit-like and there was room for their packs and boots.

Will made up a couple of their freeze-dried dinners—chicken and dumplings—and they ate right out of the pouches with their backs against some nearby pine trees, serenaded by birds and the bustling of the nearby creek.

"Hear that?" said Will.

"What?"

"That bird call." He imitated it by whistling three notes.

Kal nodded, picking the sounds out of the many chirps and bird calls. "I hear it. What is it?"

"Flycatcher. Some people say that call, those three notes, is the flycatcher saying, "Quick! Three beers!""

"Daa...ad."

"Listen, you'll hear it."

They listened, and Kal grinned. It did sound like, *Quick! Three beers!*

After they'd eaten Will took the empty pouches and the

rest of their food and went out to hang their supplies from the branch of a tree to keep it from bears. When he returned the sun was settling against the distant ridges. They sat in the twilight and Kal talked about her school and her favorite class, which was history as taught by Mrs. Liebowitz, and how she always pictured Mrs. Liebowitz as "sort of stout and meaty" on account of the deep, resonant sound of her voice and the authority with which she moved around the classroom. Then one day the class played a history game sort of like *Jeopardy!* and Kal won and Mrs. Liebowitz had given her a brief hug and Kal was amazed at how "tiny and bony" her teacher actually was.

"You can't judge a book by the sound of its voice," advised Kal.

After a while they decided they'd be more comfortable stretched out in the tent. They crawled inside and got out of their boots and socks and their camp beds felt luxurious. They were quiet, then Kal said, "Tell me the Kalmiopsis story."

"Again?" The Kalmiopsis story had been one of Kal's bedtime favorites when she was little.

"Yes. Please."

Will closed his eyes. "So there was this botanist," he began. "Her name was Lilla Leach. She was a woman who lived here in southwest Oregon like a century ago. She was really smart and pretty adventurous. Kind of like you. She was a real brainiac about plants. I mean, she knew a ton about plants. And one of the things that she really loved to do was hike around in the mountains and look for rare plants—plants you might not find anywhere else in the world. And that's because this place, where we are right now and around this whole part of southern Oregon, which is called the…?"

"The Klamath-Siskiyou region."

"Right on. She knew that the Klamath-Siskiyou region

had unusual soils…"

"Which you love."

"I do. I like rocks almost as much as I like you. Although you might come in second to a nice chunk of serpentine."

"Ha ha."

"Okay. So Lilla Leach knew there were things here—plants and animals—that couldn't be found anywhere else. So she and her husband, and his name was John, would hike all over southern Oregon looking for rare species. And they hiked with their burros…"

"Pansy and Violet."

"Yup, Pansy and Violet, two of the sweetest little donkeys you could want and darn good pack animals—sure-footed, strong, tireless. The four of them, the Leaches and their donkeys, hiked more than a thousand miles all over the Siskiyou Mountains, over deer trails and bushwhacking and always searching, looking for plants, keeping an eye out for something new and exciting.

"And one of the things they found was this little shrub with pretty flowers. Lilla would say in her writings that it was the prettiest thing she'd ever come across. And to top it off, it was a whole new species, a plant that nobody knew existed.

"Now at first, Lilla Leach thought she'd found a new kind of laurel, because there's a lot of laurel in these hills and it wouldn't have been too far off to think that this little shrub was related. But it wasn't, it was all new and Lilla got to name it. So she started with the genus name for laurel, which is…"

"*Kalmia.*"

"And she combined that with a Greek word…"

"*Opsis.*"

"Jeez, you got a memory like a steel trap."

"That's what everybody says."

"And *opsis* means?"

"Okay, wait. Ah, it means 'very much like.' And that's

where we get that really nice name, *Kalmiopsis*."

"And the full genus-species name is *Kalmiopsis leachiana*, named after Lilla Leach."

"So cool."

"It is. So in the spirit of Lilla and John Leach…"

"And Pansy and Violet."

"…and Pansy and Violet, we are off to search for rare things."

"Do they have a nice smell?"

"Pansy and Violet?"

"No! Jeez! Kalmiopsis flowers!" Kal already knew the answer. When her father was away she'd listened to a version of the Lilla Leach story on her audio encyclopedia a dozen times. The narrator mentioned that *Kalmiopsis* had a nice fragrance. But the best version of the story was her dad's, always just a bit different each time he told it.

"Yes," said her father. "They have a wonderful smell."

And here they were, going on a wilderness adventure, searching for a rare plant. Her dad had said they were late in the season and that *Kalmiopsis* might not be blooming, but Kal had said that was all right. Everything was all right. Deep down, she didn't care if they found any *Kalmiopsis* at all.

Sunday, June 21
Rogue River-Siskiyou National Forest

ON A ROUTINE charter flight from Crescent City to Medford the pilot of the Cessna turboprop noticed that a small, low-lying cloud off in the distance had the columnar shape and dirty amber hue of woodsmoke. Given the dry conditions and their current position over the heart of timber country, the pilot decided to confirm the sighting. He had a single paying passenger on board, a doctor who was ferrying between a clinic in Crescent City and his private practice in southern Oregon. The doctor had chosen to sit up front and wear a headset and listen to in-flight chatter. The pilot reached over and tapped the doctor on the arm and pointed out the side window.

"I think we'd better take a look at that smoke," he said over the headset. "Okay? It'll just take a couple of minutes."

The doctor nodded. It was Sunday; he had no time commitments. He peered at the distant horizon. "I don't see it. How far away is it?"

"I'm going to put it on our twelve o'clock," said the pilot as he guided the Cessna into a banking left turn.

As the horizon settled into view the doctor nodded. "Ah."

The pilot toggled air traffic control. "Control, this is Mountain Air one nine seven inbound from Crescent City."

"Go ahead, one nine seven."

"Fifteen minutes out of Medford at 160 knots and eleven-thousand feet. I'm requesting deviation seven, eight miles to the north to check out some smoke. Looks like right about the eastern edge of the wilderness area."

"All right, one nine seven. You're cleared for deviation. Maintain altitude. Let us know what you see."

"Roger that. One nine seven, out."

In a few minutes they were over the area. It was a fire. Dirty smoke was snaking out of a stand of conifers and the burning edge of flames had spread to form a sparkling orange necklace.

The pilot circled his plane twice more before toggling air traffic control. "It's a fire, all right," he reported. "Looks like half an acre or so. Here's the coordinates."

"Okay Mountain Air one nine seven. We'll pass it on to the Forest Service and ODF. Thanks for the heads up."

The pilot banked right to return to his flight path. As he did, he caught a faint glint in the distance—sun reflecting off a car or truck somewhere far away. There were people out in the forests, all the time. In fire season, you just hoped that if anything big happened, they'd get out.

SUPERVISOR OATES and FAO Hudek studied the big wall map of the area—two sprawling green splotches of Forest Service jurisdiction bisected by white-and-yellow-checkered swaths of private properties and BLM lands. In the heart of the western splotch was a ragged oblong of darker green—the Kalmiopsis Wilderness. Hudek noted the approximate location that the commercial pilot had reported. Another fire in the Kalmiopsis, probably a sleeper left over from the recent storm.

Similar to the one they'd had just a week or so ago, this one was small, remote, not immediately threatening to life or property. There was a road to the north and one into the wilderness to the south, but the fire was located a good seven miles from either. No direct access for engines. They would get after it with rappellers.

It was late evening, nearly 2000 hours. Too late to launch an attack. It was a young fire; it would burn slow as nighttime temperatures dropped. Might even burn itself out.

Oates rang the DDO and ordered a spotter plane to be in the air first thing. Chances were the fire wouldn't be a problem. But fires in these extreme conditions sometimes didn't play by the rules. She texted Matt Murphy and told him to have the crew ready for an early morning operation in the Kalmiopsis.

Monday, June 22
Rogue River-Siskiyou National Forest Headquarters, Medford

BY 0800 THE SPOTTER plane had confirmed the burn and had radioed dispatch that the wildfire was three-quarters of an acre with light winds pushing the smoke toward the southwest. Already at his desk, FAO Ken Hudek reviewed the Weather Service report and noted northwesterly winds up to 15 mph moving through the area. Air movement was starting to pick up. He called the rappelling base manager on his cell phone to give him a confirmation for the initial attack. "Matt, I'm working up the TARO," Hudek advised.

Two minutes later Hudek got a call from the Incident Operations Chief overseeing the three-week-old blaze in the Fremont National Forest, 150 miles east. The Tomcat Fire had burned 40,000 acres and was thirty percent contained. There were already 400 personnel involved.

"We're maxed out," said the IC. "We'll take whatever you can send us." From the noise of equipment in the background and the throaty sound of his voice Hudek knew the IC was calling from his fire camp and that he was probably sleep deprived.

These requests weren't unusual. Battle-weary ICs often radioed neighboring agencies for help. There wasn't a Fire Officer around who wouldn't lend a hand to a nearby district if possible, even if it meant reducing local resources. Southern Oregon might have fewer active fires than other districts, but the fire potential was alarming.

In fire years like this one budgets were getting squeezed all the way up the line—local, state, district, and federal. Requests for more bodies and equipment made for tough decisions—who was really in need? What fires could be put out quickly so that the trucks and crews and aircraft could be routed somewhere else? What budget got dinged to exhaustion? Hudek figured the Tomcat Fire IC had probably already called the GACC and the GACC had probably relayed the fact that the Rogue River-Siskiyou had just gotten severity funding and was sitting on additional resources. He couldn't say *No*.

"We can get you four engines, possibly half a dozen ground crews." Those were resources from the Rogue River side of the National Forest. For now, he'd keep the districts on the Siskiyou side fully equipped.

"That's a help," rasped the IC. "Thanks."

"They'll be there tomorrow a.m.," said Hudek.

After he hung up Hudek called dispatch and gave the orders to route the equipment and crew to the Tomcat Fire. He turned to his computer and brought up the Northwest Interagency Coordination Center website and registered the new Kalmiopsis burn. Then he worked up a Tactical Air Response Order for the rappel team and sent it out by fax and email, knowing they'd be on site within the hour.

On the TARO the new fire was listed as "Incident 395."

Monday, June 22
Rogue Rappellers Team base, Grants Pass

LOU PEDERSEN grabbed the big Viking horn and bellowed out the news. By 8:45 the initial helitack was en route to the sleeper fire. John Deluth was strapped into the spotter's harness. Bob Penny was the team IC and Danny Cravell was aboard as IMED.

Because she'd been on the previous mission, Corby Jones' name had been cycled to the back of the rotation. She bounced listlessly between the monitors in the main room and the refrigerator scrounging for snacks, drifting past the control room so she could listen to radio coms. Waiting around during an active burn was harder than anything, harder than grubbing around on hands and knees searching for hot spots in the ashes or humping out in the heat of the day with ninety pounds of gear.

She happened past the control room when she heard John Deluth's voice crackling over the radio talking with dispatch. "We're over the fire now, looks like it's moving to the southwest through new growth. Moving pretty good. We're going to need another two sticks up here."

"Roger that," said the voice from dispatch.

"Oh man," said Corby, who was practically in Murphy's hip pocket.

"Corby, go tell Lou to sound the horn for second load."

Corby hustled into the operations room to find Pedersen in front of a computer screen. "Lou! Second load!"

Pedersen grinned and made for the door. A few moments later the big horn bellowed and then Murphy came on over the loudspeaker *Second load!* and the next four-person team listed on the duty board headed for the tree cooler to gear up.

Corby returned to the radio room where Murphy was listening to the spotter adjust the helicopter into a drop position.

"Matt," she said, "do you think they'll need a third team?"

"Corby," he said calmly. "Go cut the grass."

"Cut the grass?" She was incredulous.

"Duty calendar says it's your turn."

"Matt, jeez, the grass is all dried up. There's no grass."

"There's grass in the shady spots, and now would be a really good time to cross that little chore off your list before it gets too hot."

"Oh crap," she said quietly but loud enough, and she went out to the machine shed. The sky overhead was the color of bleached denim and a scattering of buzzards rode thermals through the whiteness. The sun came down hard and hot and the far horizon was blurred with summer haze and the returning helicopter emerged in the distance, wavering and distorted by heated air. Corby hauled the ancient LawnBoy out of the shed. "If you're gonna give up the ghost," she spoke to the dusty machine, "now would be a really good time." But it started on the first pull, as always, and she set out on a meandering route, the grass too short and stubbed off by heat to provide any way to track progress, quietly cursing the base manager.

As she made her way around the compound the helicopter landed and powered down for refueling as the pilot took a moment to walk around and stretch his legs. The second crew stomped out of the tree cooler in their yellow Nomex shirts and dark green pants and red belly bags, carrying initial attack boxes full of supplies. She didn't notice Matt Murphy come up behind her until he tapped her on the shoulder, which made her jump and lose her grip on the deadman's switch. The faithful LawnBoy choked to a stop.

"Corby," he said, "get geared up. You're going with the second team."

"What's going on?"

"Danny sprained his foot or maybe broke it when he landed. He's at the drop zone. I'm sending in Tom, too. You go in, see what's happening with Danny and what kind of extraction we need. John says there's no place to land nearby, so he's going to recon a place maybe Danny can walk to with Tom's help. I know there's a pair of crutches around here somewhere. Lance says there's a landing spot about two miles due east of the fire. I'll get a helicopter from ODF or a contractor to pick him up so we can rig up our aircraft with the bucket and start making water drops. You'll stay on the burn."

"Got it."

"For the time being, that makes you the only team IMED. Get going."

She happily stowed the lawn mower in its shed and sprinted for the tree cooler to gear up. Tom Su was already there. "Hey," said Su, "here we go again. Except I've got to babysit Danny." He shook his head.

"Beats cutting grass," Corby smiled as they suited up. Walking to the landing pad they passed the two disappointed team members who been bumped out of their rotation. "Tell Danny to keep his stupid knees up, would ya?" said one.

Corby shrugged and pointed at the lawn mower shed. "If you need something to do how about finish cuttin' the grass for me? I'm going to be busy for a couple of days."

"Ha ha."

Out near the landing pad the crew went through their safety checks and then climbed aboard. Corby and Tom Su sat on the inside of the bench with Lucas Bowden and Mike Krazinski to the outsides. The Huey began spooling up and at the sound she felt the adrenalin tingling. *It never gets old.* The blades reached their manic takeoff speed and the aircraft began to lift and then they tilted forward and hurried into the sky. The spotter John Deluth described the fire and the plan of attack. The burn was hot and moving as winds were picking up. They were cutting a line in front of the active fire but the IC was saying that they were having to really hustle to stay ahead. As soon as Corby had attended to Danny she'd be needed on the line.

They did a fly-over and Deluth got the team oriented, pointing out the active edge of the burn and the spike camp location and then the drop zone. The first team went in and as Corby got out on the skid she looked down and could see the first team wiggling out of their harnesses with Danny Cravell sitting off to one side with his legs stuck out straight in front of him. A quarter mile distant smoke was lifting out of the mountainside and she could see the ribbons of flame dancing and twisting. Deluth gave the signal and she and Tom Su were on the ropes and sliding away from the helicopter.

On the ground Corby cleared the rope from the descender and unbuckled her harness. Danny was looking up at her with a rueful smile.

"Goddammit," he said.

Corby crouched by his side and studied his face for signs of shock. "What happened?"

"The chopper got pushed down just as I was about to touch. Kinda rammed me into that fuckin' thing." Danny pointed at a large rock with a pyramidal crown sticking out of the ground. "Stupid rock."

"Yeah. John says they caught a downdraft. You're lucky Lance is a good driver or it could have been worse. All right, let me see what's going on, then we'll get you out of here." She nodded at Tom Su who stood nearby.

"Heads up," said Mike Krazinski as an IA box made its

way down from the helicopter. Then the spotter released the ropes and they fell from their great height and collapsed into loose piles on the ground like things that had been shot dead out of the sky. As the chopper took off Krazinski asked, "How's it look?"

"It's a bad sprain, could be a break," said Corby. "It's not fun but it's not serious. The really bad news is that he's probably gonna live."

"Says you," said Danny.

"You handle it all right?" asked Krazinski.

She nodded. "I'll get it stabilized."

Krazinski cut open the IA box and pulled out the crutches. "Tom, take a radio. Danny, if you think you can hike out with Tom, let me know. If you can't make it, we'll figure a plan B."

"I'll duct tape him into a ball and roll him down the hill," said Su.

"Corby, we'll get your bag to the camp. It's about a hundred yards up and to the left, right? When you get Danny stabilized up and if he can move okay then meet us at the burn. Stay near the ridge on the way over. Keep your eyes open." Then he and Bowden hefted the gear and headed off.

Corby got Cravell's boot off and sock off and inspected the ankle which was already purplish and beginning to puff up. She gave him ibuprofen and worked quickly to tape the ankle before it swelled up too much to get his boot back on.

The radio crackled and the crew IC, Bob Penny, came on telling the base that the fire was on the move. "It was going to get around us on the downhill side so we're moving to the ridge and cutting a line there," said Penny, his radio voice crackling. "We need to get some drops on the southern edge."

A moment later John Deluth radioed coordinates for an extraction point and Tom Su plugged those into his handheld GPS. Then he helped Cravell get to his feet and adjusted the crutches for his size. "You okay?" he asked, holding Danny's forearm.

"I'm fine, other than it hurts like hell and now when I get back down to the base I'll probably have to fill out some dumbass accident report."

"Yeah you, me, Corby, Lance, maybe John. Something to look forward to. Try those out."

Cravell practiced a few halting steps with the crutches. "It'll work. Won't be very fast, though."

Su got on his radio and relayed the message to dispatch that he and an injured rappeler were starting out to the extraction coordinates with an ETA of two to three hours. Dispatch said a contract helicopter was standing by.

"All right," said Corby. "Be safe, you two."

"You too." Tom Su hoisted the two belly bags and he and Danny began making their way down the slope, moving with slow, deliberate caution over the scree. Corby watched until they'd disappeared into the trees. Suddenly, she was very alone. The chopper was Dopplering off into the distance and fire team was a quarter mile away. She was in the wilderness without a radio. In a live operation, being isolated from the group wasn't a good thing. *Better get to it.* She took a good mental picture of the camp location and the terrain that led from the camp to the fire and she picked up her Pulaski and headed out.

She made her way up to the rough crest of the ridge and worked her way toward the fire. The ground was rocky and loose and in places the underbrush threw up an almost-impenetrable matrix of branches. Rough rock outcroppings channeled her left and right. The woodsmoke was dusked with the smell of boiling resins and the haze thickened and she could hear flames snapping. The curling edge of the fire was eating its way into the brush one hundred yards away.

INCIDENT 395

Corby found the team cutting a line just behind the ridgetop where the vegetation was sparse and a line would hold. She switched out the Pulaski for a McCleod rake and fell in line and began scraping duff down to mineral soil. Seven rappelers bent to cutting a break and their arms and torsos pumped up and down like the camshaft of some living engine and the dust of their work rose to meet the drifting smoke. The sun baked on their backs and the tools chunked and clanged and sweat dropped off noses and chins and fell into the dirt and instantly evaporated.

The IC Bob Penny was constantly moving, monitoring the front and rear of the line, telling the crew when to bump up, scrambling onto outcroppings to survey the firescape on the other side of the ridge. The fire had moved out of the bigger timber and had taken hold in the brush and snags and it was on the move, burning hot and pre-heating the fuels in its path. The smoke column rose and then bent to the southwest. He didn't like this fire's behavior and the way it had shifted and was now moving in the general direction of their camp and exit route. The alternative route meant heading down a drainage that everybody would rather avoid.

The best option would be to keep cutting a line along the ridge toward the camp, maybe do a burnout inside the line, make water drops on the south flank, and let the wind move the fire into the control where it would burn itself out. Another option would be to bug out entirely.

The helicopter arrived with the big bucket and Penny directed the release from below, aiming at the fire's widening front. He watched as the looser parts of the deluge got shunted sideways by the wind and the tops of the trees bending to the increasing velocity. Embers flew out of the leading edge and he watched some of them get lofted by the wind so that they fell further and further in front of the head of the main fire. Spot fires began to appear fifty yards in front of the churning flames. He radioed dispatch for a targeted weather update and two minutes later got a reply saying that winds in the fire area would be variable coming from the north-northeast with speeds of fifteen to twenty mph and gusts to thirty.

The sun beat down and sweat ran past his ears. Penny stared at the fire and swore, *C'mon you fucker, slow down and let us box you in.* No IC liked to lose control of a fire, but it happened. The best course was to not fool yourself into thinking you could beat it with muscle and will power. The fire was moving fast—too fast. Tongues of flames licked at the unburned trees and scrub. Bursts of wind ripped through the underbrush.

He got on the radio and told dispatch, "The fire is moving faster than we can keep up. I'm calling in a Type Three and we are heading for the exit."

"All right, Bob. Stand by."

In a few moments Penny's radio crackled and a new voice said, "Bob this is Ken Hudek. I understand this burn is moving fast and you're calling it in as a Type Three. Over."

"Roger that. It's outflanking us, Ken. Winds are picking up and it's starting to head for our camp area. We're not going to stay in front of it. Over."

"Understood. I'm going to get another rotating wing and bucket in the air for support. Are you safe and heading for the exit? Over."

"That's affirmative. The crew is heading for the exit. Out." Penny holstered his radio and hustled back to the crew. "We're packing it up and moving out," he yelled through his cupped hands. He held up his index finger and twirled it.

They knew the deal. Nobody liked giving up on a burn they'd been called to, but sometimes you regrouped. They all nodded and began to gather up tools.

All except one. Lucas Bowden was furiously working his Pulaski, throwing up billowing dust.

"Lucas," called Penny. "Hey Lucas!"

Bowden didn't look up. He shuffled sideways, his tempo unabated. Dried duff flew up around his knees.

Penny trotted over and leaned down and said, "Lucas, hey! We're pulling out. Like now. The fire's getting out of hand."

"Bullshit!" spat Bowden.

Penny was confused. Was this the new guy's attempt at humor? If so, it wasn't funny. "Okay, Bowden, knock it off. We're out of here. They're going to get after it from the air for now."

Bowden kept digging. "We can beat this thing," he growled. Then he raised his head and shouted at the rest of the crew, "C'mon, keep at it!"

Penny turned and saw the crew had paused, watching. The fire was moving past them to their downhill side, putting them in a dangerous position. "Get moving!" he barked to the rappellers. "We're going to decamp and head for the exit."

"Keep working!" Bowden yelled with such ferocity that Penny took two involuntary steps away from the man.

"Jeez, Bowden, calm down. It's okay. We lost this one for now. They're gonna do recon and they'll figure it out. Maybe we'll be back on it. So let's get going before we get cut off."

Bowden stood. Six-foot-four and broad-shouldered, he was an imposing figure. He held his Pulaski with the working end toward Penny, like a blunt-topped lance. In just the last fifteen minutes the sound of the burn had intensified from a snarl to a roar. Whipped by winds, the flames were lashing out horizontally. In the big timber, fire was boiling up into the crowns. Flames appeared over the ridgeline.

"Bowden," Penny tried to speak calmly, even though he had to raise his voice to be heard. "We're outflanked. Get moving." He turned to the crew and shouted, "Go!" and they moved but hesitantly, unsure what kind of strange rebellion they were witnessing.

Bowden's eyes were wide and glassy. He shouted *No!* and spittle flew from his lips. The heat where they stood was beginning to intensify, the burn billowed into the surrounding brush not ten yards away. Bowden looked past Penny and saw the rest of the crew watching over their shoulders as they retreated, mesmerized, their tools in hand. He found Corby's eyes under her white hardhat.

"Lucas," yelled Corby.

Bowden couldn't hear her, but he saw her mouth form his name. A memory was trying to push its way forward and he choked it back. He lowered his Pulaski until the steel head touched the ground. Suddenly couldn't get enough oxygen and he took gasping breaths. "I..." he swallowed. "I..." His head hung down; he leaned on the Pulaski to hold himself upright. He swayed slightly. Then he shifted the Pulaski to a conventional carry grip and bent down and with his other hand picked up two of the Mcleods near his boots. Penny tensed, unsure what was to come next. With his head down, Bowden walked past Bob Penny and fell in line behind the crew as they began to make their way toward the camp and the exit.

"CLOSE THE DOOR," said Matt Murphy.

Bowden shut the door to the base manager's small office. Normally, the only door on the base that might be closed was the door to the bathroom. All the rooms stayed open to each other. A shut door to the manager's office was a big deal.

"Have a seat."

Bowden sat.

"You want to tell me what was going on up at the burn?"

Bowden took in a long breath. "Well, ah, I thought we could get a line around the fire if we just kept at it."

Murphy scratched behind his ear. "Were you watching the head?"

Bowden shifted. "I could tell how it was burning from our position. It didn't look that bad."

"Well, in a way it doesn't matter what you thought you saw. It's the IC's job to keep an eye on the big picture. When the IC calls it, it's called. It's a done deal. Any hesitation creates risk not only for you, but for everybody. Now, you should know that. You've been on a lot of rappels. You've had some that got past control."

Bowden nodded.

"But that's not what concerns me. What concerns me—and several people have told me this—is that you seemed to threaten Bob Penny."

Bowden shook his head. "Maybe it seemed that way, but I didn't, really. I guess I just got caught up. Got a little too excited."

"You don't seem like a guy that loses his cool."

"I'm not."

Murphy tapped in finger on his desk. "This is what I'm going to do. I'm taking you out of the rotations for now."

Bowden started to say something then stopped.

"I'm not going to write up a letter of reprimand. And I'm not going to suspend you. I'm going to keep you on the base, see how you manage yourself, how you get along. There's plenty to do around here, keeping up with the indices and the gear. And we'll see how it goes."

Bowden got up.

"Lucas. You know we got counseling services if you

need. I can request that you get them, but I'd prefer to keep this all unofficial for now."

Bowden nodded. "I'll keep it in mind."

"You're a good rappeller. I'd like to get you back in the air."

Bowden nodded, opened the door and walked out.

THE HEAT HAMMERED down in the late afternoon. The air was a pall, dirty with typical summertime haze and drifting smoke from the wildfire some thirty miles away. Hot air rose off the land and turned the dark distant mountains into undulating waves.

Lucas Bowden watched the swaying ridges from the shade of the big oak tree. He seemed to be part of the haze, the warping of everything. He felt untethered. He already missed going out on missions and coming back filthy and tired enough so that even the devil inside would be too exhausted to torment him. The adrenalin and dopamine. Chemicals. Always trying to keep the juice going, stay one step ahead of the thing that wanted him.

He stared at the base helicopter as it ferried a bucket of water to the fire front, a dark dot against the hot sky, watched the Huey and its tethered sack until it was swallowed by the vapors.

He walked to the tree cooler. Inside, the weight room was silent. The window that Sven had broken had been replaced and it glinted in a slice of overhead sun. Motes spun lazily through the light. He sat on one of the padded benches and leaned forward, his arms on his knees. He clasped his hands and as he did so he found himself in a classic pose of prayer. He thought about praying, to what or whom he wasn't sure, but then he thought somebody might walk in suddenly and find him praying and it would be weird. So he didn't.

If he knew how to pray, he'd ask to be allowed to step out of himself, like a molting snake. Only not shedding the outside part; that would remain. But get rid of the eroding core, replace it with something new and clean. How does somebody really do that?

He got up and went to the tool cabinet and took out a file and sharpening stone. He gathered up a half dozen Pulaskis and carried them outside to the lunch bench to touch up their cutting edges. He set the tools on one end of the tabletop, then took a single tool to the other end so he could work on it. He examined it all over, the dual-headed blades as well as the handle itself. Then he set it on the table so the blade protruded just enough so he could file the edge, taking out nicks and scars and honing the cutting edge.

He was filing an axe when Corby Jones came out of headquarters, caught sight of him, and walked over.

"Hey," she said.

"Hey."

"Pretty damn hot."

"I guess."

Corby sat on one of the bench seats. A long minute passed to the rasp of the file against steel. "You doin' okay?" she asked.

He shrugged.

"I hear you got bumped out of the rotation."

He didn't stop working.

She nodded. "Won't last. Did they give you an idea of how long?"

"Nope."

Corby sighed quietly. "You wanna tell me what was going on up there? On the line?"

"Got a little excited. I guess you're not supposed to display enthusiasm."

"Well, I gotta admit, it was kinda weird."

"Just call me the rotten apple of the bunch."

"You doin' drugs?"

He stopped filing and scowled. "What makes you say that?"

She held up a hand and extended her fingers one at a time. "Mood swings. Dilated eyes. Skin pallor. Profuse sweating..."

"I'm a fireman. It gets hot."

Corby put her hand back down and stared at him. "Lucas, I don't give a shit. I mean, everybody's got issues, I understand that. I think you're a good guy. I think you got a good heart. But the bottom line is keeping each other safe. You know that. And you can't jeopardize that, ever. Because I'm pretty sure nobody else would do that to you—knowingly put you in jeopardy. So if you can't pull that off, then I definitely think you should reconsider what you're doing here." She got up and made as if to walk off but she stood there and dusted off the back of her jeans to give Bowden space for a reply.

Bowden looked off. "I won't be in the air any time soon."

She squinted. "What do you think about that?"

"I don't know." He looked down at the ground between his boots. "Sucks."

"So? Are you?"

"Am I what?"

She gave an impatient snort. "Doing drugs? Have you got an issue there?"

"What, you want to report me?"

"No, not really. It's an option, though. The reality is I'd like to see you be whole. Get some help if that's what you need."

"Damn." Bowden got to his feet. "Everybody's askin' me if I need help."

"Maybe people care about you."

"I can take care of myself." He sucked in his cheeks and nodded. "I can do just fine." He tested the blade edge of the Pulaski with his thumb. "But thanks. For the thought."

"I'm not shittin', Bowden. I got med training. I can help you find somebody to talk to."

"Were you shittin' when you told me about being half Umpqua?"

She frowned. "No. Why you are asking me that all of a sudden?"

He shrugged. "I don't know. I think it's pretty cool. Being connected to the original People."

"Are you trying to change the subject?"

He briefly smiled. Then he put the file to the tool steel and returned to his chore.

Tuesday, June 23
Kalmiopsis Wilderness

IN THE MORNING they put on hiking boots, shouldered their backpacks, adjusted trekking poles and locked the SUV. Will held out one of his poles and said *Let's go* and Kal knew the little ritual and she reached out with one of her poles and found her dad's and tapped it and said, *We gone!*

The plan was to hike in the morning when the temperatures were coolest, make a deliberate, unhurried pace of three to four miles per day, stopping in early afternoon to set up camp before it got too hot. Then they could explore a bit or just relax in some shade.

The first day would be a short hike of a couple miles into a designated botanical area where they'd camp and scout around for *Kalmiopsis* plants. On the days following, they'd follow a ridge trail for about eight miles, then take a spur trail that descended to the river and looped back to their parking spot. At their relaxed, measured pace, the whole trip would take six or seven days.

With Will in the lead, they walked along a dirt path lined with star thistle and the fifteen-foot-high skeletal remains of fire-killed rhododendrons. He set an easy tempo, calling out, *slight veer to the right* and *little hump coming up* to preview her on what was just ahead. It took Kal a good hour to get a feel for the rambling, uneven footpath under her thick-soled boots. She stumbled a couple of times but caught herself with her poles before she faceplanted. At the sound of her faltering Will would stop and turn around to find her stretched out over her poles like a ski jumper taking off. Before he could ask if she was all right she'd say, *I'm good, I'm good* and then she'd walk herself upright and Will would extend one of his poles and say *Let's go* and she'd click poles and say *We are gone.*

They left the river behind and followed the trail northwest, hiking steadily in the growing heat of the day. As they climbed the sound of the river settled into a distant murmur and the cadence of their trek became more prominent—their boots crunching on gravel and muted on soft dirt; the counterrhythm clicking of their trekking poles; the random chimes of a loose buckle bouncing against one of their stainless-steel water bottles. She tracked her father carefully, fine-tuning herself to the subtleties of his movements—the location of each of his pole strikes and the swish of his nylon pants—trying to anticipate subtle changes in pace and direction. They were careful with idle chatter that might distract from audible cues and aside from her dad saying, *tree root on the left*, their hike was a steady rhythm. The backpack was heavy and for sure was going to test her endurance, but she knew that coming in. *Kalmiopsis or bust*, she thought. The sweat that ran down her back felt wonderfully well-earned.

When they stopped for breaks and to take drinks of water Kal asked her father to describe what he saw. "Details," she requested.

"Well, there are ridges rising to the west, toward the sun," he said and Kal turned so that the sun's blaze fell full on her face. "Like three big dinosaur backs, one right after the other. There's a big patch of old trees that didn't get burned down to our right, and beyond that through a crease in the land is the river. Two sparrows just flew by, chasing each other."

These little narratives could be difficult for Will. When she was younger she was always asking for descriptions of things, often taking him by surprise. What kind of truck did they just pass and what was it carrying? What does the school parking lot look like? What is so-and-so wearing? He'd tell her as best he could because she loved to hear it, to have the words blossom in her imagination as patterns and sprites he couldn't fathom. But sometimes these narrations were painful reminders of what his daughter could not see, as if visual things denied to her were his fault, some defective gene that he'd passed on to his daughter: some DNA code not twisted into proper alignment, an out-of-kilter nucleotide. He knew Joss had the similar pangs of guilt. And although Kal's blindness was now well-integrated into all their lives, there were moments, like this one, when he would have done anything, anything…

She did see things, but in her own way. Within her blindness phosphene things melted and swirled, came bright and flashed and hovered and dissolved. Trees were magical beings composed of shimmering auras of gold and blue; rivers were ribbons of white effervescence. Dogs were boundless pink; birdsongs were rainbow microbursts. The house where she lived was warm chocolate and the taste of real chocolate itself caused cascades of silvery stars that waterfalled along the edges of her mind. Mountains caused feelings rather than visual sensations; they were swellings inside her chest cavity, straining against containment.

"More," she said softly.

"Well, when we were closer to the river, the water was so clear you could see every rock and baby trout. But where the shadows of trees fell across the river the water was so dark and you couldn't make out anything. It was like black doorways cut into the water, and everything disappeared inside of it."

"Black," she said. Black was slick, sharp-cornered, cool to the touch. Black was the edge of her laminate-covered computer desk at home.

Will scanned their surroundings. The land unfurled around them as if boundless, dark brown ridges swathed in shawls of dark green firs and cedars and open wounds of upright dead tree trunks, their bottoms swathed in manzanita and coffeeberry bushes and poison oak and everywhere new conifers beginning to muscle their way into the mix, their crowns prominent. It wasn't the most photogenic wilderness area you could wander into, but Will loved it for its rugged persistence and its ultramafic heart—the strangely complex geology that had produced such a mysterious ecosystem.

"All around us here are big trees. They're dead snags and they're all grey, like an older person, because their bark has fallen away and the exposed trunks are bleached by the sun. But it's like they're standing guard over the new forest that's growing up around them. Like old souls watching over new little souls."

She came to his side and put her arm around him. "Any *Kalmiopsis?*"

"Not that I can see. Not yet. We'll check out that botanical area. If nothing's there, we'll eventually move down close to the river. Maybe in spots where's there's more moisture we'll find them."

They clicked poles and set out. They hiked through the heart of the morning and as they made their way along the trail Kal tracked the sun as it swung through the sky, radiating from different parts of the overhead. At last Will announced they arrived at a good camping spot and Kal wiggled out of her shoulder straps and let her backpack fall heavily to the ground. "Whew."

Will guided her to a spot where she could sit down with her back against a big rock and he handed her a water bottle. "You rest," he said. "I'll set up the tent."

"I can help, you know."

"You just hang out. It's been a long day. You can help set up tomorrow."

Kal eased gratefully against the rock and listened to her dad and the rustling of the nylon tent and the whack of him pounding stakes with a rock. She drank the warm water with its metallic tinge and felt the longed-for backpacking ache in her legs and she decided that she was ridiculously happy. As the sun settled Will heated water on the tiny propane backpacking stove and made spaghetti and meat sauce from a freeze-dried packet and Kal said it was about the best meal she'd ever tasted in her life and she meant it.

"A good day's backpacking will do that to your taste buds," said Will. He got his cell phone out of his backpack and checked it. "I'm looking at my phone," he said, "and we have no bars. No reception. We are officially in the wilderness and out of touch with civilization."

"Yay!" said Kal. Then she sighed. "I wish we could have a campfire, though."

"Well, not this year. Maybe next year we'll go earlier in the season. Would you like that?"

"Serious?"

"Of course. Have campfires, the whole thing."

"Oh, we are so gone."

Tuesday, June 23
Rogue River-Siskiyou National Forest headquarters, Medford

THE 0900 BRIEFING took place in Conference Room Three on the second floor of the administrative building that the Forest Service shared with the Bureau of Land Management. The window shades were down to block out the intense morning sun but slices of light came in at the bottoms and sides of the shades and struck across the room hot as branding irons.

Supervisor Oates and FAO Hudek sat at one end of a plain laminated table with the duty officer, an assistant station manager, and the public information officer and the Fire Officer from the Bureau of Land Management. In the middle of the table was a squat conference phone speaker that connected Conference Room Three with the National Weather Service station in Medford, the fire managers from Bureau of Indian Affairs, National Park Service, Oregon Department of Forestry, Oregon State Fire Marshall's office, and the duty officers for all six ranger districts in the Rogue-River Siskiyou National Forest. Spread out next to the phone was a map that showed the National Forest and its surrounding area, and beside that lay a detail map of the Kalmiopsis Wilderness. A quad map of the area was pinned to the wall.

The current topic was Incident 395 in the Kalmiopsis Wilderness, now dubbed The Tincup Fire after a nearby mountain peak. Overnight the Tincup had grown to five-hundred acres and although relatively small, conditions were ripe for a blowup. After the rappellers retreated, Hudek had directed helitack operations to continue aerial water drops at the head of the fire, and the Northwest GAAC had authorized contracting two more helicopters from a private company in Medford. It was the most practical way to attack the Tincup, but it was also one of the most expensive when it came to bang for the federal buck. Having ordinary ground crews hike to the fire over the extremely rugged terrain wasn't a good option and any local Hotshot crews—who could have made that hike—were all deployed to various incidents throughout the Northwest. With the fire broken out past the initial attack and no available tanker support, the room held a quiet sense of urgency.

The meteorologist on the call gave a sobering forecast. "We've had an upper-level ridge over us for the last week," he reported, "and this hot, dry weather is going to continue. We've got a strong thermal trough that's developed along the coast, and winds are gonna blow offshore from the northeast as they're pulled into the low pressure at the coast. That'll cause wind speed to be much higher than we've seen in the last few days. As winds flow downslope, they'll warm up and dry out even more. Expect highs near one hundred, afternoon humidity below ten percent, and winds of twenty to thirty mph with gusts to fifty, even stronger in northeast to southwest aligned drainages. We'll also see considerable eddying in the lee side of mountains with swirling winds pushing in all directions. Today is going to be a very critical fire weather day."

Everyone nodded—this was a conundrum that had bedeviled fire response in the Kalmiopsis for generations: A burn that was too remote for engines and ground crews but had unfettered access to hundreds of square miles of bone-dry fuel and was about to get whipped by strong winds. Hiking hand crews into the area as far as possible and then cutting and burning out control lines was possible, but burnouts in the Kalmiopsis had a bad history. After the mammoth Biscuit Fire of 2002, some post-fire analysts concluded that the Forest Service's strategy of setting extensive burnouts and backfires had contributed to the destruction of more than half a million acres of wildland. Although it had happened decades ago, the damning conclusions still haunted the Forest Service.

The nearest defensible natural fire control was the Illinois River to the east and north. But if the fire got that far it would have burned a minimum twenty thousand acres and dumped smoke all over southern Oregon. The locals would be howling. If the fire went west it would burn into one of the most rugged, remote areas in the state. Once there, the only way to stop it would be to pray for rain. To the south was another river, the Chetco, which was too narrow to be a reliable natural control. If the fire got past the Chetco, it could run all the way to the towns that dotted the Redwood Highway.

One of the district managers came on the speakerphone and cited a study at Oregon State University that said new growth burned hotter than expected and that old burn scars were prime candidates for intense and erratic fire behavior. Someone else said they'd like to see the study and there were murmurs of *Yeah me too* and the district manager said he'd send everyone the link.

If there was any good news it was that the fire was still relatively small and isolated, and that the rappelers had managed to establish a partial control along the upper edge of the ridge before they'd pulled out. The latest surveillance confirmed that the blaze was not yet hopping over into the next valley, but spot fires were continually popping up ahead of the blaze as it headed south along the eastern flank of the ridgeline.

The Kalmiopsis itself was basically roadless except for rutted remnants that once led to miners' cabins. Two Forest Service roads approached the upper part of the Wilderness from Highway 199. One road approached the wilderness from the north and stopped a few miles from the border. If the fire ran that direction, ground attack would have access. The other road was a decent one-lane, asphalt-paved road that ran alongside the Illinois River, passing by several small campgrounds along the way. After ten miles the asphalt stopped and the road became a narrow gravel track that wound up into the mountains, following the course of the river glistening a thousand feet below. After another ten miles this rough road descended to rejoin the Illinois, ending at a small campground at Panther Bar.

If needed, that would be the way to bring crews and equipment in on the fire's eastern flank. Supervisor Oates turned to the duty officer and said, "Have Wild Rivers get a ranger and a truck up there and clear out the campgrounds along the Illinois."

LATE THAT MORNING Doug Doty climbed into the cab of one of the green Ford F-250 brush trucks that had been assigned to the Wild Rivers Ranger Station in Cave Junction. Ranger Doty was headed up the Illinois River Road toward the Kalmiopsis to let civilians know about the fire and to politely insist that they leave the area. It was a great day to be on the back roads, motoring alone in the mountains on a special assignment with no time constraints except to be back at the station before 5 p.m. With slow and careful driving, Doty reckoned he'd return somewhere around quitting time. Hopefully, he'd get lucky and not have to confront any beer-soaked knuckleheads skinny dipping and defying the river's ban on alcohol.

At the first campground Doty saw a handful of cars and pulled into the lot. A path led down to a sandy spit of beach, and Doty could hear laughter and yelling coming from below. He got out and tucked in his shirt and got his official Smoky-the-Bear-style, wide-brimmed hat set just right and walked on down. Sure enough, eight or so teens in swimsuits were lounging on lawn chairs and swimming noisily in the river. He could smell pot. There was an open cooler nearby, and a couple of kids had cans of Coors.

It was a beautiful spot, with the green-glass river stretched out and hobbit-like rocks heaped up and deep pools of clear jade. What kid wouldn't want to come up here on a hot day and cool off? He walked up and they didn't register him until he was only a few feet away and then they looked up startled as rabbits. "Hey there," he smiled.

"Um," was the collective reply.

"You know there's a no-liquor policy here on the river, don't you?"

Everyone looked at their beers as if the cans had appeared in their hands by magic. "Um, there is?"

Doty looked off and nodded. He didn't go for a hardass approach; he knew to just let the uniform do its job. He said, "Well, there's a wildfire happening not too far from here and we're telling people to pack up and leave the area."

"Oh wow. You mean like, close to here?"

"Yes. You see that cloud?" They followed his pointing finger and nodded. "That's not a cloud, it's smoke. You folks need to leave immediately."

"Right."

There was a pause as the teens wondered if they were about to be busted for having beer on the river. Doty let them stew in their paranoia for a few moments, then said, "And you know, on the drive down? You wouldn't want somebody behind the wheel who might have been tipping a frosty, right?"

"Oh for sure, right."

"I'm going to the other campgrounds," Doty jerked a thumb over his shoulder, "then I'm coming back to make sure everyone's out of here."

Ranger Doty visited all the remaining camps and waysides except one. The last remaining campsite to check was at Panther Bar, ten miles distant up the rocky, unpaved portion of the single-lane, and Doty settled in for a drive that would take the better part of an hour. The truck was getting retrofitted with a new water pump but the equipment had yet to be installed so it was light in the rear end and skittered on the loose gravel and washboard ridges and it trailed great balls of road dust that rolled forward to overtake him whenever he slowed down. The plume of the Tincup Fire burn hung on the western horizon. From its looks, Doty judged it to be a thousand acres. He didn't sense it was a worrisome fire—he'd seen worse.

At its high point the corniche clung to the side of a ridge with vertical rock walls to the right and a precipitous drop off to the left. This was a tricky piece of road but he'd been on it several times before and the fact that it might be dangerous hardly registered. But as he came around a hard bend he was surprised by a big object in his path and he slammed on the brakes and there was a heart-stopping moment as the Ford skittered a bit sideways before coming to a halt. He turned off the engine and got out and he could feel his heart thumping as the dust swirled. There was an enormous rock in the roadway. It was curved on one side and flat on the other and it looked like a gigantic, overturned turtle. Doty looked up the face of the cliff and saw the clean, shiny place where the knob had recently sheared off. Rocks tumbled onto the backroads all the time, but this definitely was the biggest single piece he'd ever seen. It was surrounded by chunks and shards of newly cracked serpentine that glinted in the light.

"Son of a bitch," said Doty. He went to his cab and got on the radio to dispatch. "Hey this is Doug. I'm on the River Road and I'm up past Deep Gorge and there's been a slide and there's a big rock blocking the road. Over."

"Ah, roger that. How big is that rock, Doug? Can you maybe move it with the truck? Over."

"No way. I mean, it's the size of a refrigerator. It's four, five tons easy. It's gonna take a dozer. Over."

"All right. Well, head on back and we'll get a road crew to take care of it. Over."

"Roger that. And out." Doty sighed. Now he'd have to carefully back down the road until he found a spot to turn around. He studied the roadway and decided there was a decent turnout about a hundred yards away. He got in the cab and micro adjusted the side mirrors so he could keep close watch on the distance between the edge of the road and the rear tires, then he put the truck in reverse and started to ease back down. The first bend was a challenge and in the brief fraction of a second it took to check the passenger-side mirror he felt a sickening slump from the rear end and the truck started to slide. He pumped the brakes for all he was worth and the truck tilted and slid another foot which took an eternity of time and then it stopped. A tire had gone off the edge. Doty clutched at the steering wheel and stared at the driver's side rearview. How the hell had that happened? He was being so careful. He put the truck in forward gear and hoped the four-wheel drive would pop him free but when he touched the accelerator the wheels skipped on loose gravel and the truck slipped incrementally sideways toward the precipice. *Shit.* He turned off the motor and set the parking brake, then undid his seatbelt and carefully inched his way to the passenger side door. He got out and stepped clear and for the second time in the last fifteen minutes his heart was thrumming like a hummingbird.

The driver's side rear had indeed caught a soft spot along the edge and had slipped off the road and the truck was lopsided and looked to be resting on its rear differential.

Of all the dumb-ass stupid things. Doty peered over the edge. The tire was on loose scree and the slope was seventy degrees and if the truck had gone over it would have tumbled some one hundred feet before rock outcroppings and dead snags stopped it. Maybe. It would not have been pretty.

It was going to take a tow truck now and they'd have to get that up here before the bulldozer arrived but he realized with a shit-on-top-of-shit feeling that he'd have to get back into the cab to use the radio and he was not inclined to do that. He worked his jaw back and forth and finally decided he didn't have a choice—he'd have to radio dispatch and tell them what happened. Just then the truck gave a little shudder and moved another inch or so and that was that. He was not getting back in the cab.

He could walk out or wait for help to arrive. The worse that could happen was he didn't make it back by five and dispatch would try to raise him by radio and when he didn't respond they'd send another truck up to see why.

He looked down along the valley and saw the brown line of the road etched vaguely against the far ridges. It would be a long hot walk. The mid-afternoon sun was blazing and his mouth had gone dry. At least he had his wide-brimmed hat. Maybe he'd luck out and meet a vehicle coming up, or maybe a dozer truck was already on its way. At least the walk would be mostly downhill. He started off, shaking his head at how things can suddenly go wrong and at the same time knowing they could have been worse. As he walked he took in the fire plume in the distance, noting its shaggy color and the fact that it looked much bigger than earlier in the day.

AT ABOUT 1800 HOURS Ranger Jan Bergholtz found Ranger Doty walking down the Illinois River Road with a wobbly gait. She stopped her truck and Doty opened the passenger door and climbed inside.

"Jesus, Doug, where the hell have you been? You didn't respond to any calls. And where the hell is your truck?"

Doty licked his lips. They were dry and flaky. "Man, I'm thirsty. You got any water?"

Bergholtz rummaged in the back of the cab and came up with a metal thermos. "It's cold coffee from this morning. It's all I've got."

Doty unscrewed the cap and drank the remains in two large swallows. "Whew," he said, wiping his mouth on the back of his hand. "What a day."

So he explained the situation, finding the big rock and then slipping off the road and the fact that the rig was in a precarious position and he was reluctant to climb back in the cab to use the radio. Telling it now, he wondered if he sounded chickenshit, so he emphasized the fact that the road had been poorly maintained over the years and had been allowed to erode and that he had been extremely lucky to escape with his life. "Give that truck a good stiff breeze and it would have gone right over," he said. "No way I could get to the radio."

Bergholtz clucked in sympathy and reached for the radio to call dispatch. "Yeah, I got him. He, ah, had an accident with his truck and it's still up there."

"Roger that," said the dispatch operator. "We'll see if we can get a tow truck up there in the morning."

"Copy. Out." Bergholtz replaced the mike in its cradle and peered out the windshield at the smoke plume as it rose up to catch the lowering sunlight. "It's starting to blow up pretty good."

Doty followed her gaze and nodded.

"Let's get down to one of the campgrounds so you can get some water," she said. "You look about dried out."

"What I could use," said Doty, "is a beer."

"Roger that."

Wednesday, June 24
Wild Rivers Ranger Station, Cave Junction
Rogue River-Siskiyou Forest Service Headquarters, Medford

IN THE MORNING Doug Doty recounted his adventure on the Illinois River Road to the Fire Management Officer at the Wild Rivers Ranger Station. The FMO directed the Duty Officer to request a local tow truck operator to retrieve the disabled brush truck. Then he called Forest Service dispatch to say that Wild Rivers was handling the blockage on the Illinois River Road.

The DO called an auto repair shop in Cave Junction that offered tow services and was on a list of local contractors who worked for the Forest Service on a regular basis. There was no answer, only an automated answering system, so the DO left a detailed message about the location of the brush truck and that it should be removed as soon as possible. He hung up assuming that the message would be heard and the truck soon retrieved. It was not. The mom-and-pop owners of the auto repair shop, Zach and Gloria Richardson, had taken the day off. Zach had scheduled a colonoscopy at a hospital in Grants Pass, and Gloria had agreed to drive him there and back. It was his first colonoscopy. There wasn't anything wrong, but his doctor said it was routine medical maintenance for those over 50. Zach made butt jokes for days leading up to the actual procedure.

After it was over and the anesthetic had worn off, Zach announced he was ravenous on account of the high-powered laxative he'd been required to take the night before. He wanted to chow down at the local Black Bear diner, which they did. When the waitress handed them their bill at the end of the meal, Zach grinned up at her and said, "Hey, I just paid off my colonoscopy bill and now I'm in arrears. Get it? Like, in the rear?" The waitress wrinkled her nose and confessed she didn't get it. Gloria said, "Oh don't mind him."

The Richardsons didn't get home until late that evening. Gloria, who was responsible for tracking appointments for the repair shop, took one look at the blinking, insistent message light on the office phone, shook her head, and said, *I'll catch up tomorrow.*

AT 0900 HOURS Supervisor Olympia Oates conferred with Fire and Aviation Officer Ken Hudek to review the latest reconnaissance reports, satellite imagery and fire perimeter overlays of the Tincup Fire along with data from the National Weather Service. The burn had grown to 3,000 acres and, abetted by dry conditions and increasing wind velocity, was projected to triple in size by noon the following day. The fire had quickly outpaced local firefighting capacity.

"We're calling this in as a Type Two," said Oates. The GACC in Portland could now give the go-ahead for mobilizing an extensive fire response, pulling in prearranged resources from all over the region.

Shortly after the briefing the Deputy Forest Supervisor was on his way to the Interagency Office in Grants Pass to coordinate the process of establishing the fire camp—a location big enough to accommodate dozens of firefighting engines, water tankers, skidgens, bulldozers, and crew transports along with helicopter staging areas, command centers, as well as food and shelter needs for 200 to 300 firefighters. By noon the Logistics branch of the Type 2 incident command structure had procured an open, ten-acre site just outside the small town of Selma and was already dispatching construction crews to build tent shelters, a food commissary, washing and shower facilities, and to position the dozens of Porta-Pottys.

Wednesday, June 24
Medford

JOSS SPENCER WENT grocery shopping at Albertson's. It was a small luxury to be able to shop in the early afternoon when the store was practically empty. She bought several frozen dinners—freedom from real cooking was another small luxury—and as she cruised the aisles she found herself reflexively adding items that were her daughter's favorites—whole grain breakfast flakes, sustainably-sourced chocolate chips, organic mandarin oranges that would hopefully last until Kal returned from her adventure.

Joss was thinking of the sharing arrangements she'd made with Will. Her ex would get Kal every other weekend from Friday afternoon until Monday morning, various three- and four-day weekends, plus a summer vacation. The backpacking trip was in addition to everything, sort of a daddy's-home bonus. She didn't know if she was being too generous or not generous enough with the custody agreement. How did anybody really know these things? How do you reconcile what's right for the child with what's right for each of the parents?

She was lost in thought and also walking while trying to read the ingredient label on a container of salsa when someone touched her on the arm, startling her. It was Heather Franklin, the mother of one of Kal's friends, Betsy. Although lately Kallie didn't have much to say about Betsy.

"Hi Joss."

"Hey Heather."

"I haven't seen you in a while."

"Well, we've been pretty busy."

"I hear Kallie's dad is back in town from the Middle East."

"Yeah. He's back." It was an effort to keep uncertainty out of her voice. "She likes having her dad around."

"I hear they're on a backpacking trip."

"That's right."

"Isn't that dangerous for Kal? Not being able to see?"

Joss suppressed a sigh. "Not really. They've got a system worked out and Will takes it easy. They've hiked before. They're fine."

"I hear there's a big fire up in the Kalmiopsis Wilderness. Isn't that where they are, the Kalmiopsis?"

It took a moment for the information to sink in. Joss blinked. "There is?"

"I heard about it a couple of hours ago. They say it's getting big. A thousand acres? Ten thousand? I forget exactly. But big."

"Huh." Joss frowned. "You sure it was in the Kalmiopsis Wilderness?"

Heather nodded. "Positive."

"Well, I'm sure they're okay." Joss began to push her cart along. She'd gone several feet when she realized she was simply ignoring the woman and she turned and said over her shoulder, "Nice to see you."

Joss slowly made her way to the front of the store and the checkout. She didn't get in the checkout line but feigned interest in the end-of-counter magazine rack while the clerk leaned on the conveyer belt with both hands and waited for her. Then without acknowledging either the clerk or her groceries she abandoned her cart and walked out the automatic doors to her car. She got in the front seat and closed the door and put the key in the ignition so she could roll down the windows. *It's Forest Service land. They'll be fighting the fire. They'll have warned everybody to get out. Kal and Will are probably headed down right now.*

She got out her cell phone and called her ex-husband

but there was no response. Will had said they'd be out of cell range so they probably wouldn't get any messages until they came down out of the mountains. She left a message, *Will, call me as soon as you get this.*

She drove home and went online and looked up the local news and found a video clip about the fire. A Forest Service spokesperson was quoted as saying the fire was nine-hundred acres but it was isolated and didn't threaten any homes or people and was being controlled with firefighting rappelers and helicopters. *Okay, good. Those were good words: controlled, people weren't threatened. That most likely included campers and backpackers.*

She relaxed a bit, then looked up the phone number for the Medford office of the Forest Service. After about eight rings somebody finally answered.

"I was calling about the fire in the wilderness area. The Kalmiopsis."

"Yes ma'am, how can I help you?"

She wasn't quite sure what to ask so she said, "How big is it?"

"The Tincup Fire is in a remote area and is currently about three thousand acres."

Three thousand? Wasn't it nine hundred about five minutes ago? "My husband and daughter—my ex-husband—are backpacking up there. Are there people, Forest Service people, going up and warning people?"

"Yes, ma'am, that's standard procedure. The rangers go to all the campgrounds and make sure folks evacuate if necessary. Where exactly did your family go, do you know?"

"They were going to some botanical area."

"There's a whole lot of botanical areas up there. You know which one?"

"They were going to a place called, ah, Panther Bar. That's it. Panther Bar."

There was the sound of a creaking chair and then the voice of the Forest Service desk attendant sounding far off as he called to a colleague, "Hey Jerry? How far is that Kalmiopsis burn from Panther Bar? Okay, thanks." The voice returned to normal. "That fire is a good ten, twelve miles away."

"Um, is that far in terms of a forest fire? Do they travel fast?"

"Oh, ten miles would take quite a while. They'll have crews notifying folks at the campgrounds. Your family will be fine."

After the call Joss felt better. With a twinge of guilt, she thought about going back to retrieve her abandoned grocery cart. She wondered how long it takes grocery store employees to recognize an abandoned cart and if abandoned carts with groceries still in them were pretty high on the list of Annoying Things That Customers Do and she decided that she'd go shopping tomorrow at a different store.

At five in the afternoon Joss poured herself a glass of chilled white wine and called Will and there was no answer and she left another message. She watched the local evening news and it was a good twenty minutes into the broadcast before there was coverage of the fire. They said it was four thousand acres and zero percent contained. There was aerial footage of billowing smoke leaning out of a mountainside.

By the 10 p.m. local news broadcast Joss was three glasses into the bottle of white wine and coverage of the fire had moved up a notch in the hierarchy of the day's stories. They showed the same aerial footage and the news anchor said the wildfire in the Kalmiopsis Wilderness had a name— the Tincup Fire—and that it had grown to eight thousand acres and remained zero percent contained. The broadcast noted that the Kalmiopsis fire was one of several dozen burning in the Northwest, and that high winds, dry conditions, and limited resources were making firefighting extremely difficult all across the West.

Something about her phone call to the Forest Service was bothering her. She remembered the man had said that the rangers would clear out any campgrounds near the fire. But Will and Kal weren't camping—they were hiking. Hadn't she told that to the Forest Service man? Hiking? They could be miles away from the campground. How did the Forest Service find hikers and warn them? The wine remaining in the bottom of the bottle looked pitifully low. Had she ever consumed an entire bottle of wine by herself? She drank what was left straight from the bottle.

Wednesday, June 24
Kalmiopsis Wilderness

IN THE MORNING Will retrieved the bear bag and made breakfast from instant oatmeal packets. He sat with Kal on a gray, bleached-backed log and they ate while the sun lifted over the eastern horizon and warmth began to bake the coolness out of the nighttime mountain air. It was the third day of their adventure and they'd hiked five miles into the wilderness. The goal was to continue heading west along the ridge to where the trail forked. They'd camp there, then take a return loop that swung down toward the river and back where they'd parked the Land Cruiser. At their measured pace, Will figured another four days completing the loop, just as he'd promised Joss. They were in no hurry, and Kal seemed to be having a hell of a good time. He definitely was.

After breakfast they crammed sleeping bags into stuff sacks and rolled up the tent and hoisted their backpacks, clicked poles and headed out. The trail grew rugged and where it was especially rocky and steep Will had Kal stash her poles and hang onto his backpack for guidance and support. It didn't take long for the temperatures to move from moderate to blazing but a steady breeze had come up and made the heat bearable. The heat baked the scent out of the trees and the air was fragrant with the sweet smell of pine and cedar.

It was almost noon when Will spotted *Kalmiopsis* growing in the sturdy soils just a few feet off the trail. "There it is!" he yelped.

Kal knew exactly what her dad was hollering about. "Where? Where!"

"Just a little bit off trail."

"I want to touch."

"Let's take off our packs so we can get down close." They shimmied out of their packs and he took her hand and led her to where a one-foot-high plant huddled in the shadow of a rock outcropping. They knelt and both reached out to take the short, waxy leaves in their fingers.

"All right," Kal said softly.

"There's no blossoms right now. We're a little late in the season."

"That's okay. It's so cool just to be here and feel it. Get to know it." Gently massaging the little leaves between her thumb and forefinger. "Hi *Kalmiopsis*. Guess what my name is? Kalmiopsis! Jane Kalmiopsis Spencer. Hey dad, maybe my name should be Kalmiopsis Jane, like Calamity Jane."

"Well, that's a thought."

"Look out boys, Kalmiopsis Jane is here." She smiled, marveling at the sound of her namesake.

Will looked around and was surprised to see more *Kalmiopsis* nearby—he'd been so focused on the one plant. "There's more *Kalmiopsis* plants around here."

"That's good. Say, do you think Lilla Leach camped here, on this same spot?"

"Very likely." Will smiled. His daughter's face, with its forthright nose and gentle spray of freckles, was so full of contentment. Satisfaction. And something else. Something new had grown there since he'd been away. A raw-quarried confidence. The determination of youth. She knew she was headed in the right direction, that she was at the beginning of becoming.

He'd have to tell Joss there was some good mothering was going on.

They hiked into the heat of the day and as they picked their way along the trail they were buffeted by increasingly strong winds. Some gusts were brawny enough to stop Kal in her tracks and when she'd hear one galloping toward her through the underbrush she'd pause and plant her poles so she wouldn't be knocked off balance. After an hour they decided to call it quits for the day. Will picked out a campsite under the thin shade of two Ponderosa pines and they pitched the tent as the pines swayed and made squeaky sounds where their branches rubbed against each other.

In the evening Will built a little wall of rocks to protect the camp stove from the unabated wind and when the dinner packets were ready they retreated to the shelter of the tent to eat. Just before the sun went down Will went off to clean the plates and hang the bear bag. Then he and Kal sat outside in the lee of the tent as the western sky ebbed into strata of pink and purple and darkest cobalt blue and he felt the familiar guilt of witnessing something beautiful that his daughter could not see. He wondered if he should try to describe it but in this moment he was overwhelmed with feelings and the words were elusive. The air seemed unwilling to cool down so they sat and listened to the restless choral of the wind in the trees and all around. Just before midnight they got into the tent and lay on top of their sleeping bags and soon Kal was asleep.

Sometime in the night she awoke and shifted around and she could hear her dad's husky breathing and it made her feel full and content. Before she drifted off she caught a brief whiff of a tantalizing smell. Woodsmoke. *There must be other campers out here,* she thought. Some lucky stiffs had broken the rules and made a campfire. Kal knew it wasn't right, but she envied whoever it was who had flaunted the official guidelines. *They're so lucky!*

FROM THE AUDIOBOOK, "Our Amazing Forests," by Heidi Anderson and Vince DiMarco:

A key trigger for intense wildfire behavior is low relative humidity—the amount of moisture in the air. Extremely low humidity occurs regularly in our Western forests during hot summer months when rain showers are few and far between. Not only does the air become dry, but the entire forest dries out. Leaves, twigs, trees and bushes become so dry that they will easily burn if ignited. The parched forest floor—a mat of dead organic material that has accumulated over years called duff—adds a layer of highly flammable detritus to the mix. Firefighters refer to all these combustibles as fuels—the materials that "power" a wildfire.

Fire Burn Analysts, or FBANs, are essential firefighting personnel. Their job is to make reliable predictions about what direction and how fast a fire will move. They constantly monitor factors such as wind speed, wind direction, terrain, relative humidity and the dryness of fuels to predict how the fire will behave. During a wildfire incident, an FBAN works closely with an IMET—an Incident Meteorologist who forecasts critical weather information.

One particular variable the team will analyze is the "probability of ignition," or POI, meaning the predictive chance for the fuels to catch fire if a source of ignition is present. Ignition sources may include a spark from an engine, a dropped cigarette, or a windborne ember from a nearby fire.

In extreme conditions, probability of ignition may be eighty percent or higher. Think of eighty percent this way—if one hundred burning embers would touch the forest floor, eighty of them would start new fires.

Thursday, June 25
Medford

TIM WRIGHT GOT the call at his home at 6 a.m. An incident meteorologist was needed to staff up the Tincup Fire, which had grown to twelve thousand acres and was being upgraded to a Type 2 incident requiring a major response organization. He was to report to the fire camp that was being assembled in Selma. There, he would join with the other Incident Response Team managers and some four hundred firefighters to try and corral the Tincup.

This would be Wright's seventeenth fire as a specially trained IMET and he knew the drill. His Ford Explorer was prepacked with a printer, mobile satellite setup, fresh batteries, various office supplies, extra clothes including Nomex shirt and pants, and camping gear. His laptop was fully charged, as always, and he slid that into a daypack pre-provisioned with a solar charger, hand soap, a washcloth, deodorant, and a toothbrush. *Screw shaving for the duration.* His wife, Lisa, had already put ice packs, oranges, four beers, homemade fudge brownies and handfuls of elk jerky sticks into the standby cooler. She, too, knew the drill. By the time her husband arrived the Logistics Branch would already be setting up a field kitchen, but a few special items helped ease the stress. She handed him the cooler and they kissed and she said, *Good luck, stay safe* and he smiled and said *Thanks I will.* Eighteen minutes after getting the call Wright was on the interstate and headed for the Redwood Highway to Selma.

He'd attended fires all over the West but working one that was relatively close to home had a special urgency. He'd grown up in the Rogue Valley and the land was as familiar as his own skin. The towns changed, buildings and businesses came and went, roads turned from two to four lanes, trees came down and trees grew back up. But the land remained as before: huge, impressive, impassive. He knew the place on the highway where the ridges opened to views of the peaks of the Red Buttes and he knew the horizons where the sun rose and set with the changing seasons and he knew every bend in the Rogue River where it ran near the highway, twisting and glistening in the sun. *There are things you know and things you don't. And you better know the difference.* That's what his dad used to say.

By the time he arrived the fire camp was in the throes of getting organized. Out in the open field the long food-serving shelters were being set up and the big ten-person sleeping tents were being spread out on the ground. Engines and tenders and buses of various sizes and heritages and colors stood in neat rows opposite more haphazard lines of parked personal vehicles—trucks, cars and SUVs. Firefighters in the yellow, green and brown shirts of their respective agencies were walking around and many were gathered in small groups hearing the latest fire news and talking attack strategies. In the western sky hung the hulking, grayish-brown smoke plume.

Wright noted that toward the end of the field was a scattering of smaller camping tents. He'd brought his own tent and air mattress and planned to camp off by himself—in the past he'd endured his share of snorers and grunters in the group tents and he'd found going solo was the best way to get a few hours of real sleep. Many felt the same and before long there would be a hundred or more individual tents scattered around.

He parked and made his way to the wildlands learning center that had been turned into a temporary command headquarters for the incoming Type 2 Incident Management Team. A handful of managers was there, including the NF Supervisor, Olympia Oates, who was the acting IC for the smaller and more localized Type 3 team. Everyone shook hands and the new team members introduced themselves. Computers were being set up on a couple of folding tables and fat wires running out a nearby window indicated satellite links were being established just outside.

Oates waved her hands to get everyone's attention and said, "The Type Two Commander and his team are on their way, they'll be here in a couple of hours, and we should have most of them here by this evening. We'll have the official transfer of command in the morning. Meanwhile, here's the situation."

Oates walked to a large area map pinned up on a wall. She pointed to a blot-shaped piece of clear red plastic mylar that had been fixed over a portion of the dark green wilderness area.

"We've got the burn divided into four divisions: A, B and C here to the south, and D to the north. Winds have shifted almost one-eighty and are beginning to increase to twenty miles an hour plus. They're coming from the southwest and right now recon is having a hard time getting a good look at Delta, but we know there are spots out in front of the head. The fire is moving upwards of twenty chains per hour. It has yet to make a serious move to the west. We've been a little hamstrung without tanker support but with the upgrade to Type Two the GACC has two DC-6s headed our way so we can put down wet lines.

"The current plan is to put bulldozers and ground crews in here and build a control line to the south. We want to make sure the fire can't head toward the populated areas if it decides to turn around. There's a bridge here and we've got an engineer en route to make sure it can hold a D9 or whatever else we'll need. We have a request pending to access the wilderness with heavy equipment. When the new commander gets here, we'll see if that's the plan going forward. I see our IMET."

Wright nodded and raised his hand.

"The FBAN is Roger Markle. You know him?"

"I know him."

"We got your tent outside around the corner towards the back."

"I'll be set up in an hour."

"All right," said the Supervisor. "Let's meet back here in two hours and we'll update with any new folks."

THE WORK TENT Wright would share with the Fire Burn Analyst was a canvas, eight-sided yurt-type structure and a generous fourteen feet in diameter. The roof was vaulted on slender wood rafters and there were four screen windows with roll-down canvas shades. Three laminate tables had been placed around the perimeter along with several folding chairs, and maps of the Siskiyou National Forest and the Kalmiopsis Wilderness were pinned to the walls. Two beefy power cords snaked inside, each ending in a four-way receptacle box. Extension cords ran from the receptacles up the walls to overhead electric lights, and the cords sagged between the spots where they'd been hastily tied to the rafters. From one of the cords the logistics crew had hung a laminated carboard sign with the words *Fire Weather and Behavior* in block letters. A freestanding air conditioner was off to one side. For a field forecasting station, it was luxurious.

Wright retrieved his vehicle and drove it up to the tent to unload his gear and set up a satellite link. When he was plugged in and powered up, he noticed the small portable air conditioner near the end of one of the tables. Good thing— it was going to be stifling in the tent. It was unplugged, so he got down on his hands and knees and found a receptacle and connected it. He flicked the On switch and the device gave a high-pitched squeak and then shuddered and stopped. He flicked the switch again with various cool settings to no avail. Son of a gun, he'd have to call Logistics and see if they could repair or replace the unit. He stood and found the FBAN, Roger Merkle, standing in the tent doorway taking stock of their temporary headquarters.

"Pretty nice digs," said Merkle.

"Hey Roger, good to see you again," said Wright as they shook hands. He pointed to the air conditioner. "Portable AC doesn't work. I'll call Logistics about it."

Wright nodded. "Gonna be a hot one." He already had a sheen of sweat on his forehead. "I'd better get set up, sketch out what we've got."

When Merkle was settled at his computer, Wright opened the Weather Service website and began to shuffle through the various indices. "We've got dry, hot unstable air and a major wind shift in the last twenty-four hours, northeast flows changing to gusty winds ranging to forty miles an hour from the southwest. Extreme burning conditions. Convection over most of the fire area. Not a lot of nighttime recovery for RH."

"Snags, tanoak, and manzanita," said Merkle. "All the bad stuff. Fuel moisture at three percent, POI is ninety percent. Steep slopes, rate of spread twenty to thirty chains per hour. Lots of wind acceleration and torching in the wind-aligned slopes which are here…" he touched a screen that displayed a color-mapped version of the area, "…here, and here. Lots of fingering in the canyons and spotting up to a mile. Looks like it wants to double in size in the next twenty-four hours. Tough one to stop."

"All right," said Wright. "Let's work up a report for the next briefing."

JOSS WAS UP by six a.m. and got a cup of instant coffee and went online to look at the local news. The Tincup Fire had grown to twelve-thousand acres and continued to burn in the National Forest and Kalmiopsis Wilderness. *Fuck!* Crews were being brought in from around the region. *Shit!* There was a video of a Forest Service spokesperson who was on-location in the small town of Selma where firefighting crews were assembling. In the background were stout wildfire-fighting trucks and beyond that were dozens of camping tents set up in a large field. The Forest Service spokesperson stood next to a vehicle with "Foam Truck" stenciled on its side. People in yellow shirts and white hard hats walked past. The air looked hazy with drifting smoke. The spokesperson was saying that there was a shortage of air support because of all the other wildfires throughout the country but that the Tincup Fire was in a remote area and that no lives were being threatened and that the fire currently was "about ten percent contained."

For Joss, ten percent was on the wrong side of the contain equation. She called Will and got his recorded message. At the tone she said, "Will, are you and Kallie all right? Do you know about the fire? Get back to me as soon as you get this, please!"

Then she called the Forest Service in Medford and was relieved to have a person pick up despite the early hour.

"Look," she began, "I'm not sure who to talk with, but my daughter and my ex-husband are out hiking in the Kalmiopsis Wilderness and I'm concerned for their safety."

"Yes, ma'am. Do you know where they went hiking? Was it an overnight hike?"

"Yes. I mean, I told someone there all this already. But they're headed to a campsite called Panther Bar on the Illinois River, and from there they were going to hike to one of the trails out there and be gone almost a week."

"Well, ma'am, we send rangers out to warn any folks at the campsites. It's standard procedure."

"Yes, I know. But if that was true they would have come home by now, and they haven't come home. Or called. Or *something*. Plus, they're not just camping; they're *backpacking*. So they probably aren't even at the campsite. Do you have a way of warning people who are hiking?"

"All right. Look, the Duty Officer hasn't arrived yet but when he does I can give him a message. Like I say, they probably already sent rangers up there to make sure folks are out of the area. But give me your name and the names of the hikers and your contact info."

Joss added, "My daughter is blind."

"What's that?"

"She's blind, she can't see."

There was a pause, then, "She's blind and she's hiking in the wilderness?"

"Yes. Backpacking. She's done it before."

Another hesitation. "Well, she probably couldn't have gone too far then."

Joss shook her head. "You'd be surprised."

THE MAN WHO took the message was Gordon Finley, a retired heavy equipment mechanic who'd worked all over the southern Oregon districts of the Forest Service for forty-two years. Occasionally he got hired part-time to answer phones when the office was depleted by vacations and holidays and like now, when many staffers were out at a wildfire. It was a job he enjoyed, being part of the group and wearing his old official FS shirt even though he wasn't supposed to. He had large hands and even after being freshly scrubbed his fingers showed crevices and cuticles turned permanently black by the oils and greases of Cummins diesels and Ford V-8s and eighteen-horsepower water pumps.

When the Duty Officer arrived half an hour later, Finley ambled into the DO's office and leaned on the doorway and said, "Some lady's been calling about her husband and daughter. She says they're out hiking near the Illinois River and she's worried about them."

The DO nodded. "Yeah, Wild Rivers got up there and cleared out those campsites."

"She says they haven't checked in yet and she thinks they're still out there."

The DO frowned. "Did she say where they were?"

"Around Panther Bar. I think there's a campsite. I been up there, but it's been a few years. I remember it's way the hell out there."

The DO did some mental cartography. According to the changing wind patterns he'd seen on the Weather Service website, the fire was moving that direction.

"Hey, get this," said Finley. "This guy and his daughter, the ones who are hiking. Well, the daughter is a blind kid."

The DO frowned. "You're kidding."

Finley shrugged. "That's what the lady on the phone says." He handed the DO a piece of lined paper torn from a spiral notebook. "Here's their info."

The DO took the paper and put it on his desktop. "Okay. Say, do me a favor, Gordon. Call Wild Rivers and make sure they sent a truck up there to look for people, okay?"

Finley nodded. He liked giving directives to the districts. "Will do."

From his station at the front receptionist's desk Finley called the Wild Rivers Ranger Station. The DO responded that they'd already sent a Ranger to warn people at the campsites along the Illinois River Road.

"Good deal," said Finley and he rang off. He punched the intercom button for the DO and relayed the news. Then he sat back in his office chair and surveyed the mostly empty corridors and offices, lots of staff gone to the fire busting out in the Kalmiopsis. He thought of his younger firefighting days when he'd worked on a fire line, the sweat and the camaraderie. Good days indeed. And he missed his regular mechanic's job, although for different reasons.

And he wasn't entirely out of the game, either. He had this job at the front desk, which was nice, but he was still a resource if they ever needed another mechanic on a big fire. He'd go in a heartbeat. He had an enviable inventory of mechanics supplies in the heavy-duty truck toolbox on the bed of his Ram, and it wouldn't take but a few minutes for him to grab his Nomex from home and get on the road. If they needed him, he'd definitely go. Not only that, but he still had his D6 cat on a trailer in his big workshop. It'd been years since that D6 had been on a fire line, but a guy could hope.

Thursday, June 25
Tincup Fire camp, Selma

PRESTON INGRAM WAS the Commander for the expansive Type 2 Incident Management Team that was preparing to take over the Tincup Fire. He was a Northwesterner through-and-through, born and raised in Yakima, only son of an HVAC-contractor father and grade-school-teaching mother. After graduating Eisenhower High, he went on to get a degree in economics from Washington State University, then did six years in the Navy, discharging from the service as a lieutenant specializing in laser cartography. His years away from the Pacific Northwest had left him longing for green forests and clean rivers, so he returned to WSU and ended up with a master's in environmental science. He paid for expenses by supplementing a meager stipend as a teaching assistant with a night job at a local foundry pouring ductile and gray iron into sand casts to make blanks for disc brake rotors. He had a USN winged anchor tattooed on his left forearm and in the foundry break room other Navy vets would come over and sit with him and wipe their sweaty, ash-streaked faces with paper napkins and show their own tats and talk shit about good oceans and prick Naval officers and why circumstances beyond their control had caused them to live so far inland. Ingram listened and nodded.

Ingram was a buttoned-up process guy who innately understood structured approaches and chain of command and wore close-cropped Navy hair under a baseball-type hat with the Forest Service logo. Over the years he'd worked up to Chief Liaison Officer on several Type 1 IMTs around the Northwest, a job that put him at the heart of incident management on several large fires, but this was his first as the top Incident Commander. It was, as they say, his first rodeo.

He'd brought several clean-and-pressed Forest Service shirts with him to southern Oregon because he believed that neatness helped establish a commander's place in the hierarchy. In his right front shirt pocket he had a small spiral-bound Incident Response Guide that provided standards for wildfire response, such as optimum dimensions for a one-way helispot and tables for calculating dead fuel moisture content. Ingram didn't need the Guide—he had it memorized—but if any differences of opinion arose about technical details, then he would be armed with definitive proof. He also carried a leather-bound notebook in which he took copious notes. The notebook had been given to him by his wife, Sarah. Glued to the inside of the cover was a decorative notecard on which Sarah had printed in her neat, san-serif hand the phrases that Ingram had told her were his leadership mantras: *There are no bad teams, only bad leaders* and *Act decisively, prioritize, and execute.*

Ingram arrived at the fire camp at eighteen hundred with his Chief Safety Officer and Public Information Officer in tow. They stood waiting quietly while the Supervisor for the Rogue River-Siskiyou National Forest, Olympia Oates, finished briefing the forty-plus captains, squad leaders, section chiefs, pilots, bosses, and a hundred or so assorted firefighters assembled outside the main building. Oates had a large area map on a display board and was explaining the current attack strategies, where they'd been successful and where the fire had been unpredictable and tough to stop. She tapped at the map with a capped pen. "We're going to be staging here along the river and use it for a control if the burn starts to head that way. Up here..." she made a circle with her pen, "...is where we're getting spotting ahead of the southern head. Unfortunately..." more circles, "...we've got significant southwest winds forecast for the next three days."

Oates went on to outline strategies for the next twelve

to twenty-four hours. "If the new IC agrees," she added. "By the way, we'll have the official transfer of authority tomorrow at the oh six hundred briefing."

When Oates had finished Ingram and his staff walked over and introduced themselves. Oates shook hands all around and said, "How much of the briefing did you see?"

"Most of it," replied Ingram. "Do you have a situation room?"

"Follow me."

Inside the wildlands center building was a large conference room that had been converted to a map-splattered response headquarters for fighting the Tincup Fire. People were talking over laptops and gathered in small groups looking at clipboards and many had cell phones pressed to their ears as the new command structure began to assume responsibility for Incident 395. It was vital to bring the newly arrived managers up to speed as seamlessly as possible.

Oates led Ingram to the largest area map and pointed out the terrain, key geographical features, the growth patterns for the burn, fuel conditions and wind-speed predictions. Ingram took it all in, letting the data meld into a singular entity, as if the fire were a living thing with a personality that could be qualified. It would be unpredictable in places, of course, but in others the tendencies—and weaknesses—would start to become known. He listened as the Supervisor recounted attack strategies and operations, and he quietly nodded approval. This was a rebellious burn, but the locals had made the right moves to this point. Now, as the wildfire morphed into something larger and more ominous, it was time for response to move to the next level.

Ingram put his hands on his hips. He subscribed to the belief that body language was an essential in effective command. He had learned to curb his impulse to fold his arms across his chest or worse, stick his hands in his front pants pockets. He said, "What's the aircraft status?"

"Six Type Two helicopters, four Type Threes, two Type Two airtankers are due to arrive in Medford tonight."

Ingram didn't let anything show on his face. He knew going in they'd be strapped, what with all the other fires requesting resources, but it was not the minimum amount of equipment for a Type Two incident. "It's a Medusa," he said.

"Sir?"

"The burn has multiple heads."

"That it does."

"Where's the FBAN?"

"Right outside."

"Let's go."

In the Weather and Fire Behavior tent the FBAN and IMET took Ingram through the energy release models, forecast data, and the current conditions for the four divisions of the burn. Ingram stood quietly looking over the shoulders of the men as they shuffled through various screen displays, occasionally asking about rates of spread and topography.

"What was the last time recon was up?"

"Fifteen hundred," said Olympia Oates.

Ingram looked at his watch and considered. It was nineteen hundred hours. Plenty of daylight remaining. *Act decisively*. This would be a good time to issue his first command. He said, "Can your AO get a fixed wing in the air right now?"

Oates nodded.

"All right, let's have them look for any spotting on that northeastern flank."

Thursday, June 25
Kalmiopsis Wilderness

IN THE MIDAFTERNOON they came to the fork in the trail and they made their camp. The wind had not abated and blew steadily and occasionally whipped stinging dust at their arms and legs. Kal had done well on the day's hike except for one faceplant fortunately into soft duff and not into the rocky trail, and one low-hanging branch to the forehead. Will apologized profusely for both and had offered to deliberately ram his forehead into a tree limb so he could have sympathy pain, which made Kal laugh and her head hurt less.

It was good to shed their packs and take off their hiking boots and socks and sit barefooted in the thin shade of a young Ponderosa pine as breezes blew across their toes.

"It's nice here," said Kal.

"Sorry about all this wind. It wasn't in the forecast."

"At least it's not raining."

"True dat."

Later that evening, after they'd eaten dinner and they'd retired to the shelter of their tent, Kal said, "Tell me more about Dubai."

So Will told of being in Dubai and how the city was full of expensive shops and amazing cars and how two hundred years ago it used to be a merchant port for spices and olives and pearls, and then how oil had made the region rich beyond imagination, and how in the 1970s they made enormous artificial ports for the big oil tankers and that those ports were now aging and deteriorating and needing repair due to shifting seabeds. That was how he got a job in the Emirates analyzing seismic data and seabed stability.

Kal nodded. "Do you think you and Mom will ever get back together?"

"Well that's a non sequitur."

"What's that?"

"When a person says something that's completely different from what was being discussed."

Kal shrugged. "You were talking about Dubai, you know."

"Okay. But no, I don't think so. I mean, it's best for everybody if your Mom and I just be good friends. And help each other raise you."

She nodded, quiet.

"It's okay to ask. Any kid whose parents got divorced probably wonders that."

"Yeah. I know. I'm not sad or anything. Just wondering out loud."

After they'd bedded down for the night and Kal had fallen sleep Will lay awake and relived the more dramatic episodes of the divorce and wondered how their separation would affect all of their lives going forward. The decision to leave the area—and his daughter—hadn't been easy. But so many things had seemed to force his hand. The divorce, well... shit happens, especially in relationships. Maybe they'd put too much pressure on themselves because of Kallie; maybe because they cared so much for her there wasn't much left over for each other. Maybe they were just incompatible. At least they'd come to the realization while they were still relatively young and they could see their lives moving ahead. There hadn't been much screaming and yelling. Just a kind of stupid sadness.

Joss had kept the house in Medford because it was a single story and didn't have stairways and the layout was familiar to Kal. He'd gotten an apartment and suffered through Recently Divorced Dad Stigma, where everyone in the complex seemed to look at him with a mix of pity and distrust, as if he was guilty of some crime.

At the time of the divorce he'd been plodding along in his job doing lidar mapping and evaluating earthquake potential for Oregon Department of Geology and Mineral Industries. It was okay work, most of it was interesting, but it was still a governmental agency and prone to sagging under the weight of protocol and endless official dipshit stuff to do. The divorce was going through its machinations when a buddy at a private engineering firm had called, saying they were looking to hire a team of independent contractors to evaluate aging shipping ports in Dubai. One year, six times his current pay. Was he interested? He thought about it for all of three seconds before saying *Yes*.

Leaving Kal was the hardest, but he squared it with a few facts. *One:* Joss was a good mother; *Two:* Kal was strong and willful child—she'd be fine; and *Three:* it was only for a year and maybe the exact right time to get beyond everything and refresh his head.

So he'd flown off for the land of sun, sand, and obscene amounts of money. There wasn't a tax on income in the Emirates and it was easy to repatriate savings back to the states. He enjoyed getting immersed in a new culture—as surreal as the glistening city of Dubai seemed at times. The traffic was nightmarish and the summer months were screamingly hot, but at least it wasn't as strict as other Islamic countries—adult beverages were available and you could go out and have a beer after work. If you ever finished with work, that is. Twelve-hour days were standard, but at least the job was engaging and challenging. Emirate officials bent over backwards to make sure everything went smoothly and the people they collaborated with at the shipping ports were gracious and accommodating.

They gave the team offices on the seventh floor of the Ministry of Trade with views to the Persian Gulf and the curved edge of the Palm Jumeirah stretching away into the distance. The year slipped by quickly. One day near the end of the contract he saw big cumulus clouds gathered on the horizon and for a startled moment he thought he was looking at the snow-covered Cascades and he knew it was time to get back home. He missed the mountains and the big green trees and the clear, cold rivers. He started applying for jobs in the West, preferably near his daughter. It felt like more than just good luck when he found a job opening teaching Geographic Information Systems at Umpqua Community College in Roseburg. He applied, did the interview on Zoom, and got the position. It didn't pay much but screw the money. He'd saved enough to put a down payment on a small house in Grants Pass and he'd only be a few miles from Kal and Joss. He'd start in the fall. He wasn't sure how it would play out with Joss but from the tone of their email exchanges she was looking forward to having another parent involved in caring for and raising Kal. Civility, he hoped, would reign.

Not starting until fall meant he had some summer months to get reacclimated and settle in. Best of all, he was getting to fulfill a many-years-old promise to Kal—taking her backpacking. They even had a quest: find her namesake plant—the rare *Kalmiopsis leachiana*. It meant hiking the rugged Kalmiopsis Wilderness, but they were taking it slow, being careful, not too ambitious. They'd hiked before, and she was totally unfazed by the idea of being in the wilderness. *Bring it on*, was her mantra. His daughter. He was so glad to be back in her life.

But now that he was back, and with his daughter next to him snoring softly, the idea of an intact family was unexpectedly powerful. Mother, father, daughter. Maybe a dog, maybe some kick-butt service dog for Kal. Through the mosquito netting above his head he could see a billion stars. He fell asleep to the sound of coyotes crying far-off, their yips and pleas carried on the winds that strummed through the treetops.

Will awoke in the middle of the night. Kal's breathing was quiet, sweet, but outside he heard an odd noise. Rain pattering down. He couldn't see any stars. Damn, the forecast had been for totally clear weather. Were they wrong again?

Carefully, he slipped out of his bag, unzipped the tent door and eased outside. The stars were gone and the air was acrid—smoky. A steady wind rippled the tent fabric and hussed in the treetops. It wasn't rain that was falling from the darkened sky—it was bits of glowing embers.

Friday, June 26
Medford

AROUND NOON JOSS found herself wandering into Kal's bedroom. It looked like any kid's room with stuffed animals on the bed and knickknacks on shelves and a laptop computer sitting on a small laminate desk, except that Kal's bedroom was regimentally neat. Where other kids might have posters of pop idols or sports heroes on their walls, Kal had extruded 3-D pieces of art—Van Gogh's "Starry Night" and "Sunflowers"—with the deeper areas of relief representing dark colors and shallower grooves as lighter hues. Joss went to one of the posters and closed her eyes and ran her fingertips along the littles hills and valleys and tried to image Van Gogh's brush dictating rise and fall.

On the opposite wall Kal had pinned a four-by-four-foot relief map of southern Oregon, with the sprawling Siskiyou Mountains to the west and the Cascades rising up to the east and the Rogue Valley nestled between. Will had sent the map to Kal in anticipation of their hike. The national forests were colored kelly green and the valley was chartreuse with some browns mixed in, and a dark green blotch was the Kalmiopsis Wilderness. Joss stared at it. She found Highway 199 out of Grants Pass—the Redwood Highway—and traced its path through the mountains to Selma. Then she went to the kitchen and rinsed out her coffee mug and filled up a stainless-steel bottle with water, changed into jeans and a tee shirt, tied her hair back in a ponytail, put on hiking shoes, grabbed her keys and cell phone and a box of whole wheat crackers and went out and got into her car for the drive to Selma.

FROM THE AUDIOBOOK, "The Planet Earth: Amazing Natural Phenomena," by Dr. Jessica Shai Nusbaum, PhD:

A wildfire can burn at temperatures approaching three-thousand degrees Fahrenheit, or about twice as hot as the inside of a cremation chamber. The hottest temperatures are usually at the fire front, as the flames consume fresh fuels along the edges of the burn. It does this in a two-step process. The first step is called preignition. It occurs when the fuels just ahead of the flames absorb heat. As twigs, leaves, bushes and trees absorb increasing amounts of heat, they begin to release flammable tars and gases that ignite easily and explosively when mixed with oxygen. As these gaseous combustibles burst into flame, the next step in the process—ignition—causes fuels to begin burning. In this way the fire perpetuates itself, rolling forward as a living wall of flames.

With the flash point of wood being just five-hundred seventy degrees Fahrenheit, a fire front so efficiently preheats the fuels in its path that flames may churn along at a steady two to four miles per hour—the pace of a brisk walk, assuming no rocks, brambles, fallen trees and inclines. But add strong winds and an accompanying torrent of fresh oxygen, and a fire front can sprint out with one-hundred-foot-high flames leaping ahead at 60 miles per hour—faster than a prayer.

Friday, June 26
Tincup Fire camp, Selma

WHEN WILD RIVERS realized that the Illinois River Road had not yet been cleared of either the disabled brush truck or the rockslide, they immediately notified Forest Service dispatch, who in turn notified Supervisor Oates, who was staying out at the fire camp. Oates relayed the information to the Ops Chief, Howard Baker, who at 0700 joined Commander Ingram in front of the big wall map that hung in the HQ. Baker pointed to a point along the Illinois River Road.

"Right here," said Baker. "They're sending up a tow truck, but then we'll still have to clear the slide with a Cat. And right now all our dozers are cutting lines."

Ingram nodded, calculating. The Illinois River was standing between the fire and the eastern flank. And spots had already been called in to the north. They needed the River Road, now. "When is the tow truck going up?"

"The contractor was out on another job this morning and he says he'll be going early afternoon."

Ingram shook his head. *How the hell was a local wildfire request not a priority?* "Howie, get a contract Cat up there right away."

The Ops Chief frowned. "What about the tow truck?"

"Call him off. Get the Cat."

"Then, what about the brush truck?"

"Have the dozer driver push the whole mess over the side, and let's get some crews and engines up into that area as fast as we can."

OPS CHIEF BAKER was going to put in a procurement order for another bulldozer but first called Supervisor Oates to see if there were local resources who could respond immediately.

The Supervisor got on the horn to the FAO, Ken Hudek, who radioed the duty officer in Medford to see if Gordon Finley still had his bulldozer and heavy equipment license.

At eight hundred hours the DO walked the message down to Finley who was already stationed at the reception desk in the agency lobby. Finley got a big grin on his craggy old mug and said, "Who'll cover the phones?"

The DO shrugged. "Don't worry about it. I'll get my cousin's eighteen-year-old daughter to come in and pick up the slack. She's been looking for a parttime."

By eight-thirty Finley was at his house in Central Point hitching his flatbed trailer to his Ford F-450 dually. On the trailer was his beloved 1977 Caterpillar D6C. Near half of the yellow paint had flaked off and everywhere was mottled with islands of brown rust like the hide of an exotic beast. The battle-scarred blade was dinged and similarly oxidized but the hydraulics were good, everything was greased, the control linkage updated and the engine was unstoppable. Finley and his Cat hadn't seen firefighting action together since the 1990s, and after that only to help friends knock down trees or cut a pad on a raw piece of property. But he hadn't sold it off, keeping it with his oft-repeated mantra that the moment after you got rid of something would be the exact time you'd desperately need it. As a result, his workshop barn was heaped with aging specialty tools and buckets of bolts and lengths of copper tubing and sagging, oil-stained carboard boxes filled with one-of-a-kind springs and gaskets and tubes of grease and in the middle of it all aboard a flatbed trailer waited his D6C.

Muted light came in through dusty panes and the smell of oil and metal was a tonic. Gordon Finley was seventy-three years old but at the moment felt the floaty vigor of a thirty-five-year-old. The knees did not ache as he stepped up on the push frame, he didn't feel his arthritic, impinged right shoulder as he swung himself up onto the track to check fluids. He stepped nimbly over the lift cylinder and perched on the top edge of the blade to check the water level, then back onto the track to check the hydraulic level. He made his way into the cab and confirmed the fuel dipstick showed nearly full, then he slid into the well-worn, mouse-eaten operator's chair. He touched each control lever, their Bakelite ends burnished to a silvery black. He smiled—he and his Cat had been requested at the Tincup Fire. He was going back into action. Then he got down and climbed into his pickup to haul the bulldozer to Selma.

AT THE FIRE CAMP the communications crew gave Finley a handheld radio set to the proper frequencies. An Assistant Fire Officer brought out a map and traced the route with a finger. The AFO was a woman and Finley wasn't sure how he felt about receiving instructions from a female who was decades his junior but then things had certainly changed since he was with the Service and this young woman seemed to be a straight-shooter and knew her job, so what the hell.

He towed the flatbed and bulldozer up the Illinois River Road to the last campground before the blockage, the big-block Ford straining to pull all that iron on the uphill climb. At the campground there was plenty of room to do a complete drive-through so he swung his rig into one of the entrances and parked. There were six Type 3 engines and a tactical water tanker already in the lot, and dozens of ground crew members in their yellow Nomex and dusty white helmets milled about and sat at nearby picnic benches or on the grass in the shade, staged at the campground in anticipation of a dozer operator clearing the road. Through the haze the plume could be seen towering up and blotting out most of the sky to the west. For a delicious few moments Finley felt the visceral thrill of being on the fire lines. But a nagging thought kept trying to make itself known. With a pang, he realized he'd forgotten his Nomex. He was wearing only his everyday flannel shirt and blue jeans. *Of all the stupid…*

His angst was interrupted by three firefighters who walked up to his truck. They were young and sketchily whiskered and they wore sunglasses and their clothes were battle-smudged, but their faces were still clean. One of them leaned into the open window and said, "Hey, man, you need any help?"

Finley blinked. His distress almost made him say *No* because they'd wonder where his protective gear was and then he'd have to confess his old man's stupidity. But he took a deep breath and said, "Sure," and climbed out of the truck and together they set up the ramp and the three young firefighters worked with a strength and quickness that reminded Finley that he was not thirty-five much less twenty-two. But he could drive a Cat like nobody. That he could still do.

One of the young men looked to the west and said, "Gettin' big."

Finley followed the young man's gaze. The plume was a living mountain, an entire continent of dirty smoke thrust into the sky. He should get going.

He climbed into the cab and took in the rusted metals bursting through the flaking paint, the tarnished bezels encircling the dials, the fissured and critter-gnawed Naugahyde arm rests. His own aging self, reflected. But he settled his bones into the seat as easily as a piston slides into a freshly honed cylinder. He checked that the transmission was in neutral and the safety lever forward. He pulled the throttle lever out one-third then twisted the starter to preheat the glow plugs. After counting to fifteen he turned the starter the opposite direction and the beast awoke and the stack belched out softballs of diesel smoke. He gave it three minutes to warm up completely, then he put it in reverse and eased the

Cat down the ramp and onto the parking lot.

A nearby firefighter waved his arms and called out above the clatter of the engine, "Hey man, where's your Nomex?"

Finley smiled and shouted back, "Never wear it. Too hot." Then he pivoted the Cat to begin what he estimated to be an hour-long trek to the blockage.

The drive up the dirt road was about as exhilarating as a bulldozer drive could be. Trees and rocks rolled past; the clanking of the tracks was the sound of the cavalry galloping to save the day, the hulking plume was his dark adversary. He ran at eighty percent for most of the run, topping out at a good seven miles per hour where the road ran straight. As it got steeper and narrower he slowed and nursed the Cat up with practiced adjustments, never too extreme, steering the lumbering beast by anticipating what was just ahead. He was hot and he rolled up his sleeves and was thankful not to have encased himself in a layer of Nomex.

At the site of the rockslide Finley idled the D6, set the brake and climbed down to inspect the blockage. He peered over the edge of the embankment—it was steep as hell and through the white haze of smoke he could just make out the river glistening far below. He checked out the rockslide and gave a low whistle when he saw the size of the boulder. Definitely a job for a big Cat. He got back in the cab and put it in gear and adjusted the blade. His aim was to ease the truck over the side and hope it wouldn't slide too far and would be recoverable at some point.

He got the blade under the right-side bumper and tilted the blade back to lift the brush truck's rear end. He pushed forward and the truck moved reluctantly and seemed hung up and then just like that without much more encouragement it shimmied over the shoulder and disappeared. He heard brutal, metallic sounds as the truck began to tumble down the slope. Dust rolled up over the edge of the road and blue jays screamed furiously as they fled the commotion. The racket went on for a long time as the truck crashed through underbrush and caromed off rocks and trees and the noise went echoing down the canyon. Then it was quiet except for the throaty gurgling of the Cat's diesel engine. *Damn.* He sighed and shrugged. He couldn't have been more careful. *Waddaya gonna do?*

The rockslide needed little finesse and he pushed everything over the side in three passes and the bigger piece slid a few feet and stopped while bowling-ball-size rocks went careening down the side of the mountain. On the third pass the thin daylight suddenly diminished nearly by half and he looked up to see the sun had been swallowed up by smoke. He could hear what sounded like thunder and in the darkness he could make out flashes of lightning. Fire storm. The burn had gotten rowdy and was churning out its own weather.

He keyed his radio and it was answered a moment later by a dispatch duty officer. Finley reported what he'd done, adding that the brush truck had "taken a pretty good tumble" but that now the road was open and as soon as he could get back down and get his machine off the road the crews would be clear to head on up.

"Roger that," responded the DO. "Be aware, winds are increasing and pushing the burn your direction so you may start to encounter some smoke."

Finley set the radio in its holder, pivoted the Cat and began to head down. It was unnaturally dark and tendrils of smoke began to appear as the DO had predicted. Another mile and the smoke became heavier and in places the road was obscured and he couldn't see more than twenty feet in front of the blade. He slowed the Cat to three miles an hour, barely more than a walk. He was terribly thirsty.

He was halfway down when a violent wind suddenly

swept in, bringing with it a burst of scorching hot air like a hair dryer held to the side of his face. He turned away and held up his collar and he could feel heat sear the back of his ears. The smoke streamed horizontally and a blizzard of burning embers swept across his path and pummeled the side of the Cat and bounced off his shoulder and the back of his head and landed on the floor of the cab where he stomped at them with his feet. A flaming ember the size of an apple landed in his crotch and he picked it up bare-handed and flung it overboard. On either side of the road embers glowed on the forest floor and a number of small fires had taken root and peppered the gloom with winking light. Below to his right he could see flames. They were on his side of the gorge—the wildfire had leapt across the river.

Acrid smoke blurred his vision and he was caught between wanting to speed up and needing to slow down. He could make out a phalanx of flames advancing up the slope. He notched the accelerator to full speed and the big Cat clamored ahead but the flames and smoke were now all around, as if someone had thrown a switch and transformed the forest into a burning hell. He picked up the radio, but it slipped out of his hand and went clattering to the floor and bounced onto the moving track and was quickly carried off toward the front of the bulldozer. Before he could brake the radio disappeared over the front of the tracks. He brought the Cat to a stop and crouched down as if by making himself smaller the fire might overlook him but it did not. It roared and leapt on him with a searing wind that scorched his forearms and his cheeks and he set the brake and left the machine idling and clambered awkwardly down out of the cab and huddled in the sheltering lee of the big machine.

Human death in a wildfire often is caused by asphyxiation as the conflagration devours all available oxygen and fills the victim's lungs with smoke. Death this way, mercifully, is less painful than having the flesh charred to the bone while the victim is still alive and conscious. When Gordon Finley's body was finally recovered it was unburnt, a heap of flannel and denim curled up beside the wide steel tracks of his D6C Caterpillar bulldozer, its seats and control knobs melted, its exterior charred black, its engine faithfully idling.

INCIDENT 395

Friday, June 26
Kalmiopsis Wilderness

WILL HAD SPENT the remainder of the night fending off embers that threatened to land on the tent. He swatted at them and stomped them into the dirt. Adrenalin was singing in his ears. How far? How big? Could a wildfire come out of nowhere and cut them off? Were they already cut off? A small fire started nearby, tiny tongues of flame tangled inside a clump of dry grass, and he rushed to crush it under his boot. How could he have brought his daughter into such a dangerous situation?

Smoke had come in erratic waves, tousled by an unsteady wind. Sometimes it was thick and cloying, other times it was twirling pale wraiths barely seeable in the darkness. The rain of embers had stopped but when he turned on his headlamp he saw flakes of ash drifting down like snow. He kept watch for any more nearby flames but couldn't see any. He heard Kal move inside the tent and wondered if the smell of smoke would waken her. Right now, it was better she slept until he figured out the right course.

Worst case scenario: There was a wildfire close by and they'd have to move quickly. That might mean leaving the tent and fleeing in the darkness, making their way by the light of his headlamp. *Extremely risky, last resort.* He took a mental inventory: headlamp and backup batteries in the outer left pocket of the pack. Take both backpacks, water bottles, trekking poles, leave everything else. The emergency beacon was in his backpack. He could send an SOS, but they should be somewhere specific. If he sent the signal and then moved away from that same spot, a search operation would be thrown off the track. Better to find a place to hunker down.

The more hopeful possibility: The fire was miles away and

they were not in imminent danger. The embers were a brief sideshow, a rare but natural event. In the morning the smoke would blow another direction and the sun would be out and firefighting crews would have any burn under control. He and Kal would keep to their original schedule and take days to hike out. *Relieved, having fun, safe.* They would have quite a story to tell.

For certain they'd head for the river at first light. Moving at their best pace, they were probably a day away. Take the tent and all the gear—not going to panic, yet. From there, they'd take the river trail back to the campground and their vehicle. If things got real crazy, they could always get into the river. Could it come to that?

He stayed awake through the night, remaining vigilant.

Dawn came as a dull amber pall. They were wrapped in smoke that shifted direction on unsure winds. He got out his cell phone and turned it on—no bars. He tapped a 911 call anyway. Maybe there was some way for authorities to pick up on a cell signal.

"Dad?" Her voice slightly muted inside the tent.

"Kallie, get dressed and stow your bag."

"I smell smoke."

The ground was dusted with snow-like ash that the wind was stirring into twirls. Ash fluttered off the top of the tent; his arms and legs were peppered with tiny white flakes. "Yeah, there's a fire somewhere. Probably not near us. But let's get going."

"Whew. Stinks. Are we having breakfast?"

"Have a protein bar. Then pack up. Stuff my bag, too."

Her father's abruptness brought her fully awake. A fire. Maybe close. She hurried into her shorts and a layered top and stuffed their sleeping bags into their sacks and rolled up the sleeping pads and secured those to the bottoms of their backpacks. She got a protein bar and ate that but even the sweet raspberry flavor couldn't erase the woodsmoke tang that invaded her nose and mouth.

"Are we okay?"

"We'll be okay. But let's get off this ridge and head for the river."

She opened the tent flap and shoved everything outside, then found her boots and got them on. Will was already pulling up the tent corner stakes.

"Drink some water," he said.

She slid one of the water bottles from a pack side pocket and unscrewed the cap and took a long drink that helped clear her throat. She held up the bottle. "Dad."

Will took the bottle and drank and put it back into her waiting hand. "Thanks."

They folded and rolled the tent with practiced efficiency and stuffed it into Will's backpack. He collapsed her trekking poles all the way and stowed those also. He told her to grab onto his backpack. "It'll be faster this way. We're going to try and make it to the river by night, so we'll need to be moving at a pretty good clip."

They set off and it was tricky going. At first she clung too hard and the straps bit into her fingers as she tried to adjust to her father's quickened strides. She had to bend forward at the waist to make sure she didn't step on his heels and several times she had to tell him to slow down, she was having trouble keeping up on the rocky downhill trail. They seemed to be moving twice as fast as their usual pace.

"Do you see the fire?" she wanted to know.

"Well, there's smoke headed our way. But it'll be better when we get down the ridge." Will could only hope that was true. Even moving as fast as possible they would still be miles from their vehicle by the end of the day. He'd been up twenty-four hours straight and his brain was dancing. Burning embers floated in his mind's eye. He needed to be calm.

Project confidence.

"Are we going to get all the way back to the Land Cruiser today?"

"We'll see. We might end up camping by the river for a night."

He heard helicopters in the distance and tried to work up trust that firefighters had a handle on the situation. They had all kinds of ways for attacking fires; they would take charge of the situation before it got out of hand. But he knew that in recent years wildfires had raged due to excessive drought and climate change. There were unprecedented big fires in Midwestern and Eastern states. The feel of Kal hanging onto his backpack was a constant reminder of what was at stake.

For Kal the downward trek was harder than the uphill climb. The trail was steeper and more strewn with hazards that her father called out continually: *loose scree here, big step down now, lots of poison oak to our left*. In places he slowed abruptly and she'd plow full-face into his backpack. After an hour of their awkward hiking she said, "Dad, I've got to take a break."

Will slowed to a stop. "Let's take five," he agreed.

Kal got out of her backpack and set it down and then she eased herself and sat on the loose-packed trail and flexed her fingers to relax them. Will followed suit and dug a compass and a map of the wilderness out of his pack. The trail they were on followed a north-south ridge and then swung southeast to meet the Illinois River. At that point they'd be about eight miles from the Land Cruiser. The wind and smoke, however, appeared to be heading north—which meant the fire was moving toward them. And the Land Cruiser, for that matter. The winds were gusty and came from different directions. Sometimes the smoke surrounded them and other times it lifted so that they hiked under a mantle of churning darkness. If the fire came near—if they were actually threatened—then the river would be their safety net. They could get in the water if they had to. *Good Christ, could it come to that?*

He stood. "Ready?" he said.

Kal nodded, stood and brushed off the back of her shorts. She got her backpack and Will helped her settle it on her back. There was no *Let's go!* ritual. She reached out her hands and her father backed up to her so she could take hold of his backpack. They set out, their pace as hurried as before. It was hot and scary and any sense of fun and adventure had evaporated. Their hike had turned into something out of *Wilderness Survival*. In the book they knew just what to do in any circumstance. She gripped her dad's backpack straps and tried to keep pace so she wouldn't be a dragging weight on his shoulders. She told herself they'd be all right because he wouldn't let anything happen to her. Ever.

Friday, June 26
Tincup Fire camp, Selma

AS JOSS DROVE down the Redwood Highway toward Selma the smoke plume hung on the horizon like a malevolent ancient god, towering and dark. It made her angry. *Why the fuck did she let Will take Kallie on some stupid fucking hike? Why the fuck are you two out there? Why the fuck am I having to drive to fucking Selma to see if anybody knows you're out there? Am I the only one who cares you're out there? Fuck!*

Selma, Oregon, population 800, was uncharacteristically kinetic. There were firefighters walking the streets and milling about in store parking lots and calling to each other over the noise of pickup trucks and dusty SUVs. She drove slowly through the town, slower than the posted limit of twenty-five miles per hour, not sure what she was looking for. Something official. She spotted a small handmade sign nailed to a telephone pole that said *Fire Camp* with an arrow pointing down a street and she did a hard right turn onto the Illinois River Road.

She drove through a small residential area and then the land opened to large level fields on both sides and the area to her left was peppered with dozens of small tents and bigger white tents beyond that. Nearby were muscular fire engines with fat hoses spooled on top and a dozen buses painted that sickly pale Forest Service green and trucks carrying water in enormous cylindrical tanks. A grassy meadow had been transformed into an impromptu parking area and was full of vehicles so she turned into the entrance and drove down the rows of cars and trucks until she found an opening where there was space to park. She turned off the engine and immediately checked her cell phone—there were no messages from Will.

About one hundred yards away was a building with cars and trucks in the parking lot and more firefighters and she figured it was some kind of official center for the firefighting response. There were several large, multi-sided tents to the side of the building and those definitely had something to do with the fire. Joss got out of her car and walked over. The air was ripe with the smell of gasoline and diesel fuel and the commotion of the camp swirled around her and the intensity of it ramped up her fears.

Joss went inside the building. There were people walking around clutching notebooks and the floor was streaked with dusty footprints. There was a front counter attended by a young man in a brown Forest Service uniform and wearing a tele-communications earpiece with an attached microphone. Two hand-lettered cardboard signs were taped to the front of the counter. One said *IC* and included a left-pointing arrow and the other said *Liaison/Safety* and pointed the other direction.

"Is there something I can help you with?" said the young man, his face impassive.

Joss said, "I'm looking for some information."

He nodded. "Such as?"

She fought back an urge to curse. He was so calm and businesslike, as if oblivious to the enormity of the situation. "The thing is, my daughter and ex-husband have gone hiking up there in the wilderness and they haven't returned and I haven't heard from them and from what I gather this fire is growing very, very fast and I'm very, very concerned and you're like the tenth person I've told and I wish somebody here would share that concern."

The young man nodded. "Okay, sure. We have regular public meetings for questions about the fire. They're just getting those set up and scheduled and there's one at…" he consulted a chart at one side of his desk, "…four this afternoon at the elementary school gym in Cave Junction." He smiled. "It's right down the road."

"I'll tell you what," said Joss, coming forward and putting both hands on the counter and staring hard at the young man, "I'm here now and you're here now and we are talking about people's lives so why don't you fucking try and rustle up somebody I can talk to?"

The smile evaporated and he licked his lips and nodded slowly, as if weighing the mental stability of the woman before him. Then he reached out and pushed a button on a console and after a moment he said into his mouthpiece, "Evelyn, this is Greg down at the HQ front desk. Can you come down here and speak with this woman who's here? Yes. Well, she says her daughter and husband are hiking in the wilderness area and she's worried about the fire. Yeah, that's what I told her. Okay, great, thanks." He clicked off and said, "Evelyn Peters is one of the Public Relations Officers. She's in a meeting right now with the weather team. But she'll be here as soon as…"

"Where's that?"

"The meeting?"

"Yes."

"Well it's in one of the tents right…"

Joss turned and headed out the door as the young man called, "Wait! You shouldn't…"

She walked across the asphalt parking lot and zeroed in on one of the larger tents. The door flaps were tied open and she went inside. The place smelled of stale canvas. There were large maps pinned to the walls and electrical cords draped everywhere. There was a sign that read, *Fire Weather and Behavior.* Two men sat side-by-side at a folding table looking at a computer monitor, and a young woman standing behind them was also staring at the screen. It was hot in the tent and Joss could see the sweat glistening on the backs of hands and necks. They were so intent on the screen they didn't notice her come in. She announced herself in a loud voice, "Sorry, excuse me."

They turned around in unison. "Hey," said one. He pointed to a large portable air conditioner off to one side that was not turned on. "Are you here to fix the AC?"

"Oh, no," said Joss. "I'm looking for, I mean I guess I'm looking for some information. Are you all with the Forest Service?"

"We're contractors," said one of the men. "We do weather and fire forecasting."

To the woman Joss said, "Are you Evelyn?"

The woman crossed her arms and said, "I'm Evelyn Peters, Public Information Officer for ODF. Are you the woman they just called about?"

"Yes, I'm, my…" For a moment Joss became unmoored, everything was so strange and unreal and she felt woozy in the sweltering tent. She closed her eyes and forced herself to concentrate and said, "My daughter is out there…" she pointed randomly, "…with my ex-husband on a hike and I haven't heard from them in days. And somebody at the Forest Service told me that they sent somebody up to the campgrounds and they got people out, but if that's true then I should have heard from them by now but I haven't and it's wrong they're out there…" pointing again, "…and she's blind and they may be in trouble."

Evelyn Peters nodded, then stopped. "Wait. What? Who's blind?"

"My daughter."

"And she's the one hiking in the wilderness?"

"Yes. With her father."

"And you told the Forest Service about this?"

"Yes, a couple of times. But I haven't heard from, from my daughter…" Joss' voice trailed off.

"The Forest Service and ODF are pretty good about clearing people out if there's a fire around," said one of the men.

"Where were they hiking?" asked the other.

"In the Kalmiopsis Wilderness. They were going to the river. Um, Panther Bar. The Illinois River Trail. To look for flowers. But that's where the fire is, isn't it?"

"No, not too near there." The men exchanged a quick look.

"So, who should I talk to? I'd like to find out if they've been contacted or if anybody knows anything. I mean, can't they get a helicopter to go find them?" Joss heaved a deep sigh. "Can you please point me in the right direction?"

"Actually," said Peters, "if you're not connected to fire-fighting operations, you shouldn't be in the fire camp. When there's a wildfire there's always a lot of folks, civilians, who get excited and concerned and they want this and that. It's understandable. That's why we schedule regular briefings for the public…" Peters stopped. Joss appeared so distraught that the PIO sighed, then said, "I'm supposed to meet with the incident team in about an hour for a briefing. I'll see if she's heard anything about the lost hikers or if they've found anybody. Okay?"

Joss nodded. "Okay." At least this was something. But it was all so disorienting, as if she had awakened inside someone else's dream. "But what if nobody has heard anything? What then?"

"There's a food commissary at the main camp," said Peters, fishing in one of her pockets and producing a business card that she pressed into Joss' hand. "Go down there and get a cup of coffee or something to eat. It'll be a little while. Anybody asks you what you're doing just show them that card and tell them I said it's okay. Let me see if anybody knows something. I'll find you down there as soon as I can.

I haven't heard about a search-and-rescue operation so that's probably a good thing."

"All right."

"Give me your phone number." Joss told her and Peters wrote it on a notepad.

JOSS WANDERED ALONG rows of food tables set out with dozens of boxes of sandwiches, bags of chips, baskets of fruit, condiments, iced bottles of juice, and regimented rows of plain and chocolate milk cartons. Commissary workers in blue shirts and smudged white aprons worked to replenish the supplies and keep the tables orderly. Firefighters, drivers, mechanics, and pilots moved along the edges of the tables piling up plates and chatting about fire escapades and Joss drifted alongside, listening. Getting an ember blown up a pants leg; grabbing a six-foot rattler by its tail as it tried to escape the fire and twirling it overhead before flinging it into the bushes; watching a hundred-foot tongue of flame leap out horizontally to torch a brush truck as the driver scrambled to get away. Joss had no appetite; anger and worry had put a knot in her gut.

After fifteen minutes she got a phone call and her heart jumped hoping it was Will but it was Evelyn Peters. Joss answered by saying, "Did you hear anything?"

"Hi. Ah, no. Not yet."

"Oh." *Then why the hell are you calling?*

"I have an idea," said Peters, sounding breathless.

"What?"

"I'm sorry, what's your name again?"

"Joss. Joss Spencer."

"Right. Mrs. Spencer, how about we get you on camera?"

"On camera?"

"Get one of the local channels to do a news video.

Maybe it'll help."

"How could it help?"

"Get the word out about your daughter and your husband."

"Ex-husband."

"Right. You never know. A little media coverage might shake things up. I mean, the fact that your daughter is blind…" she stopped herself from saying *is a good story,* "…is amazing. Maybe somebody saw them and knows they're okay. It'll put people on alert."

"How does something like that work?"

"There are news crews around, they'll definitely shoot a few minutes."

Joss looked over at the organized chaos swarming in the big field. "What do I do?"

"I'll find a news team. They'll have a reporter, they'll ask a couple of questions about your hus…, ex-husband and your daughter, what's her name?"

"Kal." She almost started to explain the nickname but stopped herself. No need for that.

"They'll ask where your daughter and ex-husband went hiking, how long they've been away."

"How does this happen? I'm not dressed up or anything."

"No, no. You'll be fine."

"Um, where?"

"We'll do it there. The food tents are good backdrops. Stay put and I'll find you."

Joss walked. Being in motion felt better than sitting down. As she walked she scanned faces, as if Kal and Will might be hidden among the firefighters who were shuffling through the commissary lines and were seated at tables, hunched protectively over their plates of food.

After twenty minutes Evelyn Peters showed up with a

man shouldering a large portable video camera and another man dressed casually in clean clothes who was the reporter. They introduced themselves as the on-site crew from KOBI in Medford and they gave their names which Joss instantly forgot. They made her stand at a certain spot and the man with the camera looked at her through the viewfinder and had her face a certain direction and the reporter came up next to her and held a microphone at chin level. The videographer switched on a light and then switched it off and said, *Natural light is better, we'll be fine,* and the man with the microphone nodded and patted his hair with his free hand and then peered inquisitively at Joss and said, "Just talk to me, not the camera." He smiled. "Ready?"

Friday, June 26
Kalmiopsis Wilderness

AROUND NOON Kal said she needed a break and they shed their packs and sat side-by-side on a level piece and ate gorp and drank water. The smoke hurried around them, urged by steady winds. Then a fierce gust came up, roaring through the underbrush and bending the trees, and a few moments later a scattering of burning embers fell all around. Will pulled Kal close and grabbed a backpack and held it over their heads.

"What is it?" she said in alarm.

He didn't answer right away—didn't want a tremor in his voice to betray him. At last he said, "Dust and pine needles and stuff." When the flurry subsided, he got up and began to stamp on any glowing bits he saw. Luckily, none had landed on them.

"What is it? What are you doing?" Her voice rising.

"Just knocking the dirt off my boots." He couldn't see any fires starting from the shower of burning bits, then the wind suddenly shifted directions and blew strongly from a different quarter. Was that good or bad? He had a brief moment of panic that they were headed the wrong way; he should have abandoned the idea of getting back to their vehicle and kept going west, deeper into the wilderness, away from the smoke and fire. But no, going this way must be the right call. It *had* to be. Head for the Land Cruiser. If things got bad, they'd be right next to the river.

He put a hand on her shoulder. "How are your eyes? Mine are burning. Should we wash them out with a little water?"

Kal nodded. She took off her sunglasses and turned her face up and her marvelously gray, troubled eyes widened expectantly. He unscrewed the top to a water bottle and held it over her eyes and dribbled water and she blinked repeatedly and said, "That feels good." He did the other eyes and she sighed and said, "Thanks, Dad. That's better."

Will rinsed his own eyes and he screwed the top back onto the water bottle and said, "Look, there's a fire somewhere but we're going to be okay. The chances of it getting real close are slim. But to be completely safe we've got to keep moving, get back to the Land Cruiser as soon as we can, and get out of the area. I'm sorry, but that's just what's happening. Understand?"

Kal nodded, then she gagged slightly and ended up with a coughing fit. Will shook a bandana out of his shirt pocket and poured water on it and folded it into a triangle. "Here," he said, "this will help with the smoke." He gently tied it around her face and knotted the ends at the back of her head.

Kal knew things weren't right at all and she wanted to cry, but she fought the urge because it would not help the situation and her dad needed her to be strong. He patted her cheek and said, *We'll be okay* and within his assurance she sensed his worry.

They walked as before, Kal clinging marsupial-like to Will's backpack. The only good thing about the smoke was that it cut the sunlight and took the edge off the heat of the day. The trail was rough in places and once Will stumbled and they both went down in a heap. Kal hit the funny bone in her elbow which stunned and paralyzed her entire arm for several minutes and Will banged his knee but he said he was okay. Any other time they probably would have laughed about it. But not this day.

The hours crept past, the hardscrabble path writhing and flexing underneath her boots, trying to throw her off balance. Her father called out obstructions and changes in the trail as before, but their hurried pace required full concentration, focusing on the rhythm of her father's strides, the slight hitches that indicated a rise, the heavier footfalls that signaled a drop, the shift of his shoulders as the trail changed direction. The noises of the land that she would normally sort into their individual pieces—different birds, wind in the trees, the snap of drying twigs—melded into the singular notes of their feet moving in lockstep.

By late in the day Kal was exhausted and tired of sucking stinky air from behind a bandana that was cloying damp from her breath. Her hands were raw and cramped from a long day of trying to hold onto her father's backpack. As they made their way down the ridge the sound of the river appeared and then vanished in the hollering wind and her strength ebbed and flowed as well.

"Dad," she said at last, "I've got to stop."

"Okay. In a little bit. Take my hand, there's a tricky part."

She could barely unfold her fingers, the muscles were so locked in place. "Oh God," she said, shaking her hands to restore feeling. She held out her hand and Will took it and guided her down large, rocky steps. They made several back-and-forth turns, her shoulders brushing walls of hard stone that pressed in on both sides. As they took another turn the sound of the river suddenly rose all around—they were getting well down into the canyon.

"Okay, there's a good level spot here, big enough for the tent if we need it. Let's take a break."

Kal unbuckled her backpack and let it fall with a thump. Being suddenly free of the weight made her slightly dizzy and she carefully eased herself to the ground. "Are we done for the day?"

"Eat a protein bar."

"Are we going to cook something?" They'd been on the move all day and she was famished.

"We'll see about that. Right now I'm going to do a quick scout and look for a way down to the river. Maybe there's a place to camp down there."

"Do you see fire?"

"It's so smoky I can hardly see anything."

"Great. That makes two of us." She had intended that as a joke, but her father didn't react. The little knot of fear that had been in her gut all day got bigger and her hunger suddenly disappeared. "Should I take this off?" She pointed at the bandana.

"Not advised," said Will. "Maybe for a little bit, but it's bad here. Put it back on in a couple minutes."

"What are you using for breathing?"

"I pull my tee shirt up over my nose. Here." He leaned down and put his face in her waiting hand. "I stretched the you-know-what out of my tee shirt."

"Does it work?"

"Better than nothing. Okay, stay put. I'll be right back. I'm going to leave my backpack here and there's rocks and stuff around so be careful if you get up."

"How far to go?"

"Maybe another seven or eight miles."

She heard her father unbuckle his pack and drop it a few feet away. "I'll be right back," he said, and he walked off and the sound of his trekking poles slowly faded away. She took off her mask but the smoke was relentless so she got out a water bottle and poured some on the bandana and retied it around her face. She used to love the smell of woodsmoke. Right now, it was about the worst thing in the world.

She sat cross-legged on the hard ground and listened to the hustling water as it cleaved itself on rocks and buried itself in falls and churned against its banks. She was glad they'd made it to the river. If there was a fire nearby the river would protect them, shield them. Rivers and fires don't mix.

She pressed her wristwatch and it responded *Seven forty-eight p.m.* It was hard to believe they'd hiked that many hours. After fifteen minutes she stood carefully and stretched her legs and arms and flexed her shoulders. Some of her hunger returned and she sat and rummaged through the pockets of her backpack and found an energy bar and she unwrapped and ate that and washed it down with a slug of water. After thirty minutes she patted the ground all around to check out her immediate area and she stood again and turned in a small circle and shook out each leg and rotated her head to stretch her neck. A whole day with a backpack sure made your shoulders sore. She decided more than anything she was looking forward to getting into her own bed at home. The hike had been fun at first but now it was not fun. She loved being with her dad but she missed her nice safe room and she missed her mom.

After Will had been gone an hour Kal stood and cupped her hands around her mouth and called out, "Dad!" but the sound was muffled behind the bandana so she pulled it down around her neck and yelled out as loud as she could, "Hey Dad!" The only reply was the hurrying river. She turned slightly and called again, and then once more in another direction. Each time her voice seemed to be swallowed up, drowned in endless river rumble and the rush of wind in the trees. She sat again on the rocky ground. *He just can't hear me. He found a way down to the river and it's just taking a while. He'll be back before long.* She listened for telling sounds: a clacking of trekking poles, the rhythm of approaching boots. The wind sighed and ached in the trees. At each rustling and snap she croaked out, "Dad? Is that you?"

Time sped past. Every time Kal checked her watch the day had skipped ahead another fifteen minutes. Every so often she called out, "Hey Dad!" and held her breath for his reply. When her watch said, *Ten-oh-five p.m.* she knew it would be totally dark. Did he have his headlamp with him? She reached out and got his backpack and felt for the pocket where he kept his headlamp and when her fingers found it an involuntary sob welled up. She stood and yelled, "Dad!" with all her might and her shout disappeared into something vast, yawning, primal, unforgiving. Another hour passed. It was terribly smoky; her nose and throat felt scorched. She stood and screamed *Dad!* so forcefully that she lost her balance and fell to her knees directly on her father's backpack. She put her arms around it and hugged it and began to cry.

Friday, June 26
Tincup Fire camp, Selma

AT 1700 THE Communications Technician came up to Preston Ingram with a pained look on his face. A typo during programming caused half of the two-way radios to go out into the field with the wrong frequencies and now many of the ground and engine crews were unable to talk with each other or get directives from command dispatch.

Ingram stood with his hands on his hips staring at the floor while the COMT explained what had happened. This was a significant setback. Communications were the heart of any wildfire operation. People's lives depended on reliable comm. "How long to retrieve the radios and get them reprogramed?" Ingram asked quietly, staring at the COMT's shoes. He did not ask who'd fumbled the keystroke—that information would come out later. All that mattered now was restoring the information network.

The COMT followed Ingram's floorward gaze. "Maybe five, six hours. But we're lucky," he added hopefully, "it's late, not too many of them are in the field right now. But they're radios all over the camp."

Ingram looked up. When he narrowed his eyes and set his jaw, it was like looking at a closed vise. *Act decisively, prioritize, and execute.* "I want communications restored by oh five hundred. One hundred percent."

"Roger that." The COMT nodded, relieved to be dismissed without direct admonishment.

"Keep me posted."

No sooner had the COMT left than the Air Ops Branch Director called to say that one of the inbound airtankers had to land in Bend with engine problems. "Too bad," said the AOBD, "we finally score a couple of tankers and one of them gets dinged before it can join our operation. No word yet on how long. Thought you'd want to hear before the morning briefing."

An hour later the AOBD called back to report that spot fires had been confirmed on the north side of the river and from what they could tell several smaller fires had joined to form a mini-complex of about three hundred acres. They were ordering retardant drops but visibility was getting iffy as the winds shifted and he wasn't sure how effective they'd be until the smoke headed a new direction.

At 2200 hours the Ops Chief called to report a fatality. A dozer contractor on his way down from clearing the Illinois River Road had been overtaken by the fast-moving eastern flank. The Division Superintendent had figured something had gone wrong when they'd lost contact but getting a quick-response team in there had been impossible. They'd sent two small video drones up the road and had lost both of them to high winds but not before the second spotted the Cat and what looked like the driver. Crews had finally gotten to the body only by fighting their way in with pumpers and laying down foam to keep the flames at bay on their way back down. The Cat had been scorched black but, strangely, it was idling when they got there. They'd shut it down but it was still up there, partially blocking the road. He couldn't say if there was room for even a brush truck to get around it.

Ingram stared straight ahead as he listened to the Ops Chief. The word echoed in his head: *fatality*. They'd entered a new phase of the operation. His wildfire had turned deadly. "Didn't the Cat driver have a shelter?"

"If he did, he didn't have a chance to deploy." Ingram was silent, so the Ops Chief went on: "Safety is working with local sheriffs about getting the news to the relatives. The PIO is going to work up a statement you might want to take a look at."

"Thanks. I will."

"You know, Preston, I don't think a shelter would have done much good."

"Copy that," said Ingram and clicked off.

BY 0300 IN THE MORNING Ingram knew he needed sleep. The fire had tripled in size and smoke was filling the residential valleys to the east. The radios. The air tanker. On top of everything, a fatality. Now there'd be inquiries, accountability, processes. The Forest Service. Maybe NIOSH. The fire had jumped the river and the natural break had been breached. Spots had started a sizeable burn to the north of the river as well. He'd been up almost forty hours straight. He thought briefly of calling his wife—hearing her voice helped put things in perspective. She would listen. But he didn't want to feel as if he needed comforting.

He wasn't a stranger to losses. Working wildfires, he'd seen it all. Houses, barns, livestock, pets, stores, vehicles, people. Marketable timber. He knew that. He also knew that ruminating about losses was an indulgence for a commander. What mattered was, *What's next?* What decisions and courses of action? What is immediately threatened? What can be saved? What are the facts that matter? Facts revealed patterns, knowable quantities and qualities. Sure, sometimes fires betrayed facts. Acted irrationally, unpredictably. But in the end, odds were overwhelmingly in favor of tested and established procedures.

He wasn't going to call his wife.

Sleep. Rest. When he was younger, he'd go sixty, seventy hours straight, no sweat. But now at forty-four and shouldering command responsibility, he knew the whole operation would benefit if he got some shuteye. Just a couple hours would do it.

He walked to the big brown tent that Logistics had set

up for him behind the wildlands center. He preferred the military feel of canvas walls over more civilized options, such as an RV or trailer. It was grittier, more suitable for the combat at hand. He got inside, zipped the outer flaps closed, and sat on the cot he'd set up with a three-inch foam mattress topper. It felt good to have his ass sink into something soft and forgiving. He took off his boots and felt his muscles begin to unknot. He knew all about stress cortisol and the effect it had on the body and brain. Rest was absolutely necessary for effective decision-making. He got up and put his shirt on a hanger and suspended it with the other shirts hanging on his small portable clothes rack. He took off his pants and folded them neatly into thirds and set the bundle on the metal folding chair at the foot of his bed. He laid down and was glad he'd bought the three-inch foam instead of the two-inch. All the difference. The noise of the fire camp melted into a subdued nighttime thrum of distant voices and engines. Before he fell asleep, he prayed, *Dear Jesus take care of that poor bastard who died and please don't let my first command end up in the toilet. Amen.*

Saturday, June 27
Kalmiopsis Wilderness

FOUR THIRTY-SEVEN in the morning and her dad had not returned. Kal didn't sleep. She sat with her back against a tree and put a backpack on either side of herself to build a fortress against the night. She took out her folding pocketknife and opened the blade and held it with both hands. The treetops sighed and sudden gusts galloped through the bushes like a thing alive and made her heart spin wildly. She was queasy with smoke. She called out *Dad!* every few minutes. If he was lost in the dark he might need her voice as a beacon to guide him.

She tried to calm herself by thinking of good things. She thought of ballet poses, how she should put together a routine to show her dad when they got home. She thought of making ginger-molasses cookies with her mom. They'd make a ton of ginger-molasses cookies and eat plenty of the raw dough between batches. She thought about what kind of service dog she'd get. She wanted a labradoodle, but she wasn't sure they had labradoodle service dogs. Whatever dog she got, she would take care of it and feed it and brush it and love it more than anything and it would love her and would keep her safe.

Kal remembered the advice from her audiobook on wilderness survival, the sturdy voice saying: *Stay put. Drink water and stay hydrated. Above all, don't panic—in the wilderness, panic is the enemy.* But she needed to do something. *Don't panic.*

She could put up the tent. When her dad came back, he'd be surprised and proud and they would have shelter. Yes, good idea.

She folded the knife blade and put it in her pocket. She stood and shook out her body—she'd been sitting for hours.

She got the water bottles out of their backpack pockets and set them on the ground. Two were empty, the other two felt to be about half full. She took a drink and as the water flushed her parched throat an insatiable thirst kicked in and she drained the contents with greedy gulps. She set the newly emptied bottle next to the others, then she pulled the tent out of her dad's backpack and unrolled it. She got on her hands and knees and spread it out flat, running her palms along the expanse of nylon to make sure the site was free of stones. A gritty wind rolled through and made the tent fold up on itself—she had to find rocks to hold down the corners. She shook the tent stakes out of their nylon sack and pounded them into the hard ground using a rock she'd found that was slightly curved and fit her palm exactly. She promised herself that she would take the rock with her—as a memento—when they finally hiked out.

She got out the shock-corded poles and started to assemble them when the wind picked up the pole bag and whipped it up into her face and she snatched it off and held it tightly, scolding herself for almost losing a piece of gear. She needed to be more focused. This was the wilderness. *Keep it together.*

She searched with her fingers for the pole sleeves sewn into the tent seams and carefully began to thread the poles through the sleeves. She stopped now and then to listen. Was that her father yelling in the distance? She held her breath, focused, but all she heard was the wind sawing in the trees and rattling through the shrubs and rippling across the fabric of the tent.

She bent the poles into their impossible curves and wrestled the free ends into their pockets, a feat that took every bit of her patience. Half a dozen times the poles sprung out of her grasp and the joints separated and she had to reconnect the segments and start again. At last she felt the tent blossom upright. She'd done it. She added the rain fly, thinking maybe it would help keep out smoke. The rain fly was a challenge, the loose ends flying in the breezes. Fitting it over the tent took forever to figure out. When it was secured, she unzipped the entry flaps and crawled inside and zipped up the doors behind her. Both backpacks were still outside, each holding one of the inflatable mattresses and a sleeping bag. She'd get those soon. For now, she just wanted to be still. Less exposed. Safer. The ferocious wind could not reach her here, although it was trying.

She sat inside the tent and listened to small things—pine needles, twigs, leaves—patter against the nylon walls. Gusts made the fabric snap like firecrackers. She'd hoped the tent would be a buffer against the relentless smoke but the dark smell of burning wood was inescapable. After a few minutes she decided to retrieve the backpacks and set up their beds. She opened up the tent door and crawled out on her hands and knees. Then she stood carefully and yelled out, *Dad!* as loud as she could. She waited but there was no response. She yelled again. Then she eased back down to the ground and found the backpacks and dragged them inside the tent. She pulled out the mattresses and unrolled the sleeping bags and fluffed the stuff pillows. This was good. When her dad got back, he would be grateful.

Kal sat on one of the beds and wrapped her arms around her knees and pulled as tight as she could, as if she could squeeze herself into another place, transport both of them home by sheer will power. She began to cry. Something awful was surrounding her, closing in. She screamed *Dad!* and buried her face against her legs. She cried until her chest hurt from heaving. Then, abruptly, she stopped. She became utterly calm. She wiped her eyes with a stuff pillow and thought, *That was dumb, all that crying.* Dad was out there, doing everything right. Figuring everything out. He would do that, her dad. It was just taking longer than she wanted. He was being careful. He was totally okay. Why be so fearful? Staying put in the tent was right. Smart. Panic was wrong. It did not help Dad. Did not help anything.

But what if he really needed her help? He was strong and smart but even strong, smart people had accidents. Maybe that's why he hadn't returned. He was in some kind of trouble. It was only the two of them here in the wilderness—no one else. If he was in trouble, she was the only one who could help. No one else.

There was a forest fire happening and the relentless smoke told her it was still burning and it could be far away but then again it might be closer than she knew. It could be heading toward her. Toward her dad. Maybe there's a time for staying put and then there's a time for when you have to do something.

Kal got her trekking poles and climbed out of the tent and adjusted the poles for length. She knew the general direction her dad had gone and that he was probably following a trail so she'd head that way. Every now and then she'd yell for him. Maybe closing the distance would make a difference. She decided she'd yell every one-hundred steps. That way, she would keep track of the distance back to the tent. She had a sudden fear of being attacked by mountain lions but she shook her head and dismissed the thought because *Wilderness Survival* said that you had a better chance of getting hit by a meteor than getting attacked by a cougar.

She started off, using one trekking pole for balance and the other like a cane to read the terrain ahead. The leading point of the pole rasped against the dry soils and chunked against rocks and occasionally got hung up in trailside brush and she moved slowly, trying to gauge the language of the trail, the feel of it, counting steps and then pausing every fiftieth step to bend down and make a little cairn of stones to mark the way back to the campsite. She kept a careful mental record of her progress: *twenty steps, thirty*, reckoning the direction from which she'd come.

When she'd gone five-hundred steps she came to a place where the path widened and the way forward was uncertain. She got down on her hands and knees and felt for the telltale traces of bare earth that might indicate a trail. She found a narrow opening that was free of grasses and seemed headed toward the sound of the river. That made sense—her dad was looking for a way down.

"Dad!"

Kal got to her feet and tapped her way forward with the trekking pole and after one-hundred steps the trail began to decline and then it twisted right and left around big knobs of rough stone. The sound of the river faded as she passed behind the rocks and then there would be an opening and the tumbling would leap out, full and clear. It was rocky underfoot and she couldn't be totally sure if she was following an actual trail. She came to a large stone step and she eased her way down and when next she reached out with the pole she could not strike anything—only emptiness. She froze. The sound of the water was wide and unobstructed. There was a void before her, a yawning that opened to the river below. She carefully got to her knees and inched forward and again felt ahead with the trekking pole and it touched nothing. She patted with her left hand and found a hard lip of rock. She reached over the edge and felt the world fall away. She had come to the edge of a cliff.

For a long moment she stayed on hands and knees, immobile, not daring to move. Then she inched backwards, dragging the trekking poles by their wrist straps. When she bumped into the big stone step she slid up backwards until she was sitting on it. The terrible possibility reached up from deep inside her body and clutched at her throat and heart and she struggled to keep it from squeezing the air out of her lungs. Her mouth had gone dry and it took her a while to work up enough moisture so she could yell out, *Dad! Dad! Are you okay?*

There was no answer.

Saturday, June 27
Tincup Fire camp, Selma

SHORTLY AFTER DAWN Incident Commander Preston Ingram came awake. He'd slept in his underwear with his cell phone on his chest, clutched in one hand. He'd passed out only moments after lying down, but his infallible internal alarm clock brought him conscious at first light. Good—he'd managed two and a half hours of sleep and awakened in time to be in the situation room before the managers arrived.

Then he remembered the fatality.

He closed his eyes and took three deep breaths. Then he arched his back and ran a hand over his short-cropped hair. He thought briefly of taking a shower but instead he changed his socks and stuck his feet in his boots and laced them up. A Navy mind trick—a fresh pair of socks in lieu of a shower. He put on a clean shirt but despite his crisp exterior he still felt rumpled inside. He wasn't sure he'd slept all that well. *There are no bad teams, only bad leaders.*

Ingram stood outside the headquarters in the cool morning air. Dawn had arrived reluctantly. A steady wind blew through the camp and the American flag in front of the HQ was waving straight out. Either some eager beaver had raised it already this morning or some knucklehead had left the flag out all night. Leaving the American flag out all night was a sign of disrespect. He'd have to look into that. He stared at the flag and knew that it would be another long day of blustery, unpredictable winds.

At 0600 Ingram met the senior staff in the situation room for an early update. They all held white Styrofoam cups of coffee. The Ops Chief reported that they'd cleared restriction protocols that governed the use of heavy equipment in wilderness areas and four bulldozers had crossed the river at a bridge located partway up the River Road. They would be joined by hand crews to begin cutting thirty-yard-wide, high-priority control lines to the south. They planned to have five miles cut by the end of the day.

"FYI," said the Ops Chief, "our engineer got up there and took a look at that bridge across the Illinois and said it was a miracle the damn thing had stood up to a D9, let alone four of them. Might not be so lucky getting them back."

"Okay," said Ingram, rubbing his forehead. He needed more coffee. "Tell engineering to work up a plan for bracing the bridge."

"North of the river in Delta that fire is now about 600 acres. The River Road is now blocked as far as we know by the abandoned bulldozer."

Ingram nodded. He noted that the Ops chief had avoided direct reference to the fatality.

"We've got a road that comes in from the north so we've got some of options there. For now, we're going to be putting in a line here, to the east. We're sending more crews up there this morning..." he looked at his wristwatch, "...they should be getting ready to head out."

AT 0800 SIX ENGINES, a tanker truck and ten hand crew buses began making their way up a Forest Service road that ran along steep mountain ridges and approached the Tincup Fire from the northeast. Their mission was to establish control lines around the spot fire complex on the north side of the Illinois River.

Included in the caravan of green Forest Service crew transports were two slightly smaller, white crew trucks with the words *Oregon Department of Corrections* stenciled in black across the sides and backs. These crew trucks carried inmates who had been trained to fight wildfires as part of the ODC's voluntary work programs. The theory was that inmates who participated in job-training programs would be better at rehabilitating while incarcerated and then—after eventually being released—have an easier, more productive integration back into everyday life.

Only low-risk inmates who were merited for good behavior could be accepted to this particular program. Those who were accepted enjoyed a certain elevated status within the prison facility community. There was a sense of pride in the fact that combating fires was dirty, gritty, and demanding manual labor. There was machismo and a bit of swashbuckling romanticism about the danger of the work. They risked their lives. They fought hand-to-hand with a fierce and inhuman adversary.

For the most part the program had been successful.

The white, ten-person inmate crew transports were specially equipped with doors that locked from the outside and a protective steel mesh screen between the driver's cab and the two rows of four seats in the back of the transport. Each seat was mildly padded and relatively comfortable, and riding in the wildfire crew truck was something of a perk, even though the back roads they travelled were usually rutted and bumpy. Inmates brought headphones and music players and books and crossword puzzles for the ride to the fire and what could turn out to be a stay of several days and nights. Some simply sat and watched the real world ooze past.

Located in cubbies above the inmates' heads was their gear—individual backpacks with essentials including extra clothes, gloves, shoes, deodorant, toothpaste, toothbrush, lip balm, three-liter hydration pack, and a fire shelter that could be deployed if fire overran their positions. Any tools, such as Pulaskis and saws, would be distributed—and carefully inventoried—only upon arrival at the fire line.

Each of the trucks was driven by a crew boss from the Oregon Department of Forestry. Riding next to the crew boss in the passenger's seat was an officer with the Department of Corrections. The ODF crew boss was distinguished by his blue hard hat; the DOC officer wore a red hard hat. Both were dressed in yellow Nomex shirts and dark green Nomex pants. Neither was armed, although the corrections officer carried a cannister of Mace in a belt holster. Each had a radio programed to the frequency used by their separate dispatch offices.

Officially, prisoners were referred to as Adults in Custody—AICs. The AICs riding in the back of the transport all had yellow hard hats with bright orange Nomex shirts and pants that visually distinguished them from other hand crews typically deployed to an Oregon wildfire. Across the back of each shirt was a sewed-on tag that proclaimed in block letters, INMATE ODC.

The AICs in the two white trucks had another distinction—they were all from the Granite Creek Women's Detention Facility located southwest of Roseburg. Sixteen female firefighters plus a pair of female corrections officers made this the largest single deployment of women firefighters in Oregon history. Both ODF crew bosses were men. Once in position, the crew bosses would direct the firefighters' efforts. The corrections officers also would pitch in, working alongside the AICs as they scratched control lines in the duff and dirt.

Seated in the last row of the second bus was Parker Mayes, DOC inmate 257408336. Mayes was in the Granite Creek facility for armed robbery, a clumsy foiled attempt to rip off the West Umpqua Credit Union two summers ago. Normally resulting in lengthy prison terms, this particular armed robbery conviction was afforded some leniency in sentencing because the "gun" Mayes had used was a red plastic toy—a not-very-convincing fake and the source of some amusement when presented as evidence at trial. The judge gave her seven years. So far, she'd served twenty-two months and six days. She was forty-two years old.

At first the time had rolled by slowly for Mayes. She didn't like routines, and there was plenty of that. She often complained in her trumpeting voice about bad food and the stale drain smell in the showers and how others were ripping pages out of magazines so that the publications were generally useless for subsequent readers. Eventually, she got kidney-punched—twice—by another inmate while waiting in the food service line. Both times the perpetrator was a large blonde woman with undecipherable tattoos on her neck. Her name was Garden. Apparently, Garden didn't like Mayes ear hustling and talking loud shit and drawing attention to herself. It was hardly the most dramatic incident that could happen inside a correctional facility, but it was a message. Mayes knew any retaliation would just lead to a stupid escalation, so she let it pass. That's when she decided to enroll in the wildfire-fighting program.

She might have had a rep as boisterous and sarcastic and just plain too loud but now, as she sat in her seat in the jostling crew transport truck, she was quiet, staring out the window. Big trees moved past, each one like a distance marker from Granite Creek to here: farther, farther, farther away. Where views opened up she saw hard tan ridges heaped up under a smoke-filled sky that was stitched with thumping helicopters and laced with birds, birds winging along, birds flying free.

The crew from Granite Creek fell in alongside the other assigned hand crews and together they began to build a control line across the eastern flank of the newly spawned complex fire. There were not a few curious stares at the women in their orange fire-resistant outfits, but before long they were all bent to the work at hand and the novelty of female crews melted into rivulets of sweat.

They were cutting along a ridge a mile and a half from the burn when a fast-moving finger roared through the underbrush in the draw below their position, outflanking them to the south and threatening to cut off the single road leading in and out of the area. The strike team leader immediately recognized the danger and didn't hesitate to radio dispatch and report he was getting all the engines and crews the hell out of Division Delta. The crew bosses ordered everyone to return to the transport trucks.

At the moment the command to retreat was given, Parker Mayes was the most uphill person on her line crew. The smoke was streaming at them from the downhill side, which she had been taught was not good—it usually meant the fire was heading their way. In the distance through the haze she could just make out the blue hard hat of their ODF crew boss and the red hard hat of their corrections officer.

The other inmates turned and started to walk down the slope toward the waiting transports. Nobody seemed to be watching her. Somehow it wasn't like she made a conscious decision—her feet just seemed to move of their own accord. They turned the opposite direction and, to her wonderment, began to take her uphill. She walked calmly, carrying her Pulaski the way you were supposed to, the head parallel to the ground so you wouldn't impale yourself if you fell. She fully expected to hear the shouts of the corrections officers, the sound of boots running after her. She would feign confusion, say she was discombobulated by the smoke. After all, she hadn't been running. She was simply walking, heading up.

But there were no shouts or footfalls. The only sound was the wind moving through the trees and crackle of fire down in the draw and the scattered chirps of frightened birds on the wing.

Saturday, June 27
Tincup Fire camp, Selma

PIO CAROL HUFF was standing in the doorway of the situation room. The place was filed with the usual undercurrent of fire management—conversations in huddled groups of three or four, computer screens glowing with phosphorescent data, people moving in and out and shouldering sideways past her. She was looking for the right person to talk with and spotted one of the Operations Section Chiefs, Vickie Whitehorse, sitting in a folding chair next to the Airtack Group Supervisor. They were looking at a laptop computer that displayed satellite images of the burn. The smoke plume from the Tincup Fire was a band of white haze that had flung itself to the northeast.

Huff went over and tapped the AOC on the shoulder. "Vickie," interrupted Huff, "have you heard anything about hikers out in the wilderness area?"

Whitehorse turned in her chair. "What now?"

"It was on one of the local stations." Huff held up her smart phone as proof. "It's a video interview with this woman who says her husband and daughter are out hiking in the Kalmiopsis Wilderness and she hasn't heard from them. It was on the late news last night and apparently some of the big markets picked it up and ran it this morning. Now I'm getting calls—all the locals want to do interviews with this woman and Fox is sending down a crew from Portland."

Whitehorse frowned. In her experience, these kinds of reports usually amounted to unsubstantiated distractions. Apparently, this one had already blown way past that. "Is she credible?"

"Hard to say. But I get the feeling this is legit, yes."

Whitehorse considered. "Did she say where these

people might be?"

"I think she said Panther Bar. Illinois River Trail."

Whitehorse turned to the ATGS. "Do you know where that is?"

"Yeah, I'll show you."

They got up and walked to the big wall map and the ATGS pointed to the Illinois River and moved his finger along it until he came to Panther Bar. "Here," he said, then he slid his finger along a narrow, dotted line. "They'd probably parked here and then they'd take the Illinois River Trail here, moving west." On the map and close to the ATGS's finger were jagged red bands that indicated the fire perimeter. "Looks like an area that's about to close in."

Whitehorse turned to the PIO. "And nobody's heard from them?"

Huff nodded. "That's what the woman says."

"How long have they been out there?"

"Three, four days."

"We've been running drops along the perimeter to the east and north," said the ATGS, "but that area right there is totally closed for recon."

Whitehorse waved to get the attention of one of the Assistant Dispatch Duty Officers. The ADO came over and Whitehorse indicated the campgrounds along the Illinois River north to Panther Bar. "Get ahold of Rogue-Siskiyou. See if they know anything about civilians hiking out in this area."

"Roger that."

Huff said, "And Vickie, one other thing…"

"What's that?"

"The girl, the one hiking with her dad, she's blind."

"What?"

"Blind. Apparently. Can't see." Huff held up her phone again. "That's what all the media hype is about."

Whitehorse looked at the big map. If it was true, if they were still out there, the whole game would change. She nodded and got out her cell phone. "I'll let the Chief know."

A GROUP OF incident managers in the *Fire Weather and Behavior* tent watched FBAN Roger Merkle click through various GIS dashboards, zeroing in on conditions for Division Delta where the missing hikers were thought to be.

"And we think they're somewhere here?" Preston Ingram asked quietly, pointing to an area near the Illinois River.

Ops Chief Baker nodded. "Supposedly."

"But we're not one hundred percent on that?"

"No."

Ingram turned to the screen. "And down here, that's where the dozer operator died?"

"Yes sir."

Ingram went to the wall map and studied the wilderness hiking trails. He traced one with his finger. "What if those hikers head west?"

The IMET, who knew the region, shook his head. "That'd be tough," said Wright. "There's a trail, but it's rugged and a long way out to any extraction point. I'm not sure how much ground they could cover, especially a blind girl. I don't think they could outrun a fire."

"But they wouldn't know that."

"Well, if they were on a six- or seven-day hike," said Wright, "my guess is they're doing this loop trail that swings around and goes down along the river. If you're moving slow, which they would be, they'd be somewhere on the return leg. The guy has gotta be aware of the fire, pretty hard not to at this stage, so he'd probably head for the river anyway, for safety."

"Bonnie, do we have a Facebook page yet?"

"It's up and running. I'll post something about these

hikers and see if anybody knows anything." The PIO headed out.

"What's available for S and R?"

"We got local rescue out of Medford and we can do S and R out of the rappel base at Grants Pass. They're standing by for a break in the smoke cover."

"We may get some help with the weather," Wright put in. "We've got a thermal trough moving in from the coast. It should bring a northeastern wind. That might clear out smoke in that area, but it'll push the complex west and right toward our missing hikers. It'll bring some humidity and maybe even some rain. But I gotta say, this burn is hotter than anything I've seen in a long time. Maybe ever. Not sure we'll get enough moisture to make a difference in the big picture."

"How much time until the fire overruns this trail area?"

Merkle turned to the computer and brought up a new page. "With this rate of spread, short-term FB says less than thirty-six hours."

Ingram looked at his watch: 1030. He felt as if he'd just entered a race that he needed to win, and he was already way behind.

"Where are we with recon?"

"We've got a fixed-wing going up in…" the Airtack Supervisor looked at his wristwatch, "…thirty minutes."

"If they can get close, have them surveil the area where that blind girl and her father are supposed to be hiking."

"Copy that."

FROM THE AUDIOBOOK, "The Planet Earth: Amazing Natural Phenomena," by Dr. Jessica Shai Nusbaum, PhD:

A pyrocumulonimbus cloud is the apex predator of wildfires. It's dark, violent, and hungry. As its name reveals, it's a cumulonimbus cloud with an appetite for fire.

A pyroCb begins as a smoke column from a wildfire. As the fire expands in scope and intensity, the smoke column becomes wider, thicker, taller. Inside, heat boils upwards, pulling with it any moisture and creating a dirty cloud of super-heated ash and smoke. The uplift of heat causes the air around the base of the plume to flow inward, supplying the fire with fresh oxygen. This influx of oxygen causes the fire to burn hotter and hotter. Winds swirl into tornadoes of fire, massive trees burst into flames. The burn sucks in the surrounding air with increasing ferocity, pulling in loose branches and pinecones and saplings and grasshoppers and ground squirrels and owls and bewildered blue jays on the wing. The excruciating heat releases hot gases that ignite unburned fuels along the perimeter, helping the wildfire grow even as air flows inward. Hurricane-force winds turn the burn into a giant seething blowtorch. Scorching smoke and flaming embers shoot skyward with volcanic intensity. Pilots observing pyroCbs have reported whole trees shooting up hundreds of feet like flaming missiles.

A pyroCb may become a massive fire cloud that towers to 50,000 feet, lording over the landscape with filthy magnificence, brushing against the lower edges of the stratosphere.

It's a monster so big and full of turbulent energy that it can create its own weather system. Heated particles, ice crystals, and moisture vapor collide with such force that electrical fields are generated, producing lightning that can strike miles away from the main wildfire, starting new fires.

As the smoke and heat and water vapor rise into the upper

levels of the atmosphere, the top of the cloud may begin to cool. This causes the upper part of the pyroCb to flatten, forming the anvil shape characteristic of big Midwestern thunderheads. Under a mantle of lightning, the cooling top of the fire cloud may spew forth rain and dirty black hail that helps douse the main fire. Unfortunately, that's rare. More often, a pyroCb puts out only enough precipitation to douse the backfires that firefighters have set in an attempt to control the burn.

In rare instances, the top of the pyroCb cools dramatically, with moisture vapor freezing and the entire top of the cloud becoming increasingly heavy until it finally collapses with such force that the mammoth inflows of air are suddenly reversed, blasting out heat and fire with a sudden fury that can obliterate control lines and overtake nearby fire crews.

Saturday, June 27
Rogue Rappellers Crew base, Grants Pass

SATURDAY MORNING a tactical air response order chattered its way out of the fax machine at the rappel base. The TARO called for a fixed-wing recon mission to search for civilians who may be hiking the Illinois River Trail in the Kalmiopsis Wilderness. At 0915 Matt Murphy climbed aboard a single-engine Cessna 182 sitting at the end of the small airstrip that ran alongside the base headquarters and served both small airplanes as well as the rappellers' helicopter. Murphy was along as spotter. Piloting the overhead-wing surveillance plane was Don Caperelli, a ten-year Air Force vet who'd flown F-16s in the Gulf and had settled into a nursery and landscaping business in Grants Pass. During fire season Caperelli was on-call to the Forest Service and ODF. Even though a Cessna couldn't come close to the visceral joy of a combat jet, he loved the military-like urgency and purpose of flying an operational mission.

The day came hot and bright and as they headed west the plume rose up into the morning sun as a splendid malfeasance. Sporadic lightning set off bursts of light inside the cloud and the top was flattening against the cooler upper strata. Caperelli knew churning thermodynamics would likely make the air near the plume unstable.

They flew at 7,000 feet. From that vantage the plume looked to be in slow motion, sprawling lazily toward the northeast. The closer they got the more the cloud towered over them. They bore northwest and as they approached the proposed search coordinates Murphy could see the area was completely obscured.

"Dispatch," Murphy said into his microphone, "we're nearing the eastern edge of the main fire and it's all smoke.

No visuals on the individuals or their vehicles. We're going to get as close as we can."

Caperelli brought the Cessna around on a sweeping turn to put the fire on Murphy's side of the aircraft and it was like flying next to a giant, sentient being that slowly flexed and billowed as it considered its options. Murphy had his laptop out with a topo maps app that showed the area below. On the screen he could pick out the location of the Forest Service roads and the course of the river but looking out the window everything was obscured by smoke.

"Let's make another pass," said Murphy.

Caperelli banked and turned right and the cloud was closer now and darker, as if it could suck the light out of the air. Murphy trained his search on the ground closest to the edge of the burn and as he did the plume in his peripheral vision appeared to shudder and roll and the Cessna tilted and Murphy felt the gut-chill that happens when you drive over a hill too fast and gravity loses its grip. The smoke column was collapsing. The Cessna, caught in the downward rush, was dropping like a stone. His laptop floated up before his face and hung there and a pencil appeared along with a crumpled gum wrapper and he could feel his arms raise by themselves and flaming things spun past the windows and the plane fell and the altimeter unwound with cartoonish ferocity and then they were swallowed in smoke. In the sudden darkness Murphy could barely make out the co-pilot's yoke mimicking the pilot's attempts to recover. He reflexively stomped his foot on an imaginary brake pedal and he saw his wife's face and he thought of his parents and he wondered if this is what it felt like to die. Everything but the hard part.

With a *whump!* the plane caught solid air and the laptop slapped down on Murphy's knees and the plane began to bank out of the tumbling smoke column and after the longest fifteen seconds of his life Murphy looked out on a pale blue morning sky and wispy clouds—real clouds—and in the distance the conical tip of Mt. McLoughlin and the ragged head of Mt. Thielsen and his first thought was that this skyscape was easily one of the most beautiful things that he could ever see and that he wanted to tell everybody he knew about it. The moment was indelibly printed on his soul. "Holy crap," he breathed, and looked over at the pilot.

Caperelli seemed unconcerned and was bringing the Cessna around on a flight path back toward the landing strip. He was chewing gum.

"Holy crap," Murphy repeated. "How the hell did you get us out of there?"

Caperelli shrugged and smacked gum. "I don't know. As long as nobody's shooting SAMs at me, I'm fine."

Dispatch broke in and Murphy explained what had happened and that they had been close to the column when it began to fall and it nearly pulled them down and *Holy shit is Don Caperelli a good pilot.* He added that getting a visual on the Illinois River Trail was impossible.

Dispatch relayed the report to the Duty Officer and the DO notified the Aviation Officer who walked it up to the Ops Chief.

"Recon says they were right near the column as it started to collapse," said the AO. "They barely made it out."

"All right," said the Ops Chief, "I'll let Ingram know."

IC PRESTON INGRAM WAS talking with the Ops Chief about the recon mission's close call when his cell phone buzzed.

"Preston, it's Bonnie. There's been a development that you should be aware of."

"What's that?"

"Well, apparently the news story with the woman, the one with her husband and blind daughter out hiking? It went national today. It's everywhere. And apparently Governor Briggs saw it and he's on his way here."

"Here? To the camp?"

"Yes. He said something about making sure the missing hikers are found. He was at some conference in Eugene and he has his road entourage with him."

"When?"

"Sometime this evening."

Ingram clicked off and held his phone in his hand and stared at it. Then he did what he promised himself he'd never do, which was to swear out loud in front of his subordinates. In a loud clear voice, he said, "Fuck!"

FROM THE AUDIOBOOK, "Wilderness Survival," by A.J. Cochran:

Cougars, like other fleet-footed animals of the mountains and forests, can easily escape wildfires. Their keen eyesight and hearing give them plenty of advance warning and, unless they are surrounded by fire, they likely will escape to safety.

But that's not all that mountain lions will do during a wildfire.

Millenia of evolution have taught these apex predators that their natural prey—rabbits, raccoons, and especially deer—also run to avoid the flames. Knowing this, mountain lions often pause at the perimeter of a wildfire, waiting for panicked prey. Flooded with the urge to flee, a deer may run straight into a mountain lion's claws, oblivious to the danger until it is too late.

Saturday, June 27
Kalmiopsis Wilderness

BY THE TIME Kal made it back to the tent it was early morning. She crawled inside and lay down on her sleeping bag and fell asleep not simply because she was exhausted but as a defense against the terror of days gone horribly wrong. She surrendered herself to a heavy, toneless slumber.

She awoke eleven hours later. She was groggy and hot and her pillow and the top of her sleeping bag were damp with her perspiration. She felt across for her father but he was not there. She was still alone. Her wristwatch said, *Eight oh-five p.m.* Wind rippled up the tent walls and keened in the trees. The world had expanded its emptiness, and within it she had become smaller and more completely lost.

Breathe, one two three.

She was thirsty and she'd left the water bottles outside. She had a pang of regret for finishing off half her water supply and knew she'd have to ration what was left. So just a sip this time. She unzipped and crawled out of the tent and found the half-full water bottle. She was about to unscrew the cap when she heard something, a noise apart from the restless landscape. She ventured, *Dad?* then held her breath and listened, hoping for a human sound, his voice, or even a groan. Again, *Dad?* It was…a snuffling. An animal-like sound.

She kept absolutely still, not wanting to startle it, whatever it was. It was close. A bear? There was food in the tent, crackers and nuts and salmon jerky. Her dad would have put their food in a bag and hung it in a tree, away from their camp. But now all their food was right here, inside the tent.

A mountain lion? It was hunting, and it had found her. She tried to remember what her *Wilderness Survival* book said about encounters with mountain lions and bears. You threw things at cougars and you cowered before bears. Or was it the other way around? She took a deep breath, focused on the spot where she'd heard the noise and she threw the water bottle at it and she screamed at the top of her lungs, *Get out of here!*

The metal bottle hit the ground and clattered away and there was an excruciating pause of several seconds and then whatever it was hustled off through the underbrush. Kal listened as the sound of its scratchy footsteps faded.

Her heart was rioting. Foul woodsmoke rolled in thick and pungent and she gagged and then she realized it was not smoke but the smell of skunk. She had thrown her bottle at a skunk and it had retaliated. The stench was awful! She batted the air in front of her face to ward off the poisoned air but it was no use. A retch worked its way up her throat and she fought to keep it down but couldn't and she got to her hands and knees and crept away from the tent entrance and threw up what little was in her stomach. She vomited in waves and finally the retching subsided as the restless air diluted the odor. She wiped her lips with the back of her hand. *At least it wasn't a cougar.*

Her mouth was full of acid taste and she needed to rinse out. The water bottle was who-knows-where. Somewhere over there. She crawled, feeling ahead with her hands as little stones and brittle pine needles stabbed her palms and bare knees. It had sounded as if the bottle had rolled off to her right. Kal gave a wide berth to the spot where the skunk had probably sprayed. *Skunks can spray up to fifteen feet.*

She patted the area in front of her methodically, sweeping her hands in a five-foot arc, then moving forward a foot and doing it again. Her fingers touched rocks, cones, grit. Where there was a bush or a tree she checked around its base. Kal could feel anxiety rising inside her—the bottle held what was left of the water and she'd tossed it into the wilderness.

The arc of her search widened. It couldn't have gone this far. She must have missed it. She began to reverse course, going back the way she'd come. But the ground, the rocks, the tree trunks were strangely unfamiliar. Hadn't she explored here only a few minutes ago? She didn't remember this squarish stone, the prominent bump on this tree. She tried to keep oriented by the sound of the river. But here, in the open mountain range, as an edge of desperation crept in, everything under her fingers felt foreign, sounds melded and swirled around, masked by the constant rasp of the wind in the trees. The river should be on her left but was behind her. The ground that should be near level was steeper.

She stopped searching and tried to calm herself. *Think, think*. People will know they were out here. Her mom would know. They would be looking for them. There would be search parties. They would see the tent; they would find her and her father.

Search parties. Of course, the emergency beacon! Her dad had brought an electronic thingy that could send out a distress beacon. When she got back to the tent she'd dig it out of her father's backpack and send the signal and they would definitely be found. She was almost giddy with relief. She'd go get the beacon and push the button right away. Then she'd get back to finding the bottle.

She crawled back toward the tent but when she got to where the campsite should have been the tent had vanished. She felt around in an ever-widening circle but the tent was not where it was supposed to be. It was not anywhere. It had been swallowed by a matrix of rough-barked trees and scraggly, mean-spirited bushes. Her palms and knees were raw. Her thirst was overwhelming. Everything felt backwards and inside out. She'd miscalculated, and now she was lost. She lay on a thin scattering of pine needles and folded into a fetal position and began to sob. It wasn't right, that she be out here alone, abandoned. This wasn't the way it was supposed to happen. Why had her dad left her? Where was he?

She lifted her head and yelled, "Help! Please help me!"

There was no response, only the wind, the trees, and the restless river.

Saturday, June 27
Tincup Fire camp, Selma

AS ASSISTANT Human Resources Specialist for the Type 2 Incident Management Team, Brad Majkowski knew he was about as low as you could go in a hierarchy that now included over 600 firefighters and agency personnel. His status—or lack of it—was why he had been assigned to the vehicle entrance for the fire camp. There, it was his duty to assess incoming traffic and decide whether they had legitimate reasons for entering. This was his first such assignment and he knew he had been plucked at random from a pool of candidates whose function at the fire camp was deemed to be nonessential. Nevertheless, Majkowski felt a great deal of responsibility and, given the drama of the ever-growing wildfire, a growing authority in discharging his duties.

Most legitimate traffic was easy: fire trucks of all sizes and types, from dazzlingly clean, chartreuse-and-white Ford pumper trucks from the Josephine County Rural/Urban Fire Department to an aging, cube-headed Ward LaFrance pumper on loan from Shady Cove Fire Department; green Forest Service crew transport buses, bulbous water tankers, jerry-rigged flatbed pickups with big nozzles bolted to their rears and enormous plastic cylindrical tanks behind their cabs where the shadow of the water splashing inside was like a thing alive clawing at the walls of its confinement. The air was ripe with the cloying, rotten-egg smell of diesel fuel as the big rigs rumbled into camp.

Individual crewmembers were easy to spot no matter what they drove. They had rough faces and calm demeanors, men and women alike. Even in the baking heat they didn't use air conditioning and they drove one-handed with their tattooed left arms resting on the door frame and their elbows crooked into the wind. They'd say they were with operations or a strike team and Majkowski waved them through and as he urged them into the camp he felt as if he personally was providing the resources that could be unleashed against the blaze. Any buttoned-up types that arrived without an official uniform and announced they were with logistics or facilities he made wait while he radioed up to the procurement office where a weary but patient voice gave the okay. Lookee-loos and curious passersby he firmly turned away and admonished them to stay off the River Road in case an emergency occurred. Invoking the word "emergency" against a swarming backdrop of firefighting resources gave weight to his de facto authority.

By 2200 Majkowski had been at his post for thirteen straight hours. Luckily, a row of blue Porta-Pottys had been installed not far away and he'd been able to scoot over, take a leak and return to his duty without too much dereliction. It was during one of these biological hiatuses that Joss Spencer had driven unchallenged into the camp.

As evening fell and the heat of the day started to loosen its grip, Majkowski began to wonder if he would ever be replaced. Perhaps the team had forgotten about him. He was hungry and tired and not sure what to do. The camp rumbled behind him, the sound of engines and the general clamor quieting in the later hours. He got out his cell phone and called his supervisor and a recorded voice informed him that the supervisor's mailbox was full. "Well that's the shits," Majkowski muttered into the phone. He radioed the procurement office and asked if maybe the HR Supervisor was nearby and received a blatant sigh and a weary, *No*.

He was about to abandon his post to get something to eat and then search for his boss when two identical black SUVs came up the road and wheeled into the entrance, their headlights cutting swaths through the persistent haze. A moment later an enormous gray RV with tinted windows rolled in behind the SUVS. Probably campers looking for a late-night RV park. Majkowski raised a hand to bring the caravan to a halt. He walked up to the first vehicle and tapped on the window. It slid down to reveal a young woman dressed in business attire who looked at him with annoyance.

"I'm sorry, ma'am," said Majkowski, "but this is a restricted area."

"Would you please tell your people that the Governor has arrived?"

"The Governor?" Majkowski was perplexed. Governors don't come to wildfires, do they? Was she jiving him? He said, "The Governor of what?"

A man in the passenger seat leaned over. He wore a blue shirt with an open collar and a loosened necktie and he appeared to be exasperated by a day full of exasperations. He pointed to the trailing vehicle and said, "The Governor of the fucking state of Oregon. Warren Biggs. *That* Governor."

Majkowski followed the man's finger and stared at the second SUV, its shape blurred behind the glare of its headlights. "Governor Biggs is here?"

"Where should we go?" asked the woman impatiently.

"Um…" was all Majkowski could muster as his mind raced to think of the correct protocol, who to contact. He was about to radio Procurement for the umpteenth time, maybe they'd know what to do, when a young woman came hurrying through the dark waving her arms.

"I'm here!" called the woman. "Here I am!" She came panting up to the lead SUV and, ignoring Majkowski, shouldered her way to the open window and stuck her hand in the driver's face. "Bonnie Tucco, Public Information Officer for the incident management team," she said breathlessly. She leaned down and said to the man in the passenger seat. "Governor Biggs, so glad you decided to come."

"I'm not Biggs. He's in the other car."

Tucco squinted. "Oh, of course. Good grief, you're not the Governor. Ha. My bad." She popped her head up like a prairie dog and took in the second SUV and waved. Then she smiled down at the driver and said, "We've got a media tent set up just across the field. There are three local TV station crews that would love to get a few words from the Governor. There's also a VIP tent, very comfortable and private. Air conditioned. Right near the headquarters where there's restrooms, showers. Anything the Governor wants." She prairie-dogged up again and sniffed. "Is that…" meaning the hulking RV, "…the Governor's?"

The driver tapped index fingers along the top of the steering wheel. "That's for him. It's donated for a couple of days from…" she looked at her passenger, "…from?"

"Jasper's RV Sales in Medford. By the way, the Governor will probably give an on-camera shout-out to Jasper's and that's not to be edited out, understood?"

Tucco blinked. These two had that edge to them. In her experience, all Governors' entourages were sort of edgy. Came with the territory. "Sure. I'll let them know. It won't be a problem. Let me call the Incident Commander and let him know you're here."

She got out her iPhone and tapped the number. She knew Ingram would be expecting the call. When the IC answered Tucco said, "Preston, the Governor is here…all right…you bet." She tapped off and said to the woman driver, "I'll take you up to the media tent."

The passenger held up a finger. He got out his phone, dialed and said, "Mark, ask the Governor if he wants to go straight to the media tent." There was a brief pause, then the passenger clicked off and said, "Okay. Let's go the media tent."

Up at the headquarters, Incident Commander Preston

Ingram pocketed his cell phone and crossed his arms across his chest, looked down, shook his head and formed the word with his lips but this time didn't say it out loud: *Fuck!*

AS INSTRUCTED by his handler, the Governor took off his suitcoat and tie and unbuttoned his top shirt button so that he came across with hardworking savoir faire. His shirt was tucked into his trademark blue jeans punctuated with a Pendleton Roundup belt buckle. The IMT's information unit set up a background of area maps fixed to large tack boards and the TV station's videographers agreed to share one light setup and they placed the key light and fill lights and a wobbly back light they hoped wouldn't catch a breeze and fall over. They put their cameras in agreeable locations so no one station had a line-of-sight advantage. For the interview they'd placed two stools in the confluence of the lights, but the Governor's handler had them removed knowing that Biggs preferred to stand so he could put his hands on his hips and look determined.

The plan was to have Incident PIO Bonnie Tucco do a brief interview with the Governor that the stations could use as they saw fit except they could not, under any circumstances, edit out anything the Governor might say about Jasper's RV Sales. Tucco had printed up her questions in advance and gave a copy to each of the news teams. Afterwards, the individual stations could set up interviews by making a request through the Governor's staff public relations officer, Cynthia Paulsen, who turned out to be the SUV driver. It was noted that Governor Biggs would certainly make himself available for those kinds of one-offs in the morning, although how long the Governor might stay at the fire camp and when he might depart were unknown.

Somebody was going over the Governor's face with a makeup brush. Tucco positioned herself where the stools had originally been and looked at her cell phone; time was growing short to make the eleven o'clock local news slot.

At last the Governor walked to the center of the small staging, smiled and extended his hand to Bonnie Tucco but said nothing. His silence was meant to say, *We know who I am. Who are you?*

"Bonnie Tucco, Governor." She took his hand and received a brief, firm handshake that didn't try to overpower. Practice makes perfect. "I'm the Incident Public Relations Officer here on the Tincup Fire. We appreciate you taking the time to come here and assess the situation."

He put his hands on his hips and the smile morphed into a furrowed brow. "I understand there's a blind girl out there…" he pointed at a far horizon, "…and she may be in danger, and we're going to try and save her."

Tucco looked at the videographers. "Let's retake that." She turned to Biggs. "Governor, if you don't mind, let's start the interview and have you say that again."

He nodded. "All right."

"And, minor detail, but if you would point with your right hand instead of your left so you'll be pointing toward the fire location."

"Sure, good catch."

Tucco turned to face the cameras. They began to roll. She said, "I'm Bonnie Tucco, Public Relations Officer for the Forest Service Incident Management Team. I'm here with Governor Warren Biggs. We're just outside of the town of Selma at the base of firefighting operations for the Tincup Fire, a devastating southern Oregon wildfire that's now estimated at thirty-thousand acres and has already claimed at least one life. Governor, what brings you here to this fast-moving wildfire?"

Biggs nodded and spoke to the cameras. "We're here to give encouragement and hope to all these brave young men and women who are fighting this fire on behalf of the people of Oregon." Then he put his hands on his hips, turned to Tucco and said, "I understand there's a little blind girl out there…" he pointed with his right hand, "…and she may be in danger. And we're going to make damn sure we save her."

Sunday, June 28
Tincup Fire camp, Selma

IN THE GATHERING darkness of Saturday night Joss found her car and without any self-debate about whether to drive back home or try to get a motel room, she opened a rear door and crawled inside and curled into a semi-fetal position on the backseat and fell asleep.

The early morning brought the clatter of diesel engines and the purr of generators and the whoops and shouts of firefighters calling to each other as they got ready to face the flames. She was chilled and stiff but the sun had come up and was streaming inside the windshield and she sat upright and the sunlight fell warm on her face.

She got out of the car and stomped her feet. The air smelled of woodsmoke and diesel fuel and bacon. To the west the massive smoke plume hung dark as Devil's breath in front of a pale blue sky. She was unsure of a plan. She wondered if anyone had heard anything and reported it. She fantasized that Will and Kallie had decided to forgo the hike and instead were hanging out in town. They'd fib. They'd swear they'd been hiking hot, dusty trails when in fact they'd gone into Medford or Ashland and were having an awesome time eating at restaurants and going to movies. *Missing father and daughter spotted walking out of the Denny's this morning. Missing father and daughter seen splashing in the pool at the Holiday Inn.* God, please....

She checked her cell—no messages from Will and one unread voice message from Private. She usually dismissed any unknowns but now—no stone unturned. The recorded voice said: *Mrs. Spencer! Hi, this is Sylvie Platt. I'm press liaison to Governor Biggs. The Governor would like you to join him Sunday morning for an eight o'clock televised media session here in the fire camp.*

I'm not sure if you're in Selma or if you've gone back home, but I hope you get this in time. It's another chance to get the message out about your missing family, and I have to say the Governor is being extremely gracious about this opportunity. Please call me back as soon as you get this message.

It was six forty-five. She looked like she'd been sleeping in the back seat of a small sedan. Twists of hair hung down in front of her eyes. Her mouth tasted like charcoal. She was hungry and wanted to vomit at the same time. She needed to find that other woman and see if there was any news. What was her name? Joss pulled the business card out of her jeans pocket. *Evelyn Peters, Public Relations Officer, Oregon Department of Forestry.*

Joss called and got a recording that asked her to leave a name and number. Then she called the Governor's press liaison. "Sylvie? Hello, this is Joss Spencer. I'm here at the camp. I can do that thing with the Governor. But I think I'm going to need a little help getting myself together for any interview in front of a camera."

GOVERNOR BIGGS had changed into rattlesnake hide cowboy boots and a white, western-style shirt with embroidered button-down front pockets, no tie. The Governor had politician's hair—thick wavy dark gray with blushes of white at the temples. With his 500-watt grin and relaxed, twangy telegenics, he looked the part of the prototypical Western governor. All that was missing was a wide-brimmed cowboy hat, which he refused to wear on account of his hair. "We don't want me running around with a damn hat ring in my hair, now do we?" he told his handlers. The next gubernatorial election was a year away and a second term was a goal he coveted and an aspiration that his staff constantly reinforced.

Sylvie Platt had begged the Staging Area Manager for temporary use of a chartreuse-green Forest Service Type 3 engine as a backdrop for the video segment featuring the Governor and the mother of the blind kid. She had them park the big truck at the edge of the meadow and the engine crew stood off to one side, eating granola bars and checking their cell phones and waiting. The crew boss had obligingly lent the use of a canvas tarp to stand on, insulating the Governor from the indignity of dusty boots.

Platt texted Joss directions to the interview, saying: *Come straight across the field to the big green truck!* so Joss did exactly that but failed to take in a tanker spill that had soaked part of the meadow with hundreds of gallons of water so that by the time she got to the big green truck she had gobs of sticky clay mud on her hiking shoes and mud spatters up her pants legs.

Platt took in Joss' arrival with a tilted head. "Well, we'll only shoot from the waist up," she gave a brave smile. "Let's see what we can do with your hair."

The Governor's makeup assistant brushed out Joss' hair and blushed her cheeks and gave her forehead a tap of anti-sheen foundation. Joss and the Governor stood on the canvas and the PIO Bonnie Tucco wiggled between them with a handheld mike. The Governor nodded at Joss and gave an *I understand your pain* smile and said, "Howdy, ma'am. Sorry about your kid being lost."

Joss was uncertain how to reply. Should she thank him for being sorry about her child? And what's with the *ma'am* thing again? She blinked as the portable spotlights came on. The production supervisor came up and looked around the makeshift studio and said, "Let's get a scoop in here."

An assistant trotted up with a roundish reflector and held it at various angles until the production supervisor was satisfied and then the videographer positioned herself with her shoulder-mounted camera and said, "Three, two, one, rolling."

Bonnie Tucco began, "I'm here with Governor Warren Biggs and Joss Spencer, the mother of the little blind girl who's gone missing in the Tincup Fire. Governor Biggs, I know you've come here to help supervise the firefighting efforts. What's your reaction to this missing child?"

"Thank you, Bonnie. And first of all, I want to thank the brave young men and women firefighters who are fightin' this fire. They're doing a fantastic job." Then he set his jaw, looked at the camera, pointed in a random direction and said, "There's a blind girl out there, and we're going to make sure we save her."

"Cut!" said Sylvie Platt, waving her arms. "Look, Governor. You can't say it that way, like you personally are guaranteeing her safety." There was a pause, then Platt turned to Joss and said, "I'm sorry, but you understand."

"Ah…" was all Joss could manage before Platt turned back to Biggs.

"How should I say it?" asked Biggs.

"Just say, *I'm here to make sure we're doing*…no, wait. *I'm here to make sure they're doing all they can to save this young girl and her father*. Be sure to say *they're doing*, okay?"

"Got it."

Platt nodded at the videographer.

"Three, two, one, and rolling."

Biggs performed flawlessly in emphasizing his role overseeing the firefighting forces, adding his desire to ensure that *they* saved the girl.

Bonnie Tucco rotated a half turn. "We're also here with Joss Spencer, the mother of the blind girl who's apparently missing. She went hiking, isn't that right? With your ex-husband?"

Joss nodded.

"And how are the search efforts going so far?"

"I don't think," said Joss, her voice rising in pitch as she pointed at Governor Biggs, "that you or anybody is doing a damn fucking thing to save my daughter and ex-husband!"

There was a stunned moment of silence, then Tucco yelled, "Cut!" She glared at Joss. "You can't say those kinds of things," she sputtered. "What are you thinking! You owe the Governor an apology!"

"Take it easy, Bonnie," said Biggs. "The woman's under a lot of stress." He peered down at Joss. "Isn't that right, ma'am?" He shrugged. "Anyway, I've heard worse said about me."

Joss narrowed her eyes. "Sorry."

They did the take again, Joss still smoldering, and when they had finished the Governor nodded at her and said, "Sorry about that little dustup. Hope that won't cost me your vote." He said it like a joke, but it wasn't.

The video segment went to the local affiliates including Portland, Seattle, and San Francisco, and all the networks and cable outlets picked it up for inclusion in the evening news. The story of the little blind girl and the Tincup Fire was becoming an everyday segment of the national media.

That was not before, however, videos of Joss swearing at the Governor went viral. Apparently, some members of the engine crew who had been waiting for the completion of the orchestrated video segment had recorded the outburst on their cell phones and had posted it to various social media, *#woman-f-offs-gov*. By noon the video had 1.2M views, 145K shares, and 298K likes.

"JESUS H CHRIST," Governor Biggs said into his cell phone. "That woman made me look like a horse's ass. You should see the crap they're posting on my Twitter feed. Now I want you to find that girl and get her the hell out of that forest so we can all be heroes."

On his end of the call Incident Commander Ingram

chewed the insides of his cheeks. As a federal employee, Ingram technically didn't have to kowtow to any state official. At the same time, this was the Governor. Local resources had been put at his disposal and he had to respect that. "I understand your concern, Warren," said Ingram, sidestepping the governor's official title. "Believe me, we're trying to find those people and get them out of there. I'm as concerned as you are." *Much more concerned,* Ingram thought to himself.

"Don't you have rescue teams that can get in there? I mean, for the love of Christ, is the federal government asleep at the wheel?"

"Right now, that location is too hazardous to attempt a search-and-rescue. We're monitoring the situation closely, and as soon as we can, we're going to get a search team in there." As accurate as that response was, Ingram knew it sounded risk-averse. But that was his job, dammit, to not deliberately put people in harm's way. You measured a good outcome not by acres lost, but by lives saved. And that was always an unknown—how many lives did you save by being mindful of dangerous situations? Already one life had been lost.

"Get in there and find those people and get them the hell out,' said the Governor, "or I'll make damn sure you never get a command position in my state again." He clicked off.

Ingram slid the phone back in his shirt pocket with a steady hand. He didn't like being threatened, but he knew the Governor had influential political contacts and could easily make good on his word.

He looked to the big wall map that had recently been updated with the outline of the Tincup Fire. The latest red mylar overlay showed two appendages of the Tincup Fire closing in on the hikers' location like a giant claw.

Sunday, June 28
Kalmiopsis Wilderness

SHORTLY AFTER she'd walked away from the work crew, Parker Mayes came upon a trail that she was pretty sure was heading west—away from the wildfire and away from the authorities. West—that sounded good. She figured four, five days of hiking and she'd make the coast. She had three liters of water that, with careful rationing, she could make last. She'd heard that you could always drink out of mountain streams and, if you did get a bug, it wouldn't kill you, just make you sicker than shit for a couple of days.

She set off along the trail, occasionally upping her pace by jogging, still holding her Pulaski the way she'd been taught. The Pulaski was heavy and awkward but it was a substantial tool and given that she was pretty much down to bare essentials, a big tool might come in handy. Now and then she'd take short, off-trail detours through heavy brush. If they set dogs after her, she aimed to make their hunt a miserable affair.

Things were definitely falling her way. Back at the fire line, they'd have cleared all those trucks and crews out of the area, so there was a good chance nobody was chasing her. Even if they'd radioed in right away to report a missing AIC, any COs or state police pursuit would be hung up by the fire, maybe for days. The smoke was heavy but it kept helicopters out of the sky. As long as she could out-distance a fire, she'd be okay.

When the sun went down, Mayes kept going, making her way by the light of her headlamp. Out here there wouldn't be a damn soul who would spot a light moving through the woods. She had to slow down in the darkness but she was still moving. That was the important thing. Make time, make distance. Give yourself some breathing room.

Around midnight she came to a fork in the trail. She wasn't sure the best way to go. The right-hand trail seemed to peel off back toward the way she'd come, so she set off in the other direction. She kept on for another two hours before her headlamp flickered, strobing nearby trees into a weird, hopping dance, and then it stopped working altogether. The batteries had given out. She thought, *Probably haven't been changed in years. Cheap bastards.* She had a spare set of batteries, but when she dug them out of her pack and began to exchange them, working by feel in the dark, she realized that the batteries in her headset were triple A and the replacements were double A. *Of all the dumb fucking things.*

She found a big tree and set with her back against it to hunker down for the remainder of the night. She figured she had a good enough lead and when dawn came she'd hit the trail hard. She was too hopped up to sleep, so she sat and watched a sliver of night sky that appeared on the far horizon, just visible underneath the mantle of smoke. She could see a few stars. Outside made her feel good, alive, the way people were supposed to be. Stars and sky and openness just there for the taking. Even the smoky air was better than the smell of prison funk. *Hell yes.* She didn't want to go back inside ever. Maybe she could just disappear. Canada. Mexico. She knew a few people who might help.

At some point she'd have to get away from the trail. If they sent out helicopters, she'd get under cover—there was plenty. But they also used drones to look for your body heat. Being under trees and stuff helped there, too, but she had a secret weapon. She had a foldup fire shelter in her pack that could really block body heat. She could get under that whenever. The orange fireproof shirt and pants might be spotted, so sooner or later she'd have to ditch them, but for now they were a layer of comfort, especially at night. The fireproof work boots were primo—a thousand times better than her prison-issue brogans or the spare skippies in her pack.

Morning light came dull and brown. It was hard to know where the sun was, but if she reckoned correctly then maybe her trail was headed south. She wasn't sure if that was good or not. Maybe the other fork would have been the way to go. She wished she had a map. Would be the shits to go to all this trouble and get caught because she made a wrong turn. *Story of my craphole life.*

Mayes got out her water and had a good long sip. Save as much as possible. She stood. She'd just decided to *goddammit* retrace her steps when she saw something not too far away. Colors that looked odd here in the forest. A yellow, but an unnaturally bright yellow. She crouched and picked up the Pulaski, raising herself up just enough to eyeball whatever it was fifty yards away. It wasn't moving. A piece of plastic? Or maybe a person?

Her first thought was to hightail it. People out here were a problem. They might report her somehow. Satellite phone or some such gizmo. They might even be armed. But it was a little whacked that somebody would be out on the forest floor, alone. Were they injured? Dead? Mayes considered. Either of those possibilities might present an opportunity.

Damning her own curiosity, Mayes crept forward. *Bitch, you just love flirtin' with trouble.* It definitely was a person, lying on their side. A small person, so no problem there. No backpack or nothing. That bright yellow color was shorts. Mayes got close enough to see that the body was moving slightly, breathing in and out.

Suddenly, the body sat bolt upright and turned to face her. It was a girl, a kid. "Who's there?"

Mayes stopped. She thought she was being dead silent, but maybe not. Her mind scurried over options. She could bug out, end of story. Or maybe find out if she was on the right trail. Could make the difference. She looked around. Was there nobody else here with this kid? *What the hell?*

The girl said, "Dad?"

To Mayes, something wasn't adding up. A kid alone, asking for her dad? What, did the shithead drop her off in the middle of nowhere and take off? "Hey there," Mayes said quietly.

"Who's that? Are you rescuing us? Oh god!" The girl stood up. Her one side was peppered with twigs and pine needles from lying down. She looked hollowed out. She had a pair of sunglasses in her hand and despite the gloom, she put them on and started to walk toward Mayes with halting steps, her hands held out in front of her. She was moving off course, headed to Mayes' right.

"Hey," Mayes repeated and immediately the girl corrected and came more directly but still with strange movements, like one of those zombie things from a movie.

"Did you come to save us? You've got to find my dad."

There was something definitely off here. Those sunglasses, the way she moved. "Hey stop." There was a downed tree trunk in the girl's path. Mayes walked over until she stood a few feet away. "Jesus, you blind? You about to go head over ass."

The girl nodded. "Yes. I'm blind. We thought you'd never come!"

At the word *we* Mayes flinched and reflexively squatted down. "Somebody else out here with you?"

"My dad," she began, then starting sobbing, slowly folding down to her knees and burying her face in her hands. "He was out here. We're together. But he got lost. I don't know where he is. You've got to find him."

"You say you're blind?"

"Yes."

"You can't see me? My face?"

"No. Are you going to look for my dad?"

Mayes licked her lips, stood slowly, scanned around for any signs of movement. There, off in the distance, was something else. Gold and blue. A tent? "How long's he been gone?"

The girl gulped, choked back her sobs, and tapped her wristwatch with two fingers. The digital voice responded, *Six eighteen a.m.* "Like, thirty-five hours. He said he was going to look for a way to the river. In case of the fire. Where is the fire? Is it close?"

Mayes shrugged, then remembered the kid couldn't see her. "Yeah, I don't know, not too far." No sense in scarin' the shit out of her. "What are you doing out here, anyway? I mean, out here lying on the ground?"

"I threw a water bottle at a skunk. It was by our tent. Then I tried to find the bottle but I got mixed up, lost. Then I couldn't find my way back to our tent. Um, do you have any water? I'm so thirsty."

"You didn't find your bottle?"

"No. Please, you have to find my father. His name is Will. Will Spencer."

Mayes reluctantly got out the hydration pack. "You can have a drink out of my water pack here. Here's the suck tube. Don't take too much now."

Kal took a big drink before she could stop herself and Mayes yanked the tube from her mouth. "Hey, take it fucken easy."

Kal nodded. "Sorry."

As she repacked her water Mayes said, "So just the two of you?"

"Uh huh."

"Is your pop packing?"

"What?"

"Did he bring any weapons, guns?"

"No, just our knives."

"That your tent over there?"

"You see it? Oh, good. Can you take me there, please? Maybe my dad's in there."

"Yeah, okay," Mayes said slowly, thinking. "But then I got to get going. Um, give me your hand." Mayes held the Pulaski in her left hand, grabbed Kal by the wrist, and half led, half dragged her back to the trail that led to the tent. "Pretty dumb to be out here when there's a fire," muttered Mayes. When they got to the trail, Mayes said, "You know where this trail leads to?"

"Back to the little campground. It's at the end of the road. Panther Bar."

Damn! Thought Mayes. *That didn't sound right. This was probably the wrong fucken way.* Lost time. Not good.

Kal suddenly called out, "Dad! Hey Dad!"

"Jesus Christ!" Mayes hissed, giving Kal's slender wrist a violent jerk. "Keep your voice down!"

"What? Why?"

"Don't ask, just do it."

Thirty feet from the tent Mayes said, "Okay. It's straight ahead. You go see if anybody is inside." Mayes let go of Kal and crouched down, holding the Pulaski with both hands.

Kal nodded. This procedure seemed strange, but at least help had arrived. She walked forward slowly, her hands held out. When she touched the tent she heaved a sigh and got down on her hands and knees and opened the flaps and crawled halfway in so she could examine the interior with her hands. "Nobody's here," she said, with a catch in her voice. She backed out and stood. "You've got to look for him. Are you a rescue person? Are there others coming?"

Mayes took in the campsite, the tent, the child standing there. How old? Six? Fifteen? She was never very good at figuring kids' ages. That part of life had more or less eluded her. She'd learned how to read faces—anger, fear, when somebody gave you cut eyes, whether you were down or outside. Reading adult faces was part of survival. But kids were a mystery. They still had trust. Why anybody had kids these days was a joke, even though most of the inmates at Granite Creek were moms. Some of them had kids that came to visit; that was good. Others had kids that didn't. That was the shits—when flesh and blood turned their back on you, it was worse than just plain having no visitors at all. She herself had a sister who turned up every couple of months, and even a no-count brother who showed up last month out of the blue. When the heat died down on her escape, she was going to surprise the hell out of them, that's for sure.

"Yeah, well, not exactly. I'm a firefighter. I got cut off from my crew. Up on the far ridge there."

"Can you find my dad?"

"Hey kid, you got any food around here?"

"Um, there's some in our backpacks. In the tent." Kal got back down on her knees and reached inside and got the backpacks. Thinking of food at a time like this seemed weird but maybe this woman was famished from working so hard at putting out fires. She pulled the backpacks out and pushed them toward the woman's voice. "Look in here. There's some granola bars and nuts."

Mayes walked over and took one of the backpacks and opened it and started to root through the contents. She pulled out the freeze-dried food pouches and set those aside along with the aluminum cookware and the camp stove and gas cannisters. She smiled to herself. All good supplies for the journey ahead. Her own firefighter's backpack contained some essentials, but here was everything she'd need to survive for days in the hills, find her way to the coast. "Jackpot," she said out loud.

"What?"

"Nothin'." She got the other backpack and started to pull out its contents. Fireproof matches, the granola bars the kid mentioned, an emergency beacon—not to broadcast her location, but to sell or trade. She knew they were expensive. A knife. Clothes she didn't need. And here, down at the bottom, the ultimate prize. A wallet.

Mayes opened it. There was Will Spencer's driver's license. Nice-looking gent. Inside, one-hundred and twenty-two dollars. She grinned as she extracted the bills and put them in her own shirt pocket and buttoned the flap. Credit cards? By the time she got anywhere to use them, they'd be cancelled. Plus, they could track her whereabouts. Then again, if this guy was really lost or maybe even dead, it might take folks awhile to straighten out the details. Will's VISA and American Express went into her other shirt pocket.

Kal listened intently. From the sound of it, this woman firefighter was going through everything they had. It didn't feel right. "Did you find the granola bars?"

Mayes nodded. "Yup. Just taking stock of your stuff make sure you got everything you need."

Kal thought that was an odd reply. "Are you going to look for my dad?"

"Sure," Mayes lied. She held up Will's backpack. It was much bigger than her compact firefighter's pack. She unhooked her pack and shimmied out of the straps and set it in front of her and opened it and began to transfer its contents into the larger backpack, then she began adding all the camping gear and food.

Kal was unsure. Some inside alarm was going off. All this sound, the rustlings, was out of line with just getting a few granola bars. "We've got everything," said Kal. "Everything we need. Why are you going through everything?"

Mayes smiled to herself. The kid'll figure out in time. "Don't you worry, darlin'."

"Please look for him. He went…" she paused, reckoning the direction her father had taken, "…that way." She pointed. "Please find him. He might be hurt."

Mayes stood, shouldered the new backpack. It felt good to be loaded up. Now, get her skinny ass in gear. She looked around, checking the sky. The fires were throwing up masses of smoke. Smoke was drifting all around. Good. No air searches for a while, that's for sure. Luck was on her side for once. Time to make time.

Kal heard the snaps of her dad's backpack being clicked into place. She moved toward where the woman had been sorting through their things and felt around. Her dad's backpack was missing. Her own backpack was lying on its side, open, its contents scattered about. "What are you doing?" Kal cried. "Are you taking our gear?"

Mayes shrugged. "Just some minor essentials."

"You're not a firefighter!"

Mayes paused. She might have shafted her inmate crew, and maybe those girls wouldn't be allowed to get out on a fire line for awhile on account of her misbehaving, but she did take firefighter training and out of her whole stinking life right now it was about the only thing she could point to that was in her personal plus column. Things worked out, maybe she could wrangle her way on a real crew someday. But for now, she was leaving stinking Granite Creek in her rearview mirror. "I am a real firefighter," Mayes said.

"Well you're not a good person if you're taking our things and you won't look for my dad! What kind of person are you?"

Mayes went over and squatted on her haunches in front of Kal. She studied the girl's face, the tight, angry mouth. The blank, untelling mask of the girl's sunglasses. "You're right, kid, I'm a no-good. In fact, I'll give you a story. When you get out of this…" she waved her hand at the landscape and the smoke flowing overhead, "...you'll have a hell of a story to tell."

"I don't want a story. I want my dad."

Mayes squinted. "I'll give you the harsh reality, kid. In fact, I'll give you a couple. First, I am a firefighter, just not the regular kind. I'm a convict. You know what that is?"

Kal nodded. "You've been in prison."

"Not *been* in prison. I *am* in prison. Up until yesterday. I was working with a firefighting crew from my lockup facility. They train us and they bring us in to fight fires sometimes. Five dollars a day. We risk our necks just like any firefighter out there. But when it's over, we go right back into our cells." Mayes looked away and took a deep breath. "You wouldn't understand. But sometimes you can only take so much of being locked up."

"You escaped."

"I escaped. I did. Got the crew boss lookin' the other way and when they were pulling us out on account of the fire had got out of hand I saw some clear ground going the opposite direction and I took off, just like that. Knew they couldn't chase me, not at that moment. Didn't plan it, just did it. Not sorry neither. And here I am."

Kal was breathing hard. She was at the mercy of this person, whoever this was. This might be a dangerous, a hurtful person. Kal was defenseless and didn't know how to respond. She said meekly, "Why are you in prison?"

"Robbery. I robbed a bank. Couple of banks, truth be told. Had a gun, so it was armed robbery." Mayes sighed. "Got a nickel and change. They don't like armed robbery, course when you think about it, how else you supposed to rob somebody? Walk up and tell 'em to bend over, you about to fuck 'em in the ass?" Mayes chuckled at her own wit. "So anyway, I've done time and let me tell you one thing for your life, stay the hell out of prison."

Kal swallowed and said nothing.

Mayes stood. "The other harsh reality is about your dad. It sure doesn't look good for him if he ain't back yet. Sorry darlin', that's the reality all right."

Kal started to cry. "Please, please look for him before you go. He's probably not far. Please!" She tried to grab onto the woman's leg to keep her from leaving, but Mayes took a step back out of reach.

"No can do, kiddo." She'd learned long ago how to block out sympathy. You just focused on what you needed right here right now. It was the basis of survival. *Pacific Ocean, here we come.*

Kal listened as the woman's footfalls moved away. This horrible person was headed up the trail, back the way she'd come, away from the river. Away from her and her dad. "No! Please look! Please!" Her last words were strangled by sobs.

Then there was nothing except the rushing wind in the trees, ruffling her hair and pushing the tears across her cheeks. She was worse than alone. She'd been found and then abandoned. A person had been here, somebody who could have helped. But they didn't. They left her and her dad. It was beyond cruel. She hated that woman, that faceless monster who'd appeared out of nowhere and made everything worse when it was already so terribly bad.

Then she heard the footfalls returning. It was the woman, the convict. She was coming back. For what? To hurt her? Kal felt for something to defend herself. Her hand found the rock she's used to pound in the tent stakes. She clutched it and tracked the approaching sounds, trying to gauge the optimum moment to throw her weapon. The footfalls stopped.

The woman said, "Don't throw that." There was menace in the tone; it wasn't a suggestion. "Drop it now."

"You come closer and I'll…" Kal's voice trailed off.

"I'm not going to hurt you, okay? So just drop the damn rock so I can get on with it."

Kal hesitated. Could you trust an escaped convict? What were the chances of her stopping this person with a rock anyway? Kal relaxed her fist and the rock fell onto the dirt. Kal was drained, defenseless. There was nothing she could do to stop whatever was about to happen. Even fear had left her. There was nothing left inside.

The footsteps approached. The woman came close. She was crouching right in front of Kal, her breath harsh even in the smoky air. Kal thought briefly of reaching for the rock. If she was quick and struck now, she'd smash the woman's face.

The woman put something in front of Kal—a thick bundle. "Those are my fireproof clothes. Pants and shirt. Give me your hand." Kal recoiled, but the woman said, "I ain't gonna bite. Now put out your hand."

Kal meekly held her hand out, half expecting something painful to happen. Instead, she felt the cool metallic of her water bottle, still half full. "Them clothes, you put those on if you can hear the fire. When you can hear a fire, it's too close."

The woman stood, her voice now seemed to come from a towering height. "That fire could be coming this way. Hard to tell. Fires are tricky. Hell, somebody'll find you. Maybe your dad too. Good luck, kiddo."

The woman turned and walked away and her footfalls faded and then were buried by the sound of the bustling winds.

Monday, June 29
Rogue Rappellers Crew base, Grants Pass

A SUMMER SQUALL rolled in about midnight. The rain hammered down, dumping almost two inches in little more than an hour, pounding the dry grasses into damp matts and sluicing down the bone-dry land so quickly that the ground barely had a chance to absorb any moisture. In a cruel twist, the swath of precipitation swept along the southern edge of the burn's perimeter, failing to dampen the blaze yet drenching the fire camp and everything in it. By Sunday morning the engines and buses and tenders had churned the center of the fire camp into a sudden swamp of mud. The good news was that the relative humidity had taken an upswing to sixty percent; the bad news was that the higher humidity meant lower visibility, further restricting aerial reconnaissance. The IMET concluded the front was an anomaly and would be quickly followed by a high pressure that would dominate the area for the next five to six days, raising daily temps and drying up the ambient moisture.

Eight Rogue Rappellers had been sent to reinforce hand crews on the major control line to the south. The dozen rappellers who remained at the base gathered at 0700 for an update on the possibility of an SAR operation. IMED boxes were stashed at the entrance to the tree cooler, and a four-person team plus a backup stick were posted on the up board. The helicopter, pilot and mechanic were on standby and the yellow-and-white Huey was fueled and waiting out on the tarmac.

Matt Murphy called the on-duty rappellers and the pilot Fernandez to the map room to bring everybody up to speed.

"The spot fires north of the river merged late Friday," he said, pointing at the area north of the river. "That complex has gotten to two thousand acres and crested the ridge, but the winds are keeping it from heading down into the canyon, for now. They tried putting in lines here and here to box it in but the fire broke here and threatened the only road in so they've pulled the crews back to here.

"The main fire has blown up pretty good and is now some forty-thousand acres. It's jumped over to the east side of the Illinois and as far as we know, it's burned through the area around Oak Flat and very likely the Panther Bar campsite where those hikers put in. Recon can't get close enough to give us a good look and this road here, the Illinois River Road, has got fire on both sides. This…" his voice had a hitch recalling his own recent close call near the collapsing plume, "…is where the dozer driver died. Here…" he rubbed his finger along the map indicating a narrow stretch along the Illinois River, "…is where we think those people have gotten to."

"Jesus," said Mike Zelinski, shaking his head. "That's…" He didn't finish.

"The latest report," Murphy went on, "predicts the fire will advance through this area in the next eight or ten hours. There may be a chance winds will shift later today. If they do, we might get lucky. It may give us a window."

"It'll be too late."

Everyone turned to the voice—Lucas Bowden. Bowden the base pariah. His insubordination during the last mission hung over him as a darkness. Since his grounding he'd kept to the background of things, quiet and sullen. But now he spoke up forcefully. "The behavior report says those winds are going to channel downstream and it's going to be a firestorm in that canyon. Even if those people get to the river, it'll be bad."

There were nods and murmurs. Shit happened. Already a heavy-equipment operator had gotten killed on the Illinois

River Road. They stared at the map.

"I say we go get them right now," said Bowden.

The pilot, Lance Fernandez, gestured. "We can't get in there. Visibility is zero. They're not even flying drones. Basically there's no air ops around the northern perimeter."

Bowden nodded. "Right. But we don't go in by air. We go by boat."

It took a moment for the comment to register. Murphy spoke for the team when he said quietly, "What are you talking about?"

Bowden stepped to the map and pointed to the area where the hikers were thought to be surrounded by fire. "If they've got any sense, they've headed for the river. The dad will figure that's their best bet if the fire gets too close. So we put in upriver, float in, we find 'em, pick 'em up and exit. There's got to be a bar or an opening downstream where we can get a helicopter in for the extraction."

"That's batshit crazy, man," said Dirk Ebbetts.

"I was watching the weather maps," Bowden went on. "I saw where that rain missed the fire, but it soaked pretty good here…" He swirled a finger around an area of the map that took in the camp and much of the area directly south. "The upper drainage for the Illinois. This time of year, with the conditions we've got, it'd be tough to float the Illinois. Water level's too low and slow. But I looked up flow predictions for today, and they're high. All that precip didn't stick to anything—the ground's too hard. The Illinois is going to be honkin' with runoff. We can make the whole run in four or five hours."

Murphy rubbed his face, said nothing.

"I used to be a river guide, in Idaho," Bowden added.

Ebbets snorted. "There's class fours and a big five on the Illinois. People have died. You gotta know what you're doing."

Bowden gave Ebbets a long, hard look. "I know what I'm doing."

Murphy took a deep breath. "Where do we get boats?"

"Kayaks. I've got one in my truck." He turned to look at Corby. "And Corby's got one. They're Sea Eagles. Two-person, eight-hundred-pound capacity, inflatable. They're tough. They're rated for class fives." This was not exactly true—Bowden knew the Sea Eagles were rated up to class four. But sometimes you pushed limits.

Ebbets gave Corby a puzzled look. "Since when do you have the same kayak as Bowden?"

Corby just shrugged. It wasn't the time for explanations.

"Look," Bowden continued, "Lance can put us in right here…" he pointed to the map, "…at Miami Bar. It's a big flat area, we can touch down and won't have to get on the ropes. If there's too much smoke we can put in upriver at the McMillan Ranch. It'll add maybe forty-five minutes to the float, but that's not too bad. The Sea Eagles pack easy and we can inflate 'em when we get on the ground."

"You'll be able to carry those people out if you find them?" asked Murphy.

"No problem. One rescuer plus one hiker in each on the way out. Keep the weight manageable."

Murphy looked over the crew. "Anybody here handle a kayak?"

"I've done a few," said Lou Pedersen.

Corby Jones wriggled forward and said, "You'll need an IMED. That's me. I'm going. Anyway, it's my boat."

Murphy knew Corby Jones would jump into any opportunity that came up. The enthusiasm was admirable, but… "You've run rivers before?"

"Yup," Corby said. "Me and Lucas just ran the Klamath, as a matter of fact." She lifted her chin and made herself the picture of confidence.

"What?" frowned Ebbets.

Murphy looked at Bowden and Bowden nodded. "If the lady says she can do it."

"Who the fuck are you calling a lady?" she retorted, keeping her gaze trained on the base manager.

Murphy was working his jaw, trying to decide if the idea was legit or harebrained. One thing was certain: They were sanctioned SAR, and lives were at stake. It was everyone's prime directive. "How do you inflate the boats?"

"Electric pump. Battery powered. Takes five minutes."

"Lance?" said Murphy. "Can you get in there?"

The pilot studied the map. "There, no problem. Little rocky, but we can get in." He looked at Murphy. "We'll need a TARO on this."

All eyes were on the base manager. Murphy clicked off the things that could go wrong: they'd miss the hikers altogether and the operation would go down as a joke. Somebody could get hurt on the river—he knew the Illinois was for experts. And there was always the fire itself—it could be a hellstorm on both sides of the river. But maybe doing nothing was worse. He thought of his own recent brush with death, the recon flight near the collapsing plume. His viscera tightened remembering the gravity-less plunge toward the unknown. He forced himself to think of the pilot who'd flown them out of danger—the skill, the coolness—and when he did his gut began to relax. Everybody in this room was a pro.

He turned to John Deluth. "John, call Oates and get her buy-in on this. If she's good, have her work up the TARO. We'll need spot forecasts every hour on the hour for the next four hours. You two…" he pointed at Lucas, "…there's a rafting outfit that runs the Illinois. I think they're the only ones that are licensed. Google them. Get somebody on the horn who knows the river and can sketch out how you run it. Ask where you can be picked up downstream. And you…" he pointed at Corby, "get the med boxes loaded and do the manifest. How much do those rafts weigh?"

"Forty pounds each," said Bowden. "They're nothing."

"Okay," said Murphy, nodding. "I'll bring the Supervisor up to speed, make sure we have buy-in. Let's get this op staged." He crooked a finger to indicate Bowden should follow him into the hallway where they couldn't be heard. Murphy's eyes searched Bowden's face. "No going off crazy apeshit," said Murphy. "Keep it together. Do the job. Understood?"

Bowden nodded. "Copy that."

INCIDENT 395

Monday, June 29
Tincup Fire camp, Selma

FOREST SERVICE SUPERVISOR Oates took the cell phone call at 0715. She listened, unspeaking, as the rappel manager described a possible river rescue operation. Did she approve? It meant putting two rappelers into the heart of the wildfire. She'd never heard of a similar op. It made some sense, given the circumstances, but it was way off the books.

"Let me kick it up to the AOC," she said. Oates stood in the corridor of the operations headquarters and stared at the phone in her hand. She ran the scheme over in her head, bringing the SAR team to the river by helicopter, the river float, finding the hikers before the fire closed in. A TARO would need to come out of Operations. She called Air Operations Chief Jack Hong on his cell to outline the plan.

The AOC's first reaction was skepticism. "Rappelers doing a river rescue?"

There was no room for *maybe*—she was either all in or not. "They're all trained SAR. They've got a woofer on staff. They're expert river runners." She didn't know if that last part was exactly true, but stuff like that was hard to dispute if you said it with enough confidence. "It's probable the hikers are seeking shelter on a riverbank, and we'll be able to access them from the water. The rescue team will pick them up and bring them downriver for an extraction."

"You have boats for this?"

"Two inflatable kayaks designed to run rivers."

"And then you pick them up downriver somewhere?"

"My thought is to use the Coast Guard out of Coos Bay for the extraction. They can come in from the west, and we can continue to use our aircraft for water drops."

"And you're confident the rappellers can pull it off?"

"Well, it's the only workable idea on the table right now, so that makes it the best idea we've got."

"Is the SAR team standing by?"

"They are. But, Jack, this whole thing is time-dependent. The burn is moving through that area and the river isn't going to stay floatable for more than half a day or so."

"Right. I'll let Ingram and the Chief know, they'll want to be on top of this one."

AT 0810 PRESTON INGRAM was on his cell phone to one of the Operations Section Chiefs. The OSC was explaining that a Strike Team Leader in the Echo Division had reported that a prisoner on one of the work-release hand crews had disappeared.

"Looks like she took off when they ordered the pullback," said the OSC.

"She?"

"All-female crew from Granite Creek Women's Facility near Grants Pass."

"Is the State Police on it?"

"Everything up there is cut off right now. There's no motorized entry or exit point. We're going to set up a meeting with OSP and the DOC about it all in about an hour."

Ingram shook his head. Unprecedented. And on his command! Just wait until Governor Biggs heard about this one. He'd be howling. "All right. Do this—get in touch with the PIO, Bonnie Tucco. Have her work with OSP and Corrections and make sure they don't put out a public notice just yet. At least not until the Governor leaves the camp. Do we know when he's taking off?"

"Not sure on that one, I'll have Bonnie check it out and get back to you."

Ingram kept his expression even. He walked to one of the wall maps and put his hands on his hips. There were people around, people who watched him—judging body language and facial expressions—to see if the operation was going well or not. His one-word outburst the day before notwithstanding, it was important for a leader to project calm, even when the trains were going off the rails. An escaped prisoner in the National Forest? What next? His cell phone buzzed and he plucked it from his front shirt pocket.

"Ingram."

"Preston, it's Jack."

"Yes?"

"The rappel team over in Grants Pass has a crazy-ass idea about how to get a search team in to get those hikers."

Ingram frowned. *Crazy-ass* meant going off-book, and he was not all inclined to indulge ideas that were not based on approved operational procedures. So much had been written and documented about the proper incident response. And it was so much clearer that way. So much more defensible. His face was impassive, but the Governor's words rang in his head, *I'll make damn sure you never get a command position in my state again.* The impunity to make that kind of threat. He lifted his chin. "All right," he said, "let's hear it."

Monday, June 29
Kalmiopsis Wilderness

CORBY JONES and Lucas Bowden sat facing the spotter, John Deluth, as the helicopter tracked toward the smoke plume. The passing storm had raised humidity levels and sitting in the helicopter in her fireproof clothes Corby felt pressure-cooked. One concession they'd made to standard gear was trading their heavy boots for their everyday sneakers. If they went into the drink, boots could become twin anchors.

She'd trained for wildfires, but maybe bravado had gotten the best of her when she'd volunteered as an expert river runner. *Me and my big mouth.* Now, as the helicopter thrummed toward the river and the eastern flank of the burn, she was giving herself a little pep talk: She was along for all the right reasons; they'd need a woofer, and she was the only one they had; she was strong, smart, she knew her shit. But the idea of running a wild river—possibly while transporting a civilian—kept bullying its way to the front of her thoughts. *Sure, I've run big rivers. Yeah, right. Way to go, big talker.*

"Eight minutes," Fernandez said over the headsets.

She scrunched up against Bowden as Deluth showed them an iPad with a Google Earth terrain view of the river. He pointed to where the Illinois curved away from its northerly direction and flowed west. "We've got bars here, here, and here. If they made it down to the river, they're probably on one of those. Just keep your eyes open. You, Air Ops, Grants Pass dispatch, the base and the Coast Guard will all be on the same frequency. Give a holler when you clear the smoke and you're at a place a rotor aircraft can approach."

Bowden turned to Corby. "Looks like there's going to be fire on both sides of the river so don't let any embers sit on the kayak. Splash 'em out with your paddle. Be sure to check behind on the rear deck. I'll lead and you can follow me through the whitewater. If I miss the hikers and overrun but you see 'em, put out and radio. I'll work back to you however I can."

Bowden seemed amped, like he couldn't wait to hit the river and be heroic. Repair his rep. He was jiggling his left knee and his eyes were wide and the pupils dilated. If she didn't know better, she'd think he was on something. Probably a combo of caffeine and adrenaline. He pointed to a downriver section. "The Green Wall," he said. "That's a class five. Ever run a class five?"

Corby nodded. Now was not a great time for a confession. *Just do what Bowden does and try like hell not to screw up.*

"Looks like we'll have twelve-fifty CFS. That's a big flow for the Illinois so it's going to be rockin'." Bowden stared hard at Corby and she thought, *He knows I'm no river rat. He sees right through me.*

"Don't slow down too much," he went on. "Anticipate. Speed can be controllable balance. Pick a good line and go for it. We'll want to move fast through the burn."

Corby gave a thumbs up.

"Coming up," said Fernandez. "One minute and less than forty. Visibility about half a mile. Looks like we're right about the edge of the heavy smoke."

The pilot fought to keep the helicopter in a steady hover over a big gravel bar as winds buffeted the aircraft, then he slowly descended until they settled on a wide expanse of river-smoothed stones. Deluth opened the door and Corby and Bowden climbed out and unloaded the IMED boxes and the bundled kayaks. They moved away as the helicopter powered up and lifted off with Deluth in the open doorway giving them a thumbs-up.

The rotor wash had cleared smoke for fifty yards in all directions but downstream the river disappeared into a featureless haze. The higher humidity made the smoke thicker, more opaque. The Illinois was rowdy from the recent rains and the normally glass-clear river was muddied from silted runoff. It boiled gray against ragged knobs of rock and where rocks hid just below its surface smooth greenish tongues of water reared up and folded back upon themselves.

As the helicopter thrummed away, they opened up the kayaks and Bowden attached the battery-powered pump and as he did he talked, the words spilling out in a rapid torrent. Corby sensed he was nervous talking, as much to himself as to her. *Maybe he's not so sure about all this either.*

"With passengers there'll be extra weight up front so stay high pointed," he said. "Keep out of the stacks. Make sure your passenger stays low so you can see ahead. Just keep your fundamentals together. Balance points even: feet, butt, paddle in the water." He looked at her. "If you go in the drink, keep your feet pointed downstream."

"Roger that," said Corby, even though that was River Running 101. She thumbed on her radio. "Matt, this is Corby. You read me?"

"This is Matt. Go ahead, Corby," came the response.

"We are a go and we're about to get into the river."

"Roger that. Good luck. Stay safe."

They got their gear stashed and lashed and they double-checked knots and clips and they put on canister-type respirators and fitted their helmets over the respirator straps and strapped battery-powered headlamps on their helmets with the idea that someone near the riverbank might see the lights and make themselves known. They carried the kayaks to the edge of the water and slid them in where it was calm and they stepped in and settled into the inflatable seats. Bowden moved out quickly and Corby jammed her lower legs against the sidewalls and dug in with her paddle and thought,

INCIDENT 395

Unreal—aerial attack on some wild-ass river.

They headed downstream with the wind at their backs as the hot breezes surged through riparian bushes and blurred the surfaces of pools and pocket water. The daylight lessened by degrees and it was as if the drifting smoke and churning water were artificial, props for some super-realistic theme park ride with boiling rapids and rocky fantasias looming up unexpectedly out of the gloom.

She found a rhythm that kept her close to Bowden as they got into whitewater and slid around stacks and bounced through chutes. He had a powerful stroke but pound-for-pound Corby was just as strong and she thought *I can do twenty-two pullups* and she attacked the water and tried to keep no more than ten yards of separation between the kayaks. She watched him closely, anticipating the water ahead by the movement of his torso—when he'd hunch forward to dig in and where he'd lean back into a reverse stroke—and she began to read the language of the river as it powered them forward. In places where the smoke thickened, she focused on his headlamp bobbing ahead, the light from her own headlamp overlaid against the pall and dancing across her hands and along the length of the kayak. Ahead, the wildfire was waiting.

Monday, June 29
Tincup Fire camp, Selma

JOSS WANDERED the fire camp, feeling unmoored and useless. Whenever she turned a certain direction the giant writhing smoke plume loomed up in her field of vision, a constant reminder. She hated it. It mocked her with its inescapable presence.

Her cell kept chiming and each tone—whether phone call or text—brought an electric shock of hope. It was Will calling to say they were okay, Kal was safe. The Forest Service saying they'd been found and were safe. Safe. But each call and text was from someone else and—even if well-intentioned—was a heartbreak. Her sister in Seattle saying she'd seen Joss on YouTube and not to worry, everything would turn out all right. A cousin she hadn't heard from in years texted, *Saw U and governor, UGG!* Somebody who identified themselves as a reporter for *USA Today* was hoping to do an interview "in the next half hour or so."

She desperately wanted to turn off her phone but she needed to leave it on, just in case. She checked the power bar—at some point she'd have to find a charger. She thought of going home where it was sane and calm and familiar and safe. The fire camp was a war machine. Noisy and noxious and bizarre. Engines roared in and roared out as diesel fumes rolled across the muddy meadow. Firefighters roamed in dirty packs, their bright shirts streaked with soot, rumpled pants held up with suspenders. They'd made a pad for helicopters at the far end of the camp and the constant thudding of rotor blades pulsed against her skin and vibrated inside her skull.

But she couldn't leave. Here, at least, she was closer to the heart of whatever this fire would bring. She didn't want to be at home. She didn't want to be safe. She wanted to scream at these crews, tell them to take their big trucks and charge up the road toward her daughter and her ex and save them. If they wouldn't do it, she thought, then she'd commandeer one herself, roll through any road blockades. *Damn this fire.*

Not far away was a large, green Forest Service fire engine. It was idling: faint puffs of sooty smoke came out of a vertical tailpipe behind the big cab. The passenger side door facing her was open, as was the driver's side door opposite. There wasn't anyone inside. She glanced around—no one seemed to be tending to the big truck.

She casually walked over. She could feel the iron heartbeat of the engine in her feet. It was a massive machine. It loomed over her. There were hoses on reels and large compartments everywhere. There were two metal steps and a handrail fixed to the chassis just to be able to climb up into the four-door cab. It was unoccupied.

She walked around the front of the truck, toward the driver's side. A big steel grill jutted up from the front bumper—good for bashing things out of the way. The massive tires were nearly as high as her waist. She peered around the other side of the truck—still nobody around.

"It's a brute, isn't it?"

The voice behind her made Joss start and she took an involuntary sideways step.

"Hey, didn't mean to sneak up on you."

Joss turned to a youngish man in the ubiquitous yellow fireproof shirt and dark green pants with suspenders. He was bearded and had a baseball-type cap on with the shield logo of the Forest Service. He grinned. "Ever driven a type four?"

"Oh, no. Just, ah, admiring."

"You a driver at all, or what? You with Planning? Maybe Logistics?"

"No. I'm, ah, with the media," she lied.

"Oh hell, the media," he mused. Then he walked up to the truck and patted its dusty flank. "Well, here's the facts. Three-hundred thirty horsepower Navistar N9 diesel," he recited. "Nine-hundred fifty pound-feet of torque. Eight-hundred gallon water tank and twenty gallons of foam. All-wheel. Allison transmission so smooth you yourself—never having driven one—could probably just climb in and take off, no sweat."

"Really?" Did she sound too eager?

He laughed. "Not really. You need training to tame this beast." He used the grab bar to vault himself up into the cab with practiced nonchalance. As he did Joss saw another young firefighter appear on the passenger's side. The doors slammed shut. The driver looked down at Joss out of the open window. "Have a good one!" he said. Then the big green truck gave a clattering grumble and started to move away.

For a long moment Joss stood and watched as the truck ambled across the field to join a phalanx of other green-painted trucks. Did she really consider hijacking a fire engine? Not only would she have removed a valuable piece of firefighting equipment from the front lines, but most likely she would have wrecked it somehow. *Get your head on straight, woman.*

She needed to do something beyond just being an on-camera ass to the governor of Oregon. She stood staring at the fire camp—everything seemed to be in motion—people, vehicles, even the scattered tents were vibrating and shimmying in the steady wind.

She should eat something. She made her way toward the field kitchen mess tents. Crew members were shuffling along the tables of food, picking out sandwiches and chips and apples, moving to nearby tables to eat. A few men in blue denim shirts were refilling the boxes of food and pouring coffee for crew members.

But instead of getting in line, Joss walked into the area where the food servers stood. She came up to one of the blue-shirted men and stuck out her hand. "Hi there," she began. "Um, I'm wondering if you need any help?"

The man frowned at her hand, then raised his gaze to meet her eyes. He seemed puzzled. Slowly, he extended his own hand. He had tattoos running along his bare forearms and also the backs of his hands. His palm and fingers were rough and calloused. "And who are you?" he asked. He did not let go of her hand.

"My name is Joss. I live in Medford," she added, as if that explained anything.

He nodded. A couple of the other helpers were watching them curiously. The man released her hand. "I suppose." He looked around. When he spotted a man in a dark green shirt, he called out, "Hey boss!"

The green-shirted man looked over, raised his eyebrows in a silent question.

"Got a lady here looking for a skid bid," he grinned. The other men in blue denim shirts chuckled and shook their heads.

The green-shirted man ambled over, peered at Joss over wire-rimmed eyeglasses. "And you are?"

"I'm Joss Spencer. I'm a...a volunteer."

"Uh huh." The green-shirted man cocked his head. "Well, we can't allow civilians to..."

"Hey!" One of the servers, a barrel-chested black man, came up and pointed a finger at Joss. "I know you." He grinned and continued to point, his enormous finger suspended at her eye level. "You're that lady on the television. You whipped a whole bunch of shit on that sorry-ass governor." He called over his shoulder, "Hey fellas. This right here is that lady who slocked the Governor! Ha!"

All the men in denim shirts smiled and nodded. It was then that Joss noticed that all the men in blue denim shirts had tattoos, with some even extending up their necks. And across the back of their shirts in block letters was the word INMATE.

The big man's smile vanished. He lowered his hand. "I heards about your girl, that little blind girl."

Joss nodded.

The man in the green shirt said, "You the mother of that blind kid out in the wilderness?"

"Yes."

"That's a tough deal. I hope they find 'em."

Any response got stuck in Joss' throat. She felt her eyes getting wet. *Dammit!*

"What are you doing here?" asked the man in the green shirt.

Joss took a deep breath. "I'm waiting for any news, I guess." She gave a short laugh. "Waiting sucks, though."

"Tell me about it," said the big man. "I been waiting nine years. Still waitin'. Hey boss, let her help out. She's, ah, you know, just trying to get by."

The green-shirted man sighed. "Okay, give me your purse."

"What?"

"I gotta check it."

"Don't lift her lipstick," the big man hawed.

"Jerome, get back to work."

"Yessir, boss."

The green-shirted man opened Joss' shoulder purse and rummaged inside. When he was done, he looked at her and said, "Anything on your person that could be used as a weapon? Any knives, pens, nail files, screwdrivers?"

"No, nothing like that. But really, if it's a problem me

being here, I can find something else to do."

"Any relatives or close friends currently incarcerated in a state or federal facility?"

"No. Not that I know of."

"C'mon, boss," called Jerome, "let her stay. Not often we get to hang with a celebrity."

"All right. Anybody tries to pass you something, like a note, you let me know. And don't take any crap from these guys." He handed Joss her purse and she put the strap over her head and slung the purse behind her back so it was out of the way.

She turned around. All the inmates were grinning at her and nodding. "You runnin' with our car now," said Jerome.

"What should I do?"

Jerome pointed. "Those boxes are full of napkins. Why don't you make sure there's enough down at the end of the line? Then grab one of those bins there and you can clean up after some of those tables. One's for trash, one's for recycling empty cans and bottles. There's some latex gloves in that little box."

Joss began to move. It was good to give her weary brain something to latch onto besides worry. She concentrated on the task at hand: stacking napkins in neat white piles. There were stones to put on top of the piles so they wouldn't blow away. When she'd done that she put on a pair of latex gloves and began to work her way around the eating area, picking up stray wrappers and discarded soda cans. She carried the bins back to the mess tent and was surprised to see that the stacks of napkins had already been reduced to a few strays fluttering in the wind. She replenished those with a sense of purpose. As if her small contributions were at least pushing things in the right direction.

After a hectic midday rush there was a break in the action and Joss noticed Jerome sitting on a folding chair, smoking a cigarette. There was an empty chair next to him. She went over and sat down. His eyes followed her without moving his head.

"This okay?" she asked, uncertain about protocol.

He nodded, blew out a perfectly circular smoke ring that the ambient wind whisked away. He said, "Five years. Second-degree burglary. I've done twenty-five months and eleven days." He kept his eyes cut sideways at her. "That's what you were going to ask, right?"

She nodded. "How did you end up here, at this fire?"

He dropped his cigarette into the dirt and ground it with his boot. "Work release program. You gotta qualify. Good behavior. No fightin'. Can't shank anybody." He made a stabbing motion and laughed when Joss flinched. "They train you. I worked fire lines, sometimes in the kitchen like now. It helps when you come up for parole. I don't know, maybe I'll get a job as a firefighter when I get out." He nodded to himself. "You can do that now down in California. Used to be they didn't let convict firefighters become real firefighters. Go figure."

Joss indicated the mess tent with her hand. "That probably feels good, to be trusted."

"Yeah. It is. Good to be out in the air. Be stupid as hell to try and walk. They'd find you, bring you back for Buck Rogers time." They were quiet for few moments, then Jerome said, "You hear anything about your little girl?"

Joss took her cell phone out of her pocket and looked at it. She shook her head. "They're supposed to call me with any news." Her voice trailed off as she said that, knowing news could be good or not.

The big man who'd recognized her from her interview with the Governor was standing nearby. He'd overheard the conversation but had kept quiet until now. He said, "Hey!"

Joss looked up.

"I'm gonna pray for you and your little girl. I'm good with the man upstairs." He pointed toward the sky. "You wouldn't know on account of circumstances. But Jesus is best thing that ever happened to me. Changed me. I got prayer power now. I'm gonna pray on you and your girl. You watch. She's gonna be fine."

Joss smiled weakly and nodded. "Thank you. I hope so."

Monday, June 29
The Illinois River

THE RIVER HUSTLED them through whitewater as the smoke streamed horizontally, swept along by hot winds. They rounded the big bend where the Illinois changed its northerly course to flow west toward the ocean, and as they did a flurry of flying embers hit the water with a sound like raw meat hitting a hot griddle. Every other stroke Corby swung her paddle against the current to send water sprays that doused embers landing on the kayak.

As hard as she tried to keep up, Bowden and his bobbing headlight kept slipping out of view ahead, one moment his orange life vest and the blue tail of his raft loomed right in front of her and the next moment he had disappeared into the miasma of smoke. After another mile the flames came down to the edge of the water for a hundred yards along both banks. Bowden and his raft were specters from a netherworld, the heavy orange firelight coming not from above but illuminating horizontally from both sides—the fiendish cinematic effects of a demon director. Firebrands big and small rocketed everywhere. Then the flames retreated from the shoreline and the smoke lifted to sudden glimpses of jutting rocks and boiling stacks of water that Bowden slipped between and around as if guided by unseen forces. Corby stroked and backpaddled and dug in. There was an ache in her shoulders and she used the pain to urge herself forward. No pause; no relaxing where the river turned calmer.

The smoke collapsed around them and clogged the air and her breathing turned to heaves and daylight evaporated when a zombie's bloody face burst out of the shadows. Its claw-like hands reached for her as she swept past. Corby cried out and it was several seconds before it registered that she'd passed a real person, probably one of the hikers. She dug her paddle in hard to slow the raft and swung it toward the rocky shore. She screamed *Bowden!* but her shout was muffled behind her respirator and lost in a cacophony of churning water and blustering wind. As she stepped ashore a fusillade of embers flew past her face and peppered the raft so she used her paddle to give the boat a quick dousing, then looped the painter around a streamside bush, grabbed her first aid pack, and started to make her way upstream. She pulled off her respirator, got out her radio and keyed it on. "This is rescue one. I've spotted one of the hikers. Bowden, I'm upstream from you!"

In places the rock wall came directly down to the water, leaving a narrow strip of slippery, rocky shore that demanded total attention. A slip here could be a disaster. Absolutely no time for fuckups. The beam of her headlamp wavered inside the gloom. Smoky heat forced her to squint through tears. She grasped at overhanging shrubs and saplings for balance. How far did she go past? Where was he? "Hey!" she shouted. "Hey, where are you?"

He was laying on a small gravel bar with his face in the water. "Oh shit," she blurted. She hurried to him and rolled him by the shoulders out of the river. As she did he gave an involuntary snort and water sputtered from his lips. *Thank God he'd managed not to drown!*

She eased him onto his back. His face was lacerated in several places and his hair was matted with blood. His shirt was torn and bloodied and he had every evidence of having taken a brutal fall, which meant internal injuries were likely. "Can you hear me?" she shouted but he gave no response. They were at the bottom of a rocky wall some sixty feet high. How the man had managed to stand upright just moments before was a biological miracle.

She snapped on latex gloves and ran through assessment

as fast as she dared. Airways clear but breathing shallow; clammy skin, definitely in shock. Pupils unevenly dilated, bruising behind the ear, possible skull fracture. She unbuttoned Will's shirt to expose his skin. Bruising and unstable chest wall indicating fractured ribs. No immediate indication of a collapsed lung. There was no getting his pants off for a close look at the rest of him but she was able to roll up one pants leg where she suspected a break and sure enough, bluish discoloration and a crook in the alignment confirmed a break of his left leg. *Jesus, this guy is a mess!*

She keyed her radio. "Dispatch, this is river rescue one. I think I've found one of the hikers. Male, six foot plus. Maybe forty-five. Looks like he's fallen off a cliff. He's alive and breathing on his own. Multiple injuries, possible head trauma. Broken ribs, leg. He's in shock. Got to evac him immediately."

"Roger that, Corby. Any sign of the girl? Over."

"Not yet. I'll look. Gotta go right now. Out."

Bowden appeared as a bobbing headlamp in the gloom. When he got close Corby could see he had a rappelling rope over his shoulder and he'd tied an end of the rope to his raft and was pulling his Seaeagle upriver with him. He was soaked to the waist from wading around rocks.

"Are they here?" he called.

"I think this is the dad," she yelled over the rush of the river. "I don't see the girl."

Bowden yanked the kayak onto the bar one-handed. "How is he?"

"Traumatic injuries…" she pointed at the rocky cliff, "…probably fell. He's messed up. We've got to get him out of here."

Bowden pulled out his radio. "Dispatch, this is Bowden. I'm on the scene. Our victim looks critical. Let me know how it's looking for an extraction point. Over."

"Bowden, Dispatch. Right now looks to be Collier Bar before you're out from under the smoke. You know where that is? Over."

Corby looked at Bowden who grimaced. "That's past the Green Wall."

"Dispatch, Bowden. Any chance of the smoke clearing? Over."

"Bowden, Dispatch. Doesn't look good. The fire is moving your direction and is probably a half mile from your position. You need to hustle, brother. Over."

"Roger that. Bowden out."

Corby pointed to the kayak and said, "Drag that over here."

Bowden pulled the kayak up the rocky shore until it was even with Will's broken body.

"I gotta immobilize his head somehow, and probably splint his leg." She pointed at some nearby saplings. "We need some sturdy sticks, three feet long." She started to root in the med kit for the inflatable splint.

Bowden unholstered the hooked raptor knife he carried in a sheath strapped to his thigh and went over and hacked off two inch-thick limbs and stripped off protruding twigs and leaves.

"Help me get him in a life vest." They gently shifted Will's limp, heavy torso—lifting one side then the other—so Corby could get Will's arms into the vest. Then she pushed the two sticks down the back of the vest so they stuck out behind his head. She snugged the vest tightly. She took off her helmet and peeled off the headlamp and returned the headlamp to her forehead and adjusted the beam. She carefully put the helmet on Will and tightened the chin strap. She took a roll of self-adhesive tape and tore off a two-foot piece and wrapped that around the helmet and the sticks, immobilizing his head. Then she got his leg as straight as she could and as she did that Will gave out a groan and suddenly sat up with his eyes closed and his head immobilized but his mouth was moving as if to speak but words never came out.

"Holy shit," breathed Corby, "this guy's on auto pilot." She and Bowden both took Will by the shoulders and eased him back down and as they did that Will's body went limp. "Take it easy, buddy," said Corby. "We're going to get you out of here." To Bowden she said, "Keep a hand on him so he doesn't do that again." Working fast, she set his leg in a flex splint and squeezed the splint tight. "Let's get him into the raft."

Bowden hooked his arms under Will's armpits so he could lift him and Corby got Will's legs and it was like hefting a giant bag of jelly. Will groaned again and his arms flopped but at least his head didn't loll about. They set him in the rear end of the kayak to keep the bulk of the weight out of the bow and they readjusted the seat position to give his legs room. Smoke careened down the narrow river gorge as flames wavered in their periphery vision. Corby felt heat on the side of her face.

"Okay," said Corby, "get going."

Bowden began to gather up the paracord. "You go. You're the IMED. This guy needs you."

Corby nodded. Of course. He was right.

"Give me your carabiners," he said. "I'll look for the girl." He surveyed the cliff face. "She isn't down here. She's probably still up top."

Corby undid two spare carabiners she had on her belt and handed them to Bowden. She knew what he had in mind. An improvised descent device. Rope threaded through multiple carabiners to create friction. If Lucas found the girl up top, the quickest way back down to the river and the kayak would be a rescue rappel.

"You much of a climber, Bowden?" She looked at him.

"We'll find out."

"Okay, good luck."

Strangely, given the circumstances, he reached out and touched her cheek. "Stay safe," he said.

They each grabbed a side of the kayak and slid it into the water. Corby settled into the seat and wedged her feet under the sides of the craft. Bowden stood behind her to give a final shove. "At the Green Wall, the big second ledge, remember—left into the chute, then hard hard right, then take a middle line over the last bump."

"Copy that."

Bowden gave a push and Corby dug her paddle into the water and the kayak vaulted into the current and amid all the heat and sound and smoke and trauma Bowden's touch lingered like a hot ember pressed against her face.

BOWDEN SHIMMIED out of his life vest, clipped the radio to his belt, and began gathering the paracord into a hank for carrying. He clipped the hank to his belt and turned to the cliff face, its upper edges blurred by hurrying smoke.

The rock face was rough and fissured and offered decent foot and handholds. He started up. He tried to push everything from his mind except the feel of the stone under his fingers and toes. The smoky wind howled down the river valley. Mixed into the churn of the tumbling river and moaning winds were the gunshot sounds of fire-weakened trees breaking and crashing. *Up. Go up. Get the girl.*

There was a billowing gust and Bowden held to the cliff as the winds pummeled him and sparks rushed over his shoulders, swarmed around his legs, found their way up his pants cuffs and inside his shirt collar, searing his calves, biting his neck and ears. Sparks settled on his hands and through teary, squinted eyes he watched them turn into tiny black dots of seared flesh as he clung to the wall of rock.

Halfway up he felt his strength starting to leave him. His hands and calves ached. His sense of balance began to waver. It was difficult to breathe. A combination of adrenalin and amphetamine was overloading his body and he felt the hollowed out quivering of a crash coming on. His nerves were frying, short-circuiting his coordination. He thought of deaths, of those he'd heard about and those he'd witnessed. If the dead waited for him at the bottom of whatever pit he might fall into. A hard, unforgiving bottom of his own making. It would be so easy. Just let go, let it all go.

The rock wall, inches from his face, mocked him, defied him. It was saying, *You can't save the girl.*

He inched upward, willing the holds to be solid. A little ledge under his right foot broke away and for an awful moment he clutched at the rock wall with his fingertips and pressed his face against rough stone to keep his weight as inward as possible. He searched for a new foothold as his fingers screamed. He found a small knob, put his weight on it. It held.

He came to the top edge of the cliff and pulled himself over and lay panting. He could hear the fire. The ground was still steep so he crawled on all fours until the terrain became nearly level, then he stood and as he did the world seemed to tilt beneath his feet and he held out his arms for balance. Flames were running in the dry duff to his right and twenty-foot-high flames were leaping out of the treetops. The fire had crowned and was moving rapidly in his direction. He could feel the heat on his cheeks. The wildfire roared.

He turned away and yelled, "Hey! Where are you?" No reply. *Damn!* The girl had to be off somewhere to the west. He began to move through the brush, yelling as he went. "I'm here! Help is here!"

Bowden came to a footpath and moved along it, calling out as he went, his headlight swinging left and right. His foot caught a root and he went sprawling and he steadied himself on his hands and knees and everything seemed to slide to his right as if the world was made of melting wax. There in front of his face was a small rock cairn. He focused on it until it became steady and solid. He stood and stumbled forward and another cairn appeared. Then the light from his headlamp crossed something oddly colored, a blush of gold inside the streaming smoke. A tent. He went to it and saw the rain fly was filigreed with burn holes. He sunk to his knees and unzipped the entry and was surprised to find a person inside clothed in bright orange Nomex. The shirt had the words INMATE ODC on the back. A prisoner? How did this happen? Where was the little blind girl?

Whoever it was laying in a heap, unconscious, next to a sleeping bag that was smoldering in several places. There were little glowing craters caused by sparks that had burned through the tent fabric. "Shit," said Bowden. He reached out and shook the person's leg. "Hey!" He leaned in and saw her face—it was a girl, a young girl. Had to be the missing hiker. How she'd ended up with prison clothing was a mystery to solve later.

"C'mon, darlin'. I need you awake."

Kal didn't move, overcome by smoke. Bowden grabbed both her legs and dragged her out of the tent. "Wake up!" Bowden implored. The girl's breathing was ragged. He reached down and pinched Kal's thigh, hard as he dared. The girl stirred and moaned. Bowden pulled her so she was sitting upright. "Up!" he pleaded. "Wake up!"

Kal's head lolled and then she coughed and her hands went up as if to protect herself. "What?" she mumbled.

"C'mon, we're out of here." Bowden took off his respirator and put it on Kal. "You can do this." Speaking to himself as much as to the girl. "Get up."

"Who?" slurred Kal, trying to pull off the respirator.

"Leave that on," he said. "I'm with the rescue team. Hang on, I'm gonna carry you." Bowden stood, reached down and pulled Kal until she was standing and before she could collapse, he hunched down and put his shoulder into her midsection and then heaved upright with her slung over his shoulder in a fireman's carry. As he did his vision blurred and he gulped air to steady himself.

"No," said Kal but she didn't squirm as Bowden began to walk back toward the cliff, high-stepping carefully. The flames were chewing their way directly at them, flinging sparks and burning embers. Small fires were taking root around them. There was little choice—he had to reckon his way back to where the kayak waited below. There was an enormous wrenching groan nearby, like a giant rusty nail being pulled, and a hundred-foot pine snag came crashing down. Bowden felt the rush of heat that billowed out as it hit the ground. Flaming branches cartwheeled through the false night and he held his breath as they spun overhead but none struck them.

At the edge of the rock wall Bowden eased Kal to the ground and to his relief the girl sat upright. "Dad," she squeaked.

"It's okay," said Bowden. "I'm going to get you out of here. Don't lie down." He tried to give his voice a commanding sense of urgency but the words came out diminished, more of a plea. He undid the hank and played out the rope on the ground in careful coils. He took out his knife and cut a twenty-foot section. "Stand up," he said but Kal simply sat, her upper body moving in woozy circles. "You've got to stand up," said Bowden, then, "your dad wants you to stand up."

Kal raised her head. "Dad?"

"Yes. He wants you to stand up so you can live. Now, stand!"

Kal struggled to her feet. *Thank God* thought Bowden. "Now be still, I'm going to put you in a safety harness." *The Swiss seat harness, how did it go?* His recall was fogged. Find the midpoint of the rope, *right, that's right,* bring it around with two wraps, both ends go under the crotch, around the butt—*shit this makes sense doing it on yourself; doing it on another person is a reverse mind fuck*—bring the ends under the wraps, make half hitches, crisscross and over the shoulders, down in front, under the waist rope again, loose ends tied in a square knot. Bowden tugged at it. *It's good, it's good* he told himself. *It has to be good. It can't fail.*

"Dad," said Kal. Embers flew and one stuck on the girl's face and Bowden swatted at it and said, "Sorry. It was something burning on your face."

She nodded. "I got burned."

"Hang tough."

"Are we going to die?"

"No. We're going to get you to your dad. I'm making a rope rappel." Bowden was already cutting off another twenty-foot piece of rope for himself. "You know what that is?"

She shook her head.

"It's for going down mountains. We're going to rappel down this cliff here, and there's a boat down below, and we're going to float you out of here."

"I don't know how."

"You don't have to…" half hitches, square knots, "…I'm going to hook you up to me and take you down. Okay?" he checked the knots. *Are these right?*

"I'm going to be sick," said Kal and she knelt down abruptly and pulled up the respirator mask and vomited.

"That's okay," said Bowden. "You'll be lighter that way." He was working up the carabiners. Two to hook the girl to his harness, and four for an improvised descent control. He was lightheaded, his breathing was labored—air movement was reversing, moving back toward the blaze as the fires were starting to suck the oxygen out of the area. The leading edge of the fire was now thirty yards away.

Bowden secured the paracord to a pine tree with a series of half-hitches. He hooked a pair of carabiners to his harness and attached two more to those to make a brake. "Stand up," he said. Kal stood. Bowden snapped two carabiners to the girl's makeshift harness. "Clip those to me," he said and turned around and pointed to the back of his harness. "Here, and here. Hurry."

"Where?"

"Here. Where I'm pointing."

"I can't see."

Right—the girl was blind. He reached around and pulled the girl close. He reached behind his back and tried to hook up the carabiners but the space between them was narrow and he couldn't bend his wrist and contort his hand to make the connection. "You'll have to hook us up."

"I'm not sure."

"You can do it. Find the carabiners I clipped onto your harness."

Kal reached down to the metal loops. She could feel the spring-loaded jaw flex open as she pressed it.

"Got 'em?"

"Yes."

"Clip those onto my harness, right where the ropes cross each other. You have to clip onto both ropes. Do one side then the other."

"I don't feel so good. I need to sit down."

"No!" Bowden barked. "You can do this. You have to do it, do it now!"

Kal leaned forward, her face pressing into the man's back, the rough cloth of his shirt against her nose and forehead. She leaned against him to keep upright. There wasn't much space between their bodies, hardly enough to do what the man was telling her to do. She searched the ropes on his back to find the place where they crisscrossed. Her fingers—her reliable instruments, her window on the world—felt sluggish, dull, as if she was trying to operate them from a great distance. She managed to open a carabiner latch with her thumb and tried to snag it onto the makeshift harness. Her attempts missed again and again until finally the hook grabbed onto what she hoped was the right place.

"Other side," Bowden shouted to be heard above the snarling fire.

Now there was even less space—no room to have her right hand help her find the proper placement. She had to hold the carabiner awkwardly sideways, her thumb pressing the jaw open, as she searched for the rope junction with her pinky finger. The fire was close; the heat pressed against the side of her face. She crabbed at the rope with the open carabiner and until she felt it snag and hold. She released the jaw and it snapped shut. "Okay."

"Okay," yelled Bowden. "Now we're going to turn around." He rotated and forced Kal to shuffle around so their backs were toward the river. He threaded the paracord through the carabiners and threw the free end over the edge. There was no way to know if the line fell clear or if it was hung up somewhere. He squeezed the makeshift carabiner descent device in his left hand and grabbed the free end of the rope in his right. He didn't have gloves and prayed he wouldn't have to use his bare hands to add friction to stop them from falling. "Walk backwards," he called. The heat was searing. Steam eased out of nearby trees.

Tethered together, they shuffled backwards. As the land began to steepen, Bowden leaned back into the rope and felt the girl hesitate.

"We're going to fall," cried Kal as they leaned out over the precipice.

"No, we're not," Bowden called out. "Put your arms around my waist." She held him in a death grip and then he felt the slight heft of her come off the ground and transfer to his waist and to the rope harness. The carabiners held. He stepped over the edge until they were nearly horizontal.

"Oh god," Kal whimpered as Bowden started feeding out rope and walking them down the face of the cliff. Somewhere in the burning forest above them another snag came crashing down. Her weight pulled the makeshift rope harness taut and the cord cut hard against Bowden's shoulders and inner thighs. The paracord eased through the carabiners. *It's working,* thought Bowden. *Two minutes. Two minutes and we're down.*

WITH WILL SPENCER'S weight aboard, the kayak was a different animal, sitting lower in the water and forcing Corby to dig as hard as she could to navigate the boiling river. They hadn't gone more than one hundred yards when a rock loomed out of the smoky dusk and caught the edge of the kayak and turned it sideways. Water billowed over the edge of the craft and for a horrible moment she thought that her unconscious passenger might roll out and be swept away and she used her paddle and with all her strength pushed off the rock and the kayak came free and righted itself and the water drained. They came to a quieter section of river and Corby leaned down and checked Will's carotid pulse and he was still ticking. *Thank God.*

Every time she heard a fresh set of rapids approaching her heart got racing. The Sea Eagle demanded that she pick her line well in advance, but the pall was a moving thing that obscured the view ahead. Several times the smoke would part and there in front of them would be a huge stack or a crashing hole and she would stab the paddle into the water to swing the kayak around, narrowly avoiding catastrophe. She tried to use the quieter sections to reset herself; focus. *How many more Goddam rapids until an extraction point?*

In another mile the river curved in a wide arc and flowed south and in so doing swung back into the heart of the wilderness and the expanding flank of the wildfire. Fire thundered along the edge of the river and wide ribbons of wind-driven flame licked out sideways and orange embers littered the surface of the water, creating a glittering carpet as they landed and winked out. Corby tried to keep the kayak to the far side of the channel and she unbuttoned her Nomex shirt and pulled it partway over her head to keep her face from getting scorched. Embers cascaded everywhere and she was navigating the channel and dousing embers that landed on the kayak and on the injured man and her arms were in constant motion. The water hurried them forward, almost too fast for Corby to make the right moves, and they struck rocks and vaulted awkwardly over stacks. For all their speed they seemed to be moving incrementally through this hellish part of the river, as if pulled deeper into a waking nightmare.

Then they were past. The fires raged behind and the ash-strewn river turned tame and the smoke parted and for the first time in forever Corby saw a swath of blue sky. She rested her paddle across the gunnels and leaned down and took Will's pulse again. *Still here.* There was a glowing spark on the man's chest and she scooped water with her hand and splashed it out and as she did the man raised an arm as if pointing to the sky.

"Can you hear me?" Corby shouted but there was no response and after what seemed to be an abnormally long time for such a traumatically injured person the arm slowly folded back down. "Hang in there, buddy! I'm going to get you out of here."

As she took up her paddle she noticed the left-side gunnel was not as puffy as it should be. The top had begun to flatten and there were alarming wrinkles appearing along its inner side. There must be a leak, probably an ember burned a hole somewhere. She pressed her hand against it and felt mild resistance. Hard to say how long they could stay afloat. There was no place to put out and even if there was, she didn't have a repair kit. Time was critical for the man in the bottom of the kayak.

The smoke closed the sky; the reprieve was temporary. She estimated they were a mile from the Green Wall. She stroked hard thinking, *I can do twenty-two pullups. Bring it.*

KAL LEANED BACK. She was floating. She held onto the stranger's waist and the ropes tightened around her shoulders and thighs and her legs dangled free. The man was grunting and panting as they descended in spurts and she could hear the river getting closer and over that a banshee chorus of hurtling wind, the sound of everything thick inside the steep canyon. Tiny firebrands bit her cheek and she turned her head away and buried her face in the man's back.

Then they were down and her feet reached solid earth and she felt as if some kind of miracle had happened, as if a magician had levitated them down and set them safely on the ground.

The man said, "Okay, unhook us."

Kal worked her hand into the space between them and felt for the carabiners and the spring-loaded openings. She undid one then the other and as she unhooked the second carabiner the sudden release threw off her balance and she sat down hard on the rocky ground.

"Ow!"

"You okay?" His voice was rough and strained. She struggled to her feet but too fast and dizziness overtook her and she held out her arms to keep from falling over and the man took one of her hands in his own hot, sweaty hand to steady her.

"You're sick from smoke. The mask will help."

"What about you?"

"Been breathing smoke half my life. A little more won't..." Bowden wanted to project confidence but his voice trembled and vertigo overwhelmed him. He went down to one knee, panting, his heart rioting. "Oh shit," he whispered. Bad mix of stress chemicals and pharmaceuticals. He was a joke. What was he doing with other people's lives entrusted to him? He looked at the small girl, her innocent face.

Kal didn't know what the man was doing but she could hear his labored breathing and it frightened her. "Are you okay?"

"Little dizzy," he wheezed. "Both of us, huh?"

Kal still had his large, gritty hand in her slender one and there was something desperate in the way he kept holding onto her and didn't let go. She took his hand in both of hers and pulled. "C'mon, mister, c'mon. Let's go!" It was like pulling on something attached to the ground, but she didn't let up and she leaned back and suddenly the resistance melted and he was up, still holding on, but up.

"The kayak...is around...the bend here." He paused, puffing, trying to put his thoughts together. "I'm going to carry you...on my back." With that he turned around and lowered himself and guided her hand to his shoulder. "Get on. Grab on to my shoulders, not my neck."

Kal hoisted herself up and held onto his shoulders and crooked her legs around his waist and he stood and grabbed her underneath her knees and began to walk with an unsteady gait along the rocky shore. Once he stumbled badly and she braced herself for a fall but he caught himself and stopped for a long moment and said, *Shit, sorry,* and then they went forward. They sloshed through water and at one point they must have been in a deep part because the water got in her shoes and the bright cold of it passed through her like an electric shock.

After a few minutes he said, "Here," and reached around and lifted her off his back and set her down on something that felt like a rubber matt.

"Is this your boat?"

"Yes. Sit here." He ushered her to a part of the kayak where there was a kind of a shelf made of taut fabric and he had her sit with her back against it. She explored with her fingertips and found the sides of the kayak were fat and round and hard and the fabric was slightly textured. "Hold out your arms." She did and the man threaded each of her arms through something—a life vest. He cinched the front snug to her body with clumsy, hard jerks. He put a hard helmet on her head and tightened the chin strap so she felt like her skull was being crushed. Then he took each of her hands and guided them to big rings attached to the top of either side. "Hold onto these."

The rings felt thick and substantial. She nodded. "Okay."

"Toes. Under the sides."

She slid her feet against each fat side and wedged her toes into where the sides met the bottom. This was good. They were going to be safe.

"You know what to do…if you go in the water?"

"Um, face the way the river is going?"

"Keep your feet up."

"What's your name?"

"Lucas. What's yours?"

"Kal. Kal Spencer."

"Okay Kal, we're out of here."

She felt the man get into the boat and he sat directly in

front of her and they began to move slowly and Kal could hear the bottom of the boat scraping on rocks and suddenly they were free in the running river.

She could tell they were moving but her sense of space had gotten all jumbled, there was just so much noise and confusion. The kayak bumped and jolted and she clung to the big rings and she could hear Lucas' breathing hard and she smelled his ripe sweat. She heard his paddle first on one side of their boat and then the other and every so often a cool splash of water sang across her face. Time had gone away—morning? afternoon? She hadn't checked her watch in hours and wouldn't let go to check now. Where did the river go to? Didn't it lead deeper into the wilderness? She wanted to ask questions, but she didn't want to be a distraction. *He's a rescue man; he must know what he's doing.*

FROM THE AUDIOBOOK, "Kayaking the Big Western Rivers," Vol. 2, by Guy Mancesco:

A vortex is a column of spinning water that rotates horizontally. It occurs just behind a large, subsurface rock or abrupt change in the riverbed. As the water flows over the obstruction, it plunges down with enough force to pummel a depression into the river surface—a hole. The water at the downriver edge of this hole is pulled by gravity so that it falls backwards. The result is a cylindrical mass of water that rotates counter to the main direction of the river's flow. This rolling water does not easily release whatever finds its way into its powerful fluid dynamics. Logs, paddles, kayaks, and even people wearing life vests can be trapped in a churning hole. A large vortex can be difficult—and sometimes impossible—to escape.

CORBY AND THE unconscious Will entered the whitewater run known as the Green Wall in the late morning. The river was engorged with runoff—pounding, seething and leaping under a dark swirling canopy of smoke. There seemed to be no defined line through a maze of whale-size boulders. Any decision-making was overwhelmed by the fury of the rapids and the speed by which the water carried the craft. Corby backpaddled for all she was worth, trying to stall the onward rush to give her time to pick a line.

An enormous rock loomed like a giant fist and she leaned and dug the paddle into the torrent but the kayak, lethargic from its loss of air, turned only partially so that the left side struck hard and the kayak lifted up edgeways and spilled her into the watery maelstrom. She managed to grab onto a bungee tie-down at the rear of the kayak just as the craft tore lose from the obstruction and careened downriver. There was no way to fight the current and bring her legs and feet up into a defensive position and her hip slammed into a rock with such force that she screamed and nearly lost her grip, then her knee took another blow so that the breath went out of her and her body twisted and as it did her wrist snared in the bungee and her head went under water. She was being dragged headfirst through the whitewater and she had no air in her lungs. She fought to bring her head up but the water would not relent. It overpowered her struggles, refused to allow her back to the surface. She opened her eyes and everything was a streaming torrent of green and white and silver. She thought of her mother, waiting for her. She could hear her mother singing, her voice clear in the water that rushed past her ears.

Then something clamped onto her wrist and she felt her hand being freed and then she was being hauled into the kayak by her arm. She flopped into the bottom of the boat and turned to see Will who was like a drenched corpse staring at her with a pale, blank face. Corby wondered if maybe they were both already dead and slamming down the river through some sort of in-between world, but Will still held her wrist in a grip so strong it hurt. Then his eyes rolled up and his fingers went limp and he slumped back onto the floor of the kayak.

She sucked in air and looked around, stunned. They were going backwards and headed for the last in the series of big rapids—a thundering four-foot drop. The paddle was gone. There was nothing she could do. She reached for the gunnel ropes, stared at the man in the bottom of the kayak. *I'm sorry,* she said aloud and then she closed her eyes and prayed, *Mila, klin nate.* Mother, hear me.

LUCAS CALLED OUT *Hang tight!* and Kal clung to the rings although she could not have held on any more forcefully than she already was. There was a violent uplift and then they came down so fast that her behind lifted off the floor of the kayak and a deluge of water struck her as if thrown from a bucket. As she sputtered to catch her breath there was more water and Lucas growled *Yeah!* as if he had won a contest.

Churning parts of river swept past to her right and left, and after an hour Kal was cold and starting to shiver even though it was summer and she was wearing the heavy clothes the prisoner woman had left. She began to doubt they would ever emerge from the river channel and be in the warm sun away from the smoke. Despite the constant pitching and bucking of the kayak she felt drowsy and wished she could lay down. At one point where the water was calmer Lucas stopped paddling and turned around and he must have taken off his shirt because he draped it over her head and shoulders and said, "We're going close to some fire but you've got on fireproof pants and a shirt and I put a fireproof shirt over your head so you'll be safe, okay?"

She nodded, so sleepy.

"Don't pass out. Hang on."

"Okay." Her fingers were so cold it was hard to tell if she was holding on with enough strength. She squeezed her fists so that the seamed edges of the rings bit into her palms. If Lucas had given her his shirt then what would he wear to protect himself from fire?

The cracking and throaty roar of burning wood grew louder and Lucas grunted and strained and leaned back far enough and she sensed his head was inches from her face. Water fell across her legs and then a flurry of grainy things pummeled the kayak from the left side and landed on her exposed hands and stung like hornets. She let go of the rings to shake them off and the kayak chose that moment to pitch and her feet came out from under the sides of the kayak and she was unmoored and for a moment floated free. Then she slammed back down exactly where she should be as Lucas called out, *Face right!* and she turned and grabbed at the right-side ring with both hands and felt another round of burning things rake the back of the fireproof shirt and drum against the side of the kayak and Lucas said *Shit!* through gritted teeth and Kal knew that he'd probably been burned and stupid crazy danger of it all and the pain of the fresh burns on her hands made her want to cry but instead she screamed out, "Shit!"

The burning part of the river went on as if it would never end, and now and then Lucas splashed her with water from the paddle, batting water at her to put out burning bits. She kept her head down and she tried to make herself as small as possible and hide under the broad, heavy shirt. The noise of the fire was cruel in its insistence, thundering at them from both sides of the river, angry at their attempt to escape.

Then the raging began to fade behind them. Lucas had stopped paddling and was breathing hard.

"Are we safe?" ventured Kal, still huddled underneath

the heavy shirt.

The man didn't answer. Kal felt the kayak list to one side and heard Lucas splashing water and snuffling wetly.

"Is there more fire?"

"What?" Lucas was wheezing, still leaned to one side.

"Is there more fire?" Kal repeated.

There was no answer. "Lucas? Hey mister." Kal reached out to touch him. He was draped over the side of the kayak. The skin of his arm felt frightfully hot. "Hey, mister!" She shook him gently. "Lucas! Are you okay?" She got to her knees and felt his feverish back and neck. She reached over the side and scooped water and gently splashed him.

Bowden mumbled something she couldn't make out.

"What? What?" Kal leaned close, scooped more water. They were moving. The sounds of the river were rotating around her—they were turning slowly in the current, going sideways to the flow, now backwards. Again she reached for Bowden to shake him and her hand found the shaft of the paddle. She picked it up in both hands, unsure. Maybe she could get them to the riverbank. She jabbed the paddle out to one side and then the other, feeling for the shore. They weren't close. She put one end of the paddle in the water experimentally and the river nearly pulled it out of her hands and the boat shifted as she did. "Please, mister. Get up!"

They were moving more swiftly now, the boat was trembling and starting to buck. There was something ahead that sounded large, ominous. Big rapids. She started to cry; she couldn't help herself. Her lower lip quivered and sobs rose in her chest. Everyone was abandoning her. "Get up!" she shouted but there was no response.

She put the paddle in the water again and the river swiftly shunted it aside but the boat rotated slightly sideways and she thought *Feet first* and she put the other end of the paddle in the water on the other side of the kayak and the boat shifted again and now the front of the craft seemed to be pointed downriver. The kayak still listed to one side under Lucas' weight and she reached out with a foot and pushed at him but he didn't move.

She nestled herself into the back of the kayak and jammed her toes under the sides and the noise of churning water became huge and swallowed everything up. The kayak swooped and cold water slapped hard across her face and made her gasp and there was a *whump!* and the boat vaulted into the air. The shock took the paddle from her hands and her body lifted up and she collided with something solid that was Lucas. She felt the fabric of his shirt pass briefly across her face and then she was tumbling in mid-air and when she came down the kayak was not there and she plunged into cold, angry, heaving water.

LIEUTENANT COMMANDER Amy Royce brought the Coast Guard helicopter to a hover eight hundred feet over the Illinois River. She spoke into her headset mic, "That it?"

In the back of the aircraft Flight Mechanic Josh Levin looked out the open door and surveyed the land below. Visible in a narrow channel of the river was a white object that looked to be one of the inflatable kayaks from the river-based rescue operation. It was on a narrow gravel bar and it appeared to be hung up on a snag—one end of the boat was in the water and pulsed in the current.

"That's got to be it," said Levin. "Can you drop down another two hundred?"

The pilot considered. The air in the channel was gusting to forty mph and the smoke flowing downstream kept visibility to less than a quarter mile. Where the kayak was positioned the channel narrowed on both sides. Getting directly above the boat would not be possible. But she could get them closer.

INCIDENT 395

"Down two hundred and hold," said Royce, and she swung the nose of the MH-65 Dolphin into the wind and began to lower the aircraft into the chasm.

"Rotors are clear," said Levin as the helicopter settled deeper into the river channel and the rocky walls reached up on either side. The aircraft rocked in the heavy air.

"Roger that," said Royce. "Power is good."

Levin, strapped into his spotter's harness, leaned out of the open door. From this vantage the kayak was clearly bottoms-up and trembling rhythmically in the moving river currents. The smell of wildfire filled the cabin and long tendrils of dirty smoke streamed downriver. "That's the kayak all right," said Levin. "There's something orange next to it. Can't make it out. Life vests maybe?"

Co-pilot Lieutenant Neil Bradford keyed his radio. "Dispatch, this is oh-six-five Delta Two. Over."

The answer from the Operations Officer 80 miles away at the Coos Bay Coast Guard Station crackled over the headsets, "Go ahead, Delta Two."

"We're above the Illinois River, near Collier Bar. I'm seeing one of the rescue boats now. Looks like it might have capsized, I don't see anyone around. Over."

"Roger that, Delta Two. Can you get the rescuer down in there to take a look? Over."

Bradford spoke to the pilot, "It's too narrow to get in there and drop a line."

"Agreed," said Royce. She called back to the flight mechanic and rescue swimmer Alan Moss, who was outfitted for a land-based operation. "Guys, we're going to pop up and look for a better spot."

The helicopter powered upward and swung downriver. Bradford said, "There's an opening and a bar about a hundred yards downriver. We can get in there."

"Copy that," said Royce.

The pilot brought the helicopter to a hover over the bar, then began to settle close enough to send the rescuer down. "This is good," said Levin, "let's stay right here."

"Holding here," responded the pilot. "Power is good."

The flight mechanic said to the rescuer, "The wind is gusty to forty; you're going to be swinging a bit. We'll make sure you don't end up in the drink."

Moss tightened his chinstrap and clipped his harness into the hoist cable. "I could use a bath anyway."

Levin grinned. "It's a rocky deck so unhook fast. Make your way back upriver to the boat and give us a report."

Moss gave a thumbs up.

"Amy, how's the fuel?"

"One-hundred twenty minutes until bingo fuel."

"Keep us posted.

Moss gave two thumbs up.

"Rescuer on the hook," said Levin. "Ready harness deployment."

"Roger that, ready for harness deployment," said Royce.

"Load check complete. Rescuer going down."

Moss edged out of the aircraft as Levin held the hoist controls and began to lower him toward the rocky shoreline. The fierce wind swung Moss back as the hoist cable played out.

"Amy, our man is drifting behind in the wind. Let's come forward fifty feet to get him on target."

"Roger that. Forward fifty and hold."

The Dolphin eased forward as Levin played out the line as he leaned out the doorway to spot Moss onto the landing target.

On the ground Moss unhooked and as he released the hoist cable the wind whipped it sideways and it flew out nearly horizontal. Levin quickly reeled it in, hoping to God it wouldn't get caught in the tail rotor. On the ground Moss gave the raised arm signal, *I am alright.* Then the aircraft lifted away.

Moss was a highly trained rescue swimmer who could hold his breath underwater for six minutes and swim for miles without tiring, but he was also a devoted backpacker who'd done the Pacific Crest Trail twice solo and was comfortable scrambling on difficult terrain. From the Coos Bay Operations point of view, Moss was an obvious choice for a rescuer who could trade swim fins for hiking boots.

He shouldered the basic med kit and set out. The going was slow over the steep and rocky river channel and in places the cliffsides plunged directly into deep pools and Moss had to climb up and over and back down again, and occasionally the pack got hung up in the heavy brush and he had to pause to free himself. It took a full thirty minutes to cover one hundred yards to the overturned kayak.

The Sea Eagle lay upside down on a narrow strip of shoreline. The rear tip of the craft lay in the river where the passing current nudged at it. A bow line from the front of the kayak ran twenty feet into the brush and had been tied to a slender tree. There was no sign of anyone—only the boat. The mysterious orange item turned out to be a little pile of clothes and some knotted ropes with a couple of carabiners attached. He picked up one of the garments—a shirt. A label on the back proclaimed, INMATE ODC. He keyed his radio. "Oh-Two, Rescue. Nothing here except the kayak and what looks like a prison outfit. Was there something about an escaped prisoner in the area? Over."

"Rescue, affirmative on an escapee. From the women's facility near around Roseburg. She was working a fire crew and went on a little solo hike."

A voice came from under the kayak. "Who's there?"

Prison clothes. Moss' hand went to his raptor knife. With his free hand he reached down and grabbed the kayak by the bow and flipped it over. Two people were underneath—a man and a woman. Check that: a young girl. The man lay on his back with his hands clasped over his chest. His eyes were closed and his face was slack, mouth slightly open; he appeared to be unconscious. He was only partway onshore—from the waist down he was in the eddied current at the edge of the river. A girl lay curled up next to the man, her head raised up off a folded life vest, her eyes wide.

"Are you Kal Spencer?"

"Yes. Can you help us? Please."

"I'm with the Coast Guard. I'm here to get you out. Are you hurt or injured?"

She shook, her head. "I don't think so."

"And is this Lucas Bowden, the Forest Service rappeller?"

Kal reached out, patting the ground until her hand found Bowden's chest. "Lucas! Lucas! Are you okay?"

At the sound of his name Bowden stirred, his eyes stuttered open. For a long moment he lay quietly, staring up. He was seeing smoke snaking through the sky; he was hearing the roar of flames. Then he crunched himself upright. "We've got to go!"

Moss put his hand on Bowden's shoulder. "Take it easy, buddy. We're safe here. The fire is miles away."

"Oh Lucas," sobbed Kal, putting her arms around his neck. "I thought you were dead!"

Bowden looked around, his eyes rheumy. He blinked hard to clear them. He reached up and touched the girl's arm. . What he'd thought was the snarl of wildfire eased into the even thrum of rushing river and helicopter rotors. He saw the orange-and-white chopper hovering. "Coast Guard?"

Moss nodded. "At your service. How are you two doing, anybody in pain?"

The rappeller and the girl shook their heads.

Moss keyed his radio. "Oh-Two, Rescue. I've got the rappeller and the missing girl. Stand by." Moss knelt by the Bowden's side and checked rappeller's carotid pulse. Low but steady.

Moss looked around. "Is there anybody else with you?"

"No."

"Let's get you out of the river," said Moss. "Don't want you to go into shock from being half too hot and half too cold." Moss took Bowden under the armpits and began to gently haul him out of the water. "Let me know if anything hurts doing this."

Bowden found himself letting the Coast Guard rescuer pull him backwards, didn't try to help, just let himself be dragged backwards a few feet. He watched river water sluice off his pants and boots.

Moss helped Bowden sit up. He indicated the prison clothes with a lift of his chin. "Where did those come from?"

"Where did what come from?" asked Kal.

"That pile of clothes."

"Where?" said Kal.

"Right over…" Oh, right. The girl was blind. Somebody had mentioned it at the ops meeting. "By your left hand," Moss finished.

Kal reached over. She knew the rough fabric immediately. "Those are from a prison lady." Kal shook her head at the thought. "I didn't like her. She was mean."

Bowden groaned. "Shit, musta fallen asleep." He stared at the hustling water before him. His hand went to the makeshift rope harness he still wore. He looked at Kal. He'd been an idiot; he'd been fried while attempting the climb. He could have gotten this girl killed. "I'm sorry," he whispered. "Really sorry."

Kal shook her head. "For what?"

"Kal," said Moss, "I'm going to give you a quick check,

make sure you're not hurt."

"Where's my dad?"

"Your dad's been taken to a hospital."

"He's okay though, right? He's not…"

"As far as I know, said Moss, "he was banged up but he'll be okay."

"I'm tired," she said.

"Are you dizzy?" Moss studied Kal's face, neck and arms. No signs of bruising, broken bones, trauma. No bleeding. The girl seemed relatively alert.

"Not really. Tired."

Moss reached for her wrist to take her pulse. He was quiet as he eyed his watch and counted pulses. Satisfied, he said, "Any pain?"

"Is my dad okay?"

"He was taken to a hospital in Coos Bay. We'll get you out of here and we'll find out more, okay?"

"Okay"

Moss nodded. Somehow the girl and the rappeller had gotten through some hellacious white water. Unreal. He put a hand on the side of Kal's face so he could hold open her eyelids with his thumb. "I'm going to check your eyes."

"I'm blind. Like, legally blind."

"Right. I know." He ran through his protocols while the girl sat with her hands folded in her lap. "How did you get here?" asked Moss. "I mean here under the kayak?"

Kal shrugged. "I don't know. I was in the river. I thought I drowned. There was so much noise, I couldn't breathe. Then I, I…" Her voice trailed off.

"That's all right. You're okay now. You're safe."

"Then I was breathing. I was in the water but my head was above the water and then, um, I found him next to me."

"This man?"

"Yes. Lucas. He was like a log, not really moving. And I

was so scared I held onto his ropes and pulled and swam and just kept swimming and pulling and then…"

"The river's still running hard" said Bowden. What the girl was talking about was lost to his memory. He could only recall the cliff; clinging to the rock race with creeping terror as the sparks rushed past and the drugs began to steal the strength from his arms and erode his will power. Even sitting on the riverbank he felt as if he was suspended in mid-air. He shook his head to clear the sensation.

Moss reached out and touched Kal's arm to soothe her but his touch gave her a start. "Oh, sorry. Didn't mean to startle you. Best you try to stay calm now. We're going to get you and your friend out of here."

Kal nodded. "I just kept pulling and pulling until I couldn't pull any longer."

"You pulled Lucas here out of the water?"

She nodded. "I just kept pulling. He's heavy, but I got his head away from the water. Then I found that rope and tied the kayak to a tree so it wouldn't blow away. Then I put the boat over us to keep away the sparks."

"You did all that?"

"Yes."

Moss keyed the radio and reported that both survivors appeared in good condition. The rappeller was sitting up, groggy but breathing normally. No signs of internal injuries. Probably exhaustion.

"Rescue, this is Oh Two. We're looking at about seventy minutes of fuel here. Alan, you probably need to hump it to the extraction point. Over."

"Oh Two, I'll give it a hell of a try." He knelt in front of Bowden. "Hey, bud. I'm going to get the girl out of here, then I'll come back for you. We'll have to get downriver a piece so the helo can get near enough to drop a line. Can you hang in there?"

Bowden took a deep breath. His nerves felt like hot wires under his skin. He stood, tried to keep his weight centered, felt water squish inside his boots. Pinpricks of light danced along the edges of his vision. "I'm good."

"You sure?"

Bowden nodded. "Let's go."

Moss licked his lips, unsure. Finally, "Okay." To Kal he said, "All right, kiddo. I'm going to carry you over my shoulder, and then I'm going to get you to a helicopter and they'll get you out of here. Can you hear that helicopter?"

She nodded. "I smell smoke. Is the fire near?" A ripple of panic welled up.

"No. We're a ways from the fire. But the wind is blowing the smoke to us right now."

"Lucas." She sighed. "Are you really okay?" Tears formed. "I tried to hang on like you told me but, I don't know. I fell out."

Bowden nodded, trying to remember.

"That's okay." Moss gave Kal a tentative pat on her shoulder. "Stand up." He helped her to her feet. "If this gets uncomfortable or you have any pain or get dizzy, you let me know, okay?"

"Okay."

"Okay, here we go." Moss bent down and picked Kal up in a fireman's carry.

For the second time in the same day, some man was carrying her like a sack of flour with her face pressed into his back. Only this one didn't smell of woodsmoke. This one smelled like the ocean.

IT WAS TOO WINDY for the litter so the helicopter crew let down a rescue harness with two fifty-pound bags of sand attached to help steady the rig in wind that was increasing in velocity as the day heated up. The heavy air buffeted the aircraft and it took a full ten minutes of maneuvering to get the rig down to Moss. "Let's get you two out of here," said Moss.

Bowden shook his head. "You take the girl tandem. I'll work the trail line. Then you can drop a harness for me." He gave the Coast Guard rescuer what he hoped was a hard, determined look.

Moss nodded. There wasn't any rank here and no use debating. "Hold the hoist cable," said Moss. "You got gloves?"

Bowden looked at his bare hands and shook his head.

The rescuer took off his gloves and held them out. Bowden nodded. In heavy wind the steel cable could rip the skin off fingers and palms.

Bowden took hold and Moss unhooked the harness to make it easier to rig up. The wind grabbed at the cable and Bowden found himself digging his heels into the gravel bar to keep the line from being yanked from his grasp. Moss got Kal and himself into the harness and Bowden attached the hook and Moss confirmed that the rigging was good and the hoist hook locked. Bowden took up the 200-foot trail line to help steady the lift from the ground.

Moss looked to the helicopter and the face waiting in the doorway opening. He raised his arm and gave a thumbs up and the hoist line began to tighten and he and Kal lifted from the gravel bar as Bowden kept tension on the trail line as he played it out. The wind bowed the hoist cable and trail line into a single long curve and several times the line jerked violently and nearly yanked him off his feet. The hoist seemed to take forever. He just wanted the girl inside the helicopter. Get her inside that dark doorway and safety.

At last Moss and the girl disappeared into the helicopter. After several minutes the mechanic appeared in the doorway with the empty harness in his hand. Bowden signaled for lowering and the as the hoist cable played out from the aircraft Bowden reeled it in with the trail line, the harness twisting in the wind like a thing alive.

Bowden knew the op was taking time and the chopper was probably running low on fuel. He snagged the harness and struggled to get in as the wind played havoc with the hoist cable and the pilot maneuvered to keep the line steady. When he was secured he gave a thumbs up and the cable began to reel in. As he lifted he could feel the heavy air swing him downriver and he thought of rescue lifts they had done in training but it was nothing like this. Without a steadying trail line from below he was a marionette played by natural forces. The canyon walls loomed and then he was looking at the smoke-streaked sky and a moment later the river below striped with grayish foam.

About a third of the hoist cable had been retrieved when a heavy blast of heated air rocked the helicopter and the cable went partially slack. He was suspended and weightless and then the line snapped taut and he was flung up and sideways toward the edge of the canyon. A giant gray snag leaned out over the precipice and the hoist cable caught on a huge lower limb and Bowden was flung around the branch like a child's tetherball. And then he was swinging back and forth at the end of the cable, looking up at a sky ripped into ragged ribbons of blue and dirty gray. He tried to clear his head. Somehow, he'd gotten hung up in a tree. Looking over his shoulder, he saw the helicopter from his strange, upside-down perspective. He could see the cable was still attached—a hard straight line from the craft to the tree. The snag cracked and groaned but did not give. He twisted around and realized that the line was pulling the craft partially over on its side. The helicopter began to arc sideways into the canyon.

Bowden screamed, "Shit!" and reached for his raptor knife. He unsheathed the big blade and swung wildly at the steel cable just over his head. He couldn't cut through it but the blow was enough to begin to release the awful tension in the line and after an agonizing heartbeat the cable ripped apart. Bowden had only an instant to see the helicopter begin to right itself. Then his end of the cable unwound from the massive dead tree and he fell one-hundred and fifty feet into the yawning canyon.

Wednesday, July 1
Providence Hospital, Medford

CORBY AWOKE in a place radiant with light. She was underwater, the sun a zillion miles above her. She fought to get to the surface but she was pinned beneath something and she struck out wildly and her arm got snagged and now she was trapped and surely would die. Then she realized she was breathing and filling her lungs with air—not water—and that it was not a blinding sun so far above her but a ceiling light. She was in a room. A hospital room. Figures came into focus. Her father's face. He was alongside her with his dark eyes under a John Deere baseball cap and a matchstick sticking out from between lips buried inside a gray, untrimmed beard. For some reason he was holding her arm by the wrist.

"Pop?" she croaked.

"Take it easy, Corb. You're okay." He slowly lowered her arm to her side. "You just woke up kinda ornery, tried to sucker punch me."

Her body still seemed to be tumbling and twisting, although she lay still in a hospital bed. She remembered the kayak plunging into the hole at the bottom of the last big rapids; how the water had closed over her head; the jet-engine roar of the river.

And then they were out, floating free, the kayak half full of sloshing water and the hiker in the opposite side of the craft staring off at god-knows-what, and she looking down to see her leg unnaturally bent. The orange-and-white helicopter hovering beautifully over the river; the basket with her in it ascending into pale blue sky.

"I'm thirsty."

Bruce Jones took a straw from a small bedside table and peeled off the paper and stuck the straw in a stainless-steel cup and made a crook in the straw and held the cup toward his daughter. Corby sucked down cool, clean water.

"Davey, go see if you can find that booze doctor," said her father.

Corby blinked. Her brother, David, had magically appeared at the foot of her bed. The only brother who hadn't joined the military or fled to Phoenix or some other sorry-ass city to try and escape a motherless hometown upbringing. David remained, and here he was. He looked different, even though she'd seen him only a couple of months ago. He was larger, squarer. He'd shaved his scrawny beard and trimmed it into a wicked Fu Manchu. He was radiantly handsome. David acknowledged her with a lift of his chin. "Hey, Shithead," he said.

"Hey."

"What the hell were you doing in a damn river anyway? Aren't you supposed to come out of the sky?"

"Okay," their father cut in. "We can get to all that. Right now, go find that doctor, whatever his name is."

David went out and her father pulled up a chair and sat next to the bed. "You're gonna have quite the story, you know that? We'll hear it in due time…" he patted her wrist, "…in due time."

Corby tried to smile, then was swept by a sudden fear. "The man. The guy who was with me. In the kayak. What happened to him? Is he okay?"

Her father rubbed his whiskers. "Well, I wouldn't say he's okay. But he's alive. He was pretty banged up I think. They flew him to a hospital in Portland."

Corby looked around at the whiteness of her surroundings, the electronic screen set up to the side of her bed with its winking lights. She saw wires leading from the machine that disappeared under the thin sheet covering her. "Where is this?"

"Medford hospital. Seems like a pretty good outfit. They got some chubby nurses around here but other than that they seem to know what they're doing." Her father took the matchstick out of his mouth. "You remember the Coast Guard picking you up out of the river?"

"Sort of. It's a bit hazy…" she shook her head, "…all we went through."

"Yah, you been pretty much out of it since yesterday. Partly on account of the drugs they gave you. You snore, you know."

She snort-laughed and when she did her body seemed to awaken and she felt aches in every part of her. "Oh shit, don't make me laugh."

David reappeared with a youngish looking doctor in a white lab coat. The doctor nodded at Corby's dad and came to the foot of the bed. "I'm Doctor Smirnoff."

Corby laughed weakly and looked at her father. "Is this the booze doctor?"

Her father shrugged. "I couldn't remember his name. But I remembered the booze part."

"Yes, like the vodka," said Dr. Smirnoff patiently. To Bruce Jones he said, "Do you mind if I get in here?" indicating the space next to Corby. The elder Jones got up and the doctor moved next to Corby and took the stethoscope off his neck. "You've had quite the adventure," he said. "I'm going to give a quick listen to your heart and lungs." He bent down and pressed the cool metal to Corby's chest as she inhaled, exhaled. He helped her lean forward and he put the instrument on several places on her back. Then he straightened and looped the stethoscope around his neck. "We don't think you have internal injuries to your organs. But you've fractured your right hip—your femur—and both the tibia and fibula below your knee. And a severe dislocation of the patella. Your kneecap." He tapped her thigh gently. "We've got you in a leg cast for now while we figure out if you'll need surgery to repair your femur, or if a replacement would be better."

Corby looked down. For the first time, she realized her right side was completely paralyzed. She pulled aside the sheet. She was not paralyzed—rather, she was held in the grip of a giant cast that ran from her foot up underneath her hospital gown to her belly. At the far end of everything were five purplish toes—her toes.

"Replace my whole hip?"

Smirnoff nodded. "These days, it's a fairly routine procedure. New hip and you're back in the game."

"How long till I'm back in the game?"

"Normally, you can begin rehab almost immediately after hip replacement surgery. But your leg fractures complicate the picture, because you can't put weight on your leg until those bones start to heal." He gave a wan smile. "There's an excellent orthopedic clinic in Grants Pass. They'll monitor your progress and when you're ready, they'll get you on some iso exercises. Then another couple of months of physical therapy until you can walk properly."

"Fuck."

Smirnoff shrugged. "That's one way to put it. The other way is to remember you're extremely lucky you didn't drown."

"We'll take care of you," said her father. "Me and Davey. You can stay at the house."

Corby stared at her broken lower body. "The girl!" she said suddenly. "The blind girl! Is she..?"

"She made it," said her father. "They don't know how, but she's okay. She's here resting."

"And where's Bowden? Lucas Bowden, the other rappeller?"

Bruce Jones exchanged a look with his son. Her father

sighed. "That fella, the other rappeller, he didn't make it."

Corby was stunned. "He didn't?"

Bruce Jones shook his head.

"But Bowden," she pleaded, "he had the girl with him. Didn't he? If she's okay…"

"He had a terrible fall during a helicopter rescue. He didn't make it."

"They never found his body," put in David. "They say the body could've gotten clean out to the ocean by now."

Corby tried to haul herself out of bed and both her father and the doctor reached to hold her back.

"Easy, hellcat," said her dad.

"Please," said Smirnoff, "you need to stay quiet and rest."

"That was a hell of a tough stretch of river you went through," said her brother. "Other people have died there I hear."

"Oh," said Corby, and then everything inside her seemed to deflate and she went limp and closed her eyes and felt pain like a sickness in her bones and then everything was whirling and confused like being helpless under water and she let herself slide back into the other side of consciousness.

JOSS SPENCER SAT on a hard, wooden chair next to her daughter's hospital bed. She was caressing Kal's fingers, carefully avoiding where bandages covered the back of her hand. Joss felt the small tender bones—how frail, how precious—and tried to hold back the emotions that threatened to bust out. For the last twenty-four hours her mind was nothing but a churning variation of *thank God, thank God, thank God.*

The nurse at the foot of the bed was smiling. "You're a lucky little girl," said the nurse. "No ill effects from what must have been a very trying experience."

"I almost drowned," said Kal proudly, causing Joss to

give her fingers an involuntary squeeze.

"That's what I hear. But you were brave and except for those minor burns on your hands, you came through without a scratch.

"When can she go home?" said Joss.

"I believe we'd like to keep her here for another day for observation. But I'll have the doctor stop in and give you an update. You take care, sweetie. And if you need anything, just press that buzzer there by the side of your bed and I'll come right in, okay?"

"Okay." When the nurse left Kal said, "She's nice."

"Yes," said Joss.

"Mom, when can we see Dad?"

"We'll see, Kal. We want to make sure we don't bother him while he's trying to get better."

"Wouldn't he want to see us?"

"Oh, sure. Definitely. But he needs to recuperate and we don't want to get him too excited and stress him any."

"What about Lucas? Where's he?"

Joss took a deep breath. She'd debated how to answer and knew being straight up was the best course. But not now. Not right away, with her child laying in a hospital bed having just survived a harrowing ordeal. But soon. For now, Joss simply wanted to savor the fact that her daughter was alive and upbeat. "You know, I'm not sure," she lied. "I'll check about him." She put her hand on Kal's plaster-casted knee. "You know he saved you. When the helicopter got in trouble. They say Mr. Bowden saved everybody."

"He's a hero."

"Yes," Joss smiled. "Yes he is."

At 11 a.m. two women came into Kal's hospital room carrying vases of flowers. One of the women was Sylvia Platt, the Governor's Chief of Staff.

"Hello, Kal!" breezed Platt. "And hello, Mrs. Spencer!

How is everybody?"

"We're fine," said Joss uncertainly.

"This is Heidi Nordstrom, she's in charge of public relations here at the hospital!" Platt made it sound as if the presence of Heidi Nordstrom was an enormous piece of good fortune.

"Hello," said Nordstrom. "So nice to meet you, Kal. You're kind of a celebrity around here!"

"These are for you." Platt held out a vase of flowers expectantly. "Oh, I forgot. You can't see them."

"Flowers," said Kal. "I can smell them. Thank you."

Joss stood and took the vases of flowers from the women one at a time and held them near Kal's face. "Umm," said Kal. "Very nice."

Joss put the vases on the small side tables. "Yes, thank you. They're lovely."

"Everyone here at Providence is so glad you're okay and doing well after such a terrible time!" gushed Nordstrom. "Oh my goodness what you've been through!"

"And!" Platt clapped her hands, "we have a special surprise! Guess who's coming to visit you?"

"Um, I don't know."

"Governor Biggs! The Governor of Oregon is coming down from Salem just to see you!"

"Oh jeez."

"Yes, and there's going to be television people here and some magazine people are going to take your picture with the Governor and it's going to be quite the event!" She turned to her companion. "Do you think we can get some more flowers in here?"

"Absolutely," nodded Nordstrom, silently assessing camera angles.

"When is the Governor going to be here?" asked Joss, frowning.

"Three this afternoon. He's got a tight schedule, he's headed for a conference of western governors in Reno and he needs to be at the reception by six, but I'm sure we can make this all happen. We just wanted to give you the heads-up in case you wanted to…" she looked at Joss, "…freshen up before the Governor arrives."

"Oh."

Platt clapped her hands again as if signaling the end of the flower-giving session. "Okay then. We'll be back here about two to make sure everything's in order."

Joss wanted to say, *What in the world kind of order are you expecting?* but she held it in.

When the two women had gone Joss said, "Do you want to meet the Governor?"

Kal shrugged. "I guess. But I'd rather just go home."

Joss nodded. "I'm going to step out for a little bit and I'll be right back. You know where the button is for the nurse?"

Kal reached over and put her hand on the call button. "Right here."

"Okay." Joss leaned over and kissed Kal on the forehead. Then she went out into the hallway and headed for the nurse's station.

"I wanted to speak with my daughter's doctor, Doctor Parks? How do I find him?"

The nurse seated at the station looked at her computer monitor. "Dr. Parks is doing rounds right now. Is there something I can help you with?"

"Possibly. I wanted to know if…"

"Oh, there he is. Doctor Parks?"

Joss turned to find Kal's attending physician standing nearby, peering at a clipboard. Parks was small and unimposing, traits he compensated for by wearing his glasses toward the end of his nose so he could peer over the rims with a condescending expression. Underneath all that, Parks was a softie. Joss spoke with Parks for several minutes, then returned to Kal's room.

"I've got the doctor's okay," said Joss. "He'll discharge you, and we can leave any time."

"What about the Governor?"

"How about this. How about we take off for Portland and go visit your father?"

"Yes," said Kal. "Yes, we are so gone!"

INCIDENT 395

August 11
Kalmiopsis Wilderness

PARKER MAYES SAT slumped against a knob of rock. She was exhausted, dehydrated, and hopelessly lost. She had lost track of the days but figured it had been about three weeks since she'd walked away from the firefighting work detail. She hadn't eaten in five days, having miscalculated the time it would take her to hike to the coast and civilization, so she'd consumed most of her purloined supplies in the first several days after her escape. As she made her way she'd diverted off the established trail and struck out overland, meaning to confound any ground-based pursuit. She'd hadn't heard any helicopters but as she trudged through raw forest she draped the reflective fire shelter over her head and shoulders to hide herself from infrared-seeking drones.

Within a couple of days it became clear that the going was a lot harder than she figured it would be. She was endlessly stumbling over deadfall and tangled understory, and steep ravines appeared with regularity, detouring her this way and that, adding time and difficulty to her journey. The stolen Pulaski was heavy and hopelessly useless and she finally heaved it into the brush with sweaty disgust and a middle finger. For every hundred yards of progress another two hundred yards of stubborn, demanding landscape unfolded in front of her. To make matters all the worse, she must have dipped her ass too close to some poison oak when pissing or shitting, and an evil, itchy rash had developed on the back of one thigh. After two days pustules had appeared and after another two days of angry scratching and cursing the pustules had broken and leaked so that the back of her pants were continually irritating and maddeningly damp.

She'd reckoned her way by the rising and setting sun but

now, as she sagged against the hard rock at her back, she realized any sense of direction had abandoned her. Whatever "west" was had not led her to the coast as she had hoped. In fact, every direction seemed identical—same fucken rocks, same damn trees, same shitty relentless heat. Maybe she was wrong all along; maybe the coast was east, not west. Or south? She licked her dry lips. Her water was gone; she'd need to find a stream before too long.

She'd begun to daydream about her prison cell. It had been warm in winter, and not too bad in summer. There was a stainless-steel toilet, right there to use any time. Clean clothes. Three meals a day. Water. A bed. People to talk to, as messed up as some of them were. How much would they add to her sentence if they found her? Three years? Eight? Did it matter? She was just about a prison lifer anyway.

She reached for the backpack and pulled it to her side. She stared at it for several minutes, as if it was animate and she could talk to it. *What do you think? Well, what the hell do you know about that? You find the fucking coast then, see if you can find it without hanging on to my back all day. Go on. Ha! That's what I thought. Bitch, you are one ugly cell warrior.*

Mayes opened the backpack and reached inside and took out the emergency locator device. It was a doorway, all she had to do was step through it, knowing full well what waited on the other side. Something concrete, safe. It could protect her as much as it protected others on the outside from her. She pried open the protective button cover, ran her thumb around the smooth plastic edge of the big red button. And pushed it.

The signal flashed up to a dedicated rescue satellite that relayed the emergency code and coordinates to a rescue co-ordination center in Houston. Within minutes, the station notified the county sheriff's office that had jurisdiction over the location, as well as the Rogue Valley Interagency

Coordination Center. Because this particular locator device was assumed to be in the possession of the escaped convict Parker Mayes, the Curry County Sheriff's office initiated the search. Within two hours of the locator button being pushed, armed officers were headed up the Rogue River by jet boat to apprehend the escapee. The coordinates from the locator beacon put Mayes location about half a mile from the junction of the Illinois and Rogue Rivers. She indeed had been traveling west.

THE TINCUP FIRE had been burning for thirty-two days when a low-pressure system formed over the upper Pacific Ocean and slowly worked its way into southern Oregon. The moisture-laden front reached inland to produce a drenching rain that finally let firefighters gain the upper hand on the wildfire. Four days after the deluge Public Information Officer Bonnie Tucco put out a press release confirming that the Tincup Fire was one-hundred percent contained.

The Tincup burned eighty-nine-thousand acres and claimed the lives of two firefighters—heavy equipment operator Gordon Finley and Forest Service rappeller Lucas Bowden. As tragic as those deaths were, the firefighting operation was deemed a success for its effective defense of the towns to the south and the rescue of the missing blind girl and her father.

As hand crews and helicopters continued to extinguish lingering hot spots in the charred black interior of the wildfire, the Josephine County Sheriff's Department was assigned a seventy-two-hour window to look for the body of Lucas Bowden.

Using a helicopter and a camera-equipped drone, the search covered from where the rescue kayakers had found Will Spencer, to where the Illinois merged with the Rogue River. If the body got that far, it was theorized, then the rain-swelled Rogue might have swept the corpse all the way to the Pacific Ocean. Either that, or the body had become tangled in some submerged obstruction that snagged the remains and for now, kept the body hidden.

THE RAPPELLER CREW kept Bowden's truck at the base because they weren't quite sure what else to do with it. Bowden had left the keys in the ignition and occasionally they used the truck to haul brush and rubbish to the landfill dump but mostly it sat off to one side of the gravel parking lot. One day a rough-looking character named John Thomas appeared saying he was Bowden's cousin from California who'd come to clear out the apartment and settle Bowden's affairs. They gave him the keys and Matt Murphy put Bowden's salvaged, folded-up Sea Eagle into the bed of the truck and Thomas drove the F-150 away and that was that.

Four months after the Tincup Fire the Forest Service petitioned the state to have Bowden declared legally dead. The idea was to have a commemorative service and bring a measure of closure to the loss suffered by the Forest Service and the Rogue Rappellers in particular. The state agreed.

They held the ceremony on the tarmac at the rappeller base. It was November and the rains had come and were forecast to last for the next two weeks so they built a small bonfire on the tarmac and took turns throwing chunks of pine and fir into the flames and there was an unspoken irony about a memorial made of fire. Rain sprinkled down and hit the flames so that they made a continual hiss as smoke swirled with steam. Supervisor Oates and the FAO Ken Hudek came and so did many of the off-season rappellers and rangers and fire officers from the various districts and locals who'd worked the Tincup and before long there were two hundred men and women clustered on the tarmac in rain slickers drinking beer and talking quietly. Corby was there and she walked with a cane and a pronounced limp and told everybody that she would be back in time for training exercises next season. The rappellers sipped Coors beer from cans and made halfhearted jokes about Bowden being an asshole but any humor was damped by the knowledge that they had lived and Bowden had not. There was also a tribute to the heavy equipment operator Gordon Finley. A friend of Finley's—a fellow dozer driver—threw one of Finley's oil-stained Caterpillar hats onto the fire and everyone watched it flame up and then slowly turn to ashes. People nodded and some cried.

They took a collection so they could make a donation to the National Fallen Firefighters Foundation and have commemorative bricks engraved with the names of Lucas Bowden and Gordon Finley placed in the Walk of Honor. They let the bonfire die down until it was a pile of orange embers and many of the attendees stayed until there was nothing left but a mound of steaming black and the winter sun slipped behind the far ridges and the day turned to a dull gray chill. Several of the rappelers dumped buckets of water on the ashes and pulled apart the ashes with Mcleod rakes and then unbidden and without exchanging a word they got down on their hands and knees and although they weren't in work clothes they searched the ashes for hot spots with their bare fingers and when they were done they stood up ash-streaked and filthy and hugged each other.

December 3
Grants Pass

IN THE MID-MORNING a small package was delivered to Corby Jones' newly rented house in downtown Grants Pass. The UPS driver rapped twice and left. Corby opened the door and picked up the package and looked it over. It was wrapped in plain brown paper and postmarked Tucson. There was no return address. It was a small package but had a bit of heft to it. She had no idea what it might be and she felt the trill of curiosity that unexplained packages bring.

Her cell phone chimed and she set the package on the kitchen counter. It was a text from Trey Ebbets—he would be picking her up in fifteen minutes. Corby had left her old boyfriend and was now hanging out with Trey and feeling good about it. Trey was vital and funny and they were a solid pair. They'd talked about whether they should be seeing each other while working at the same place and they decided to go for it, even though there was bound to be a lot of ribbing and unclever remarks from the other rappellers.

Corby peeled off the paper to reveal a small repurposed carboard box that had once held printer ink cartridges. The flaps had been secured with clear tape. She broke the tape with an index finger and opened the top to reveal a wad of white cotton. She took that out and held it up and stared at the contents. Nestled in a bottom layer of cotton were two carabiners linked together. Next to them was a stone—oblong, smooth, a luminescent silver-gray bisected by a single vein of clean pure white, five inches from tip to tip.

For a long while she did not move; could not move. The right hand remained suspended in mid-air. Something strong rose up inside her and she struggled to quell it although she was not sure what it was or why it needed to be subdued.

Her cell phone chimed again. She put the wad of cotton aside and picked up the phone and saw that fifteen minutes had passed in a heartbeat and Trey was waiting for her outside and should he come in? She texted *I'll be right out.*

She took the carabiners and walked to the closet where she kept her spare firefighting gear. Her green Nomex pants were suspended on a hook and she clipped the carabiners onto a belt loop and then closed the door.

She took the stone out of the box and held it in her hand and closed her eyes. She felt the heat of fire on her face and cold river water on her skin. She went to her bedroom window and set the rock on the sill where the morning sun would touch it. She put the box and cotton in the garbage pail underneath the kitchen sink. Then she took a deep breath and went out through her front door and closed it behind her.

John Riha

Acknowledgements

This started out as an adventure book set during a wildfire. As I researched and gained a better knowledge of fire science and firefighting techniques, the book became something of a parable—a story of a battle between good and evil. It was easy to personify wildfire as the violent, evil entity. The good were those who fought to stop the evil. They were the ground crews, medical first responders, pilots, equipment operators, rappellers, Hotshots, drone operators, fire burn analysts, communications managers, weather forecasters, food servers, and dozens of other necessary contributors who compose the orchestrated marvel that is a response to a major wildfire. Caught between these two forces were the innocent—a pair of backpackers trapped by fire.

A major event such as a wildfire is never adequately defined as good versus evil, of course. Human foibles come into play. People make mistakes; schemes fail. But what does succeed is nothing short of miraculous. In a matter of hours an entire city rises up, one that will host 500 people with sleeping quarters, showers, food, bathrooms, and internet access. Equipment will be serviced, water sources established, heliports constructed on cow pastures. The latest technology is employed—satellite mapping, drone reconnaissance, fire simulation programs. The fact that this highly coordinated effort spans multiple agencies, including local fire districts, state forestry teams, the U.S. Forest Service, Bureau of Land Management, Bureau of Indian Affairs, National Park Service, and the U.S. Fish and Wildlife Service, seems unprecedented when it comes to government agencies cooperating with each other.

Controversy will always accompany forestry and fires, especially in regions where timber has been a major economic force. Best practices continue to be debated. Can the worst effects of clearcutting be mitigated? Should old-growth trees be spared? Why are wildfires becoming so common and ever-more furious? Should we cut less and sequester carbon, or should we cut more and provide more jobs? What is the more productive result—controlling fires whenever and wherever they occur, or letting them burn to let nature's natural cleansing and restoration take place?

In this regard many agencies have been demonized as complicit in the destruction of natural habitat, of placing profit above environmental responsibility. Unfortunately, many of these accusations are not without merit. Fortunately, there are earnest and ongoing attempts to find the middle ground and create workable solutions.

But on the ground level, where boots meet dirt, in the face of one of nature's most destructive forces, these vexing questions melt away. Firefighters who risk everything to protect lives, property, and livelihoods are doing the job they were trained to do—stop the fire from spreading. It's never a perfect unfolding. Wildfires are unpredictable, racing ahead, jumping control lines, consuming entire towns, and taking lives. Fire managers are faced with an unbelievably complex set of circumstances.

In creating this book I was fortunate to be able to talk with many of the people who face these circumstances as part of their daily lives. They gave generously of their time and knowledge. It's been my privilege to have these folks tell their stories and guide my research. Hopefully, I've managed to accurately capture a portion of their experiences.

Eric Hensel, the Fire and Aviation Officer for the Rogue River/Siskiyou National Forest, was extremely helpful with information and unfailingly patient with my under-educated questions. Captain **Andrew Larrimore** and base manager **Matt Schutty** of the Siskiyou Rappellers invited me to their rappelling base located just outside of Grants Pass in Merlin, and were instrumental in providing first-hand accounts and detailed knowledge of their operations. Meteorologists **Bret Lutz, Ryan Sandler,** and **Tom Wright** of the National Weather Service in Medford succeeded in opening my eyes about the role of the weather service in firefighting strategies, especially the work of the IMET—an incident meteorologist assigned to an active wildfire location. Tom Wright is an author who wrote an apocalyptic thriller called "Dead Reckoning" that I thoroughly enjoyed. I told him I'd send him a copy of my wildfire book when it was completed (on its way, Tom). I spent a great multi-hour coffeeshop conversation with a former contract fire burn analyst or FBAN, **Steve Ziel,** who was a trove of quality info and was instrumental in helping me understand the tandem role of FBAN and IMET during a wildfire incident. **Dave Larson,** Supervisor of the Southwest Oregon District of the Oregon Department of Forestry, explained the nuances of interagency cooperation and enjoyed telling harrowing stories of firefighting, and he was the backgrounding source for a number of the close calls described in the book. **Jim Wittington,** a retired IC (Incident Commander), runs a consulting service specializing in disaster management and provided extremely interesting insights into communications and media relations during a crisis. PA1 **Cynthia Oldham** of the Coast Guard's 13th District in Astoria was invaluable in answering my questions about helicopters, gear and land-based Coast Guard rescue missions. Center Manager **Dan O'Brien** and Emergency Operations Manager **Ted Pierce** of the Northwest Interagency Coordination Center in Portland provided the big picture view of command structure and hierarchy during wildfire fighting operations. **Jason Forthofer**, a mechanical engineer at the Missoula Fire Sciences Laboratory, made sure I understood how wildfires burn and how pyrocumulonimbus clouds are formed. **Jack Methot,** a former Naval aviator for the U.S. Marine Corps, schooled me on aviation procedures and protocols.

Special thanks to fellow Ashlander and retired U.S. Forest Service employee **Wayne Rolle** who helped kick the whole idea off with a ginormous map of southern Oregon and the Kalmiopsis Wilderness, and who patiently identified Kalmiopsis flora and fauna from my blurry photographs.

In an effort to ensure accuracy and authenticity, I spent untold hours in the company of technical literature. A sampling:

- Coast Guard Helicopter Rescue Swimmer Guide
- Incident Commander's Organizer
- Incident Management and Response
- Incident Response Pocket Guide
- Interagency Helicopter Rappel Guide
- Interagency Standards for Fire and Aviation Operations
- National Interagency Mobilization Guide
- National Rappel Operations Guide
- NOAA Water Resources Web Manual
- Northwest Interagency Incident Management Team Operations Guide
- Northwest Mobilization Guide
- Operations and Safety Procedures Guide for Helicopter Pilots
- Standards for Interagency Hotshot Crew Operations
- Synthesis of Knowledge of Extreme Fire Behavior, Vol. 2
- Wilderness Fire Management Policy
- Wildland Fire Incident Management Field Guide

INCIDENT 395

Inspirational kudos to a 2015 article in *Outside* magazine entitled, "Meet the Blind Man Hiking the Country's Toughest Trails," by David Ferry. It's about Trevor Thomas, a young man who lost his sight but would go on to become a professional long-distance wilderness hiker. Trevor's forthright spirit would influence the essential plot of **Incident 395** and the character development of Kal Spencer.

A shoutout to firefighter **Bobbie Scopa** who writes the blog "Bobbie On Fire" with raw wit and wisdom. Her entertaining stories highlight the very human side of firefighting. Her book memoir, *Both Sides of the Fire Line,* will be available from Chicago Review Press.

Glossary

IA box: Incident Attack box. A box approximately 4 feet long and 2 feet wide that contains food, gear, and tools necessary to support a firefighting operation. IA boxes accompany each rappeller operation and are lowered from the helicopter once the firefighters are safely on the ground.

AIC: Adults in Custody is the official Oregon state designation for jailed inmates.

AO: Air Officers are dedicated to deployment and maintenance of firefighting aircraft.

AOC: The Air Operations Chief is in charge of aircraft deployment during large-scale wildfire response.

Buck Rogers time: A prison sentence so long that release is in the far-off future.

Car: A group of prisoners who share a common bond.

Cell warrior: An inmate who acts tough when locked in his cell, but is a coward face-to-face.

Chain: a unit of measurement equal to 66 feet.

DDO: Dispatch Duty Officer. The DDO is the hub of agency communications.

FAO: The Fire and Aviation Officer coordinates air-based firefighting, such as helicopter and airplane water and retardant drops, rappelling operations, drone flights and surveillance.

FBAN: The Fire Behavior Analyst monitors conditions such as air temperature, humidity, fuel dryness, wind speed and terrain to make estimates about what direction and how quickly a wildfire will move. An FBAN often works closely with an IMET.

GACC: Each region of the country is monitored by a Geographical Area Coordination Center that monitors firefighting operations and resource management for that area. The U.S. is divided into 10 GACCs.

IC: Incident Commander. Each level of wildfire response, from the smallest to the largest, is overseen by an IC. As an incident grows in complexity and the need for a larger response team is requested, the previous IC gives way to a new IC. At the higher levels of wildfire management, this transfer of power requires official paperwork.

IMED: Incident Medical Specialist. Someone trained to give medical treatment during a wildfire.

IMET: An Incident Meteorologist is on-site at a wildfire to provide up-to-the-minute weather forecasts. An IMET collaborates with the on-site FBAN.

IMT: Incident Management Team

NICC: National Interagency Coordination Center monitors all U.S. wildfires and allocates firefighting resources based on need.

Nickle: Prison slang for a five-year sentence.

NIOSH: The National Institute for Occupational Safety and Health includes a program for investigating firefighter fatalities.

NWS: National Weather Service

Ops Chief: The Operations Section Chief is in charge of firefighting operations, including ground crews, engines and heavy equipment, and air operations for fire suppression, surveillance, and rescue.

PIO: A Public Information Officer is responsible for providing news media and the public with the latest information about a wildfire.

POI: Probability of ignition is the chance that a firebrand will cause an ignition when it lands on receptive fuels, expressed as a percentage of certainty.

Pulaski: A basic firefighting hand tool for use in clearing brush and establishing control lines around a fire. The steel head of a Pulaski includes an ax blade and a hoe. The invention of the tool is credited to Ed Pulaski, a Forest Service ranger in the early 1900s.

S and R: Search and rescue, often abbreviated as SAR.

Shank: A prison weapon.

Spotter: During rappelling operations, the spotter directs deployment of the firefighters and tools. During surveillance, the spotter maps the location of wildfire outbreaks.

STFB: Short-term fire behavior is one of the data points available via WFDSS, the Wildfire Decision Support System.

STFB estimates the number of hours it will take a certain part of the fire to move from one specific point to another.

Stick: A team of two rappellers.

TARO: Tactical Air Response Order. No air-based mission can proceed without a TARO from a command center.

TFR: A Temporary Flight Restriction is ordered if conditions are hazardous to air operations. TFRs forbid any aircraft, including drones, from operating in certain areas.

Woofer: Wilderness First Responder, a trained medical professional specializing in administering first aid in remote locations.

WFDSS: Wildfire Decision Support System. A software-based program that analyzes all relevant wildfire behavior data to help commanders make key decisions about how, where, and when to deploy fire suppression resources.

John Riha

About the Author

John Riha was born and raised in the Midwest. He visited the Western states several times and finally resolved to stay there, among the big mountains and clear, trout-filled rivers. He lives in Ashland, Oregon, with his wife, Debra. They have two grown, wonderfully self-sufficient sons.

He is the author of *The Bounty Huntress,* an acclaimed historical novel set in southern Oregon in the 1920s, and *Rookies in the Wild,* a non-fiction book about hiking on the Pacific Crest Trail with one of his sons. He writes the humorous gardening blog, "Schiddygarden."

www.ingramcontent.com/pod-product-compliance
Lightning Source LLC
LaVergne TN
LVHW020428270425
809721LV00024B/801